HAINTS

Haints

A Novel by Clint McCown

First Edition
Library of Congress Control Number: 2011942069
ISBN: 978-0-89823-266-0
American Fiction Series

Cover design by Emily Heath
Author photo by Dawn Cooper
Interior design by Daniel A. Shudlick

The publication of *Haints* is made possible by the generous support of the McKnight Foundation and other contributors to New Rivers Press.

For academic permission or copyright clearance please contact Frederick T. Courtright at 570-839-7477 or permdude@eclipse.net.

New Rivers Press is a nonprofit literary press associated with Minnesota State University Moorhead.

Alan Davis, Co-Director and Senior Editor
Suzanne Kelley, Co-Director and Managing Editor
Wayne Gudmundson, Consultant
Allen Sheets, Art Director
Thom Tammaro, Poetry Editor
Kevin Carollo, MVP Poetry Coordinator

Publishing Interns:
David DeFusco, Andreana Gustafson, Katelin Hansen, Noah M. Kleckner, Daniel A. Shudlick, Sarah Z. Sleeper, Alicia Strnad

Haints Book Team:
Tyler Anderson, Kate Hauge, Kaitlynn Moessner, Alicia Strnad

New Rivers Press
c/o MSUM
1104 7th Avenue South
Moorhead, MN 56563
www.newriverspress.com

ƒor Dawn, healer of spirits

and for Caitlin and Mallie,
should they ever wonder about the clay

CONTENTS

Prologue
February 29, 1952

Signalman 3rd Class Ronald Dawson—*Ronnie Boy* to his dead shipmates—made his way up the aisle of the bus and eased himself into the torn seat behind the driver.

"I need to get off here," he said.

The driver looked at him in the rearview mirror. Ronald knew the man was sizing him up—passengers weren't supposed to get off between towns. But maybe the uniform would make a difference. That's all the driver was likely to see.

"You got any baggage to pull out?"

Ronald thought about the question. Everything he owned lay stuffed inside the canvas seaman's bag in the compartment underneath the bus.

"No sir," he said. "Nothing."

The driver let out a small snort, as if he'd just lost an argument, and steered the bus onto the shoulder. "I've got a kid brother in Korea," he said as he pulled the lever that folded the door aside.

A brother in Korea. That was appropriate. Rules were being broken, exceptions were being made. His dead shipmates were clearing a path for him now.

"Better get where you're going," the driver said as Ronald stepped out into the dazzling sunlight. Ronald squinted back at the driver, who was now just a shadow perched behind the wheel. "They're calling for thunderstorms."

Ronald didn't care about thunderstorms, but he scanned the sky anyway to be polite. Sure enough, a steep bank of clouds was already rolling in from the northwest end of the county.

"Thanks," he said.

The driver closed the door, and Ronald watched as the bus pulled back onto the crumbling blacktop and disappeared around a bend. An eddy of dust swirled across his shoes, softening their gleam.

He was alone again, more or less. He took a slow breath. The approaching clouds were dark and greenish, almost like the sea.

Don't watch the sky, Ronnie Boy, said his dead shipmates. *That's not your job.*

They were right, as always.

The hike to his grandfather's old cabin was a difficult one, not only for the steepness of the terrain but for the unfamiliarity, which he hadn't expected. The deer trails he'd followed as a boy had all melted back into the landscape. Maybe the herds had thinned out over the years—or just shifted away, moving to more remote ground now that every crossroad in the county had sprouted a noisy filling station or a neon-framed steakhouse. In any case, the old paths were gone.

Or maybe he was wrong about that. Maybe the deer were still there, threading their same old route up the mountain, and he was the one who had changed, the one who could no longer find his way among the sharp outcroppings of rock and fallen trees and the brown tangle of last year's vines. He'd grown used to the sea, with its overwhelming sky and its own faint and temporary trails, so broad and flat, sometimes dissolving right before his eyes. He never worried about finding his way over the water—the ship itself took care of that, giving everyone on board a common direction. But here on land, each step was once again his own, a terrible uncertainty, and for long stretches of the climb he suspected he was lost. But the voices kept pushing him forward, driving him up the rugged slope through wave after wave of budding undergrowth. When at last he broke through to the crest of the ridge, he was exhausted. But that was all right. He had little left to do.

The cabin was gone now, save for the blackened stone pilings of the foundation and a few charred boards jutting like bones from the pit. Lightning, he imagined, or maybe vandals. Years ago, from the look of it. Most of the ash had washed away.

"I know," Ronald said, before his dead shipmates could chide him. "It's none of my concern." He had no claim on this land. The TVA had seized the property before he left for the navy. *The law of eminent domain*, they'd called it. And they'd paid only enough for him to bury his grandfather, whose heart had burst over the loss.

But that's what governments did, after all: sacrifice the few for the sake of the many. The country needed hydroelectric power. Dams were being built all along the Tennessee River and its tributaries, and soon the entire valley of his childhood would be flooded. The old roads and country stores and even the forests themselves would all be under water.

He took it as one more sign. Water would follow him wherever he tried to go, even into the past. There was no point trying to escape it.

He walked to the overhang and stared across the valley as the roiling gray-green sky lowered itself over the opposite ridge. The storm would be on him in a few minutes.

At his feet he could make out the last traces of the danger line—that thick yellow stripe his grandfather had painted across the rock shelf so many years ago. Ronald had been forbidden to cross that line. Beyond it the smooth ledge tilted downward, and a clumsy step could send a boy sliding off into space, into a hundred-foot drop to the rocky creek bed below.

But he'd never been good at following orders, even then, and though his grandfather never knew it, Ronald had crossed that painted line the day he turned thirteen. Not boldly, because in truth he'd always had a crippling fear of heights. But he'd crossed it nevertheless, creeping down the incline on his hands and knees, daring himself forward, inching toward that terrifying edge until at last, shaking and prickling with sweat, he could look straight down the cliff and imagine what might be. Because, frightened as he was, he still wanted to know what it would be like to cross that next line, that final line, the one that could not be uncrossed. Dizziness had swamped him then, and he almost took the plunge.

Of course, he'd recovered himself, and, shaken by whatever devil had tempted him to crowd the edge, to push that point of no return, he'd scrambled back to safety across his grandfather's yellow line. He never crossed it again.

Until now.

You're not a sailor anymore, his dead shipmates reminded him. The sneer in their voices was unbearable.

He sighed and took off his shoes. The toes were scuffed from the climb, which disturbed him. He liked having a good shine on his shoes. The old man had always admired whatever was well-pressed and polished. Too bad he never got to see Ronald in uniform.

He spat on the shoes and buffed them with the end of his neckerchief until the gleam was again so deep and clear he could see himself in the glossy blackness—the long pale face, white buzz-cut hair. His features were distorted, but that was just as well. Ronald hadn't been able to look himself in the face for more than a year now.

One year and twenty-seven days, to be exact. One year and twenty-seven days since his mind had wandered while he was standing watch. Since he had failed to sound the alarm. Not that it was all that easy to spot mines bobbing in dark water. But he'd been trained—he knew what to look for. People had counted on him to keep them safe. And he'd wanted to—of course he'd wanted to—but he'd never been much good at holding his focus. The waters were calm and the horizon was clear, and somewhere in the long stretch of the evening, his mind just drifted away. He found himself daydreaming about what he might do after the war, about maybe finding a girl and a piece of land someplace—not in the Tennessee mountains but near the shore, where he could always look out at the ocean, which had become the place he loved the most. Maybe he could set himself up with some kind of excursion boat in Florida and take tourists on fishing trips or sightseeing tours. He could arrange a business loan to get started—he'd be a war veteran, after all, a man to be respected, the kind of man bankers would always be willing to bank on.

The first he knew of the mine was when it exploded against the hull. And that was that. Eight men dead, six wounded. The USS *Partridge* taking on water, then listing lazily to the starboard side, then sinking to the bottom of Wonsan Harbor.

Strange that all he'd lost was his cap.

Well. That and everything else.

He tucked his socks inside his shoes and set them gently on the yellow line. His neckerchief and bell-bottoms flapped in the rising wind. He took off the rest of his clothes, folding the uniform as neatly as he could. Not crisp enough to pass inspection, but respectful, at least. He placed the clothes beside his shoes, but the wind was wilder now, and before he'd even straightened up, his uniform tumbled away up the incline, the white suit billowing and flopping along the stony ground like some drunken ghost.

No matter. The navy was just one more ruined cabin to him now, one more abandoned piece of ground. He'd stood on the dry deck of the rescue ship watching the fresh crew search for bodies they would never find. His commanding officer, Lt. Clark, was among the lost. Ronald assumed that was why he was never brought up on charges—no officer to file a report. But whatever the reason, from that moment until his redeployment to the States a year later, no one ever said a word about his failure. No one suggested a court martial. No one accused him of dereliction of duty. No one said anything to him at all. It was as if he had disappeared with his dead shipmates.

Maybe that's why they talked to him now.

Ronald rose to attention and walked naked out onto the weathered slab, stopping a half step from the edge. A few large drops of rain spattered across the rock-face like the first few notes of a discordant song. He peered down at the familiar litter of boulders below. This time he felt no fear, not the smallest tremor, not the slightest chill. He looked out again at the doomed valley, hoping for one last happy glimpse of something he had once loved. Instead, he saw the angry hand of God whirling in a dark spiral, reaching down from the heavens, snatching up fistfuls of branches and stones and debris as it rampaged back and forth across the hollow. Ronald felt one final surge of dread.

Don't think this squares anything, said his dead shipmates.

"I won't," Ronald told them.

He closed his eyes and leapt.

Herb Gatlin

Deep in the hole of his own digging, Herb Gatlin mopped the sweat from his leathered neck with a frayed blue handkerchief and offered up a prayer of thanksgiving: another day half done, and he still hadn't taken a drink, cursed God for the pain in the stump of his leg, or killed Doc McKinney.

The strength to resist the latter was his greatest blessing, and he knew not to take it for granted. He'd fought the murderous urge for twenty years, and so far he'd held his ground, but that didn't mean he could relax his vigilance. The Devil was a relentless foe, relentless as Doc McKinney himself, and the temptations were as numerous as the opportunities. The Doc was always looming over him, it seemed, directing him on some menial chore, overseeing his progress, complaining about his workmanship—almost as if he were asking for that sudden pick-axe in the chest, the brick to the side of the head, even a simple stranglehold.

The current chore was especially galling. He'd spent the past week hand-digging a well on the two-acre lot where Doc McKinney was having a new house built for his daughter, and even though the well site was barely two hundred yards downhill from the pumping station on Reservoir Hill, Herb hadn't hit water.

That didn't surprise him, really. Herb was used to small failures, and he knew this job had been doomed from the start. The county was a lumpy accumulation of ragged hills, and the water table was down deep. Nobody could get there with just a shovel, especially not from halfway up a hillside. Herb might dig until kingdom come and still not make it to the source.

So where did that leave him?

He asked himself that question on a regular basis, and the answer always came back the same: stuck in a hole. In this case, stuck high and dry in the deepest hole he'd ever dug. He laughed a little at that and leaned against the cool dirt wall to take a breather, hooking an arm through the rope ladder to steady himself.

The sky had gone gray, what he could see of it, so he couldn't be sure of the time. At least three o'clock, he figured. He might knock off around five. There was a new movie playing down at the Lincoln Theatre, *High Noon*, with Gary Cooper. Supposed to be pretty good, and he'd always liked Westerns. But he'd have to clean himself up first. It was hard to work in a hole all day and not come out grubby, and even though late February was a comfortable time of year for outdoor labor, he still had a tendency to sweat through his work shirt. Maybe he could borrow Moody Smith's washtub again and have himself a good cold bath.

Or maybe his next shovelful would bring him all the bathwater he needed, right here, right now. There was always a chance he might tap into a stray spring snaking up between the levels of rock. At least it was something to hope for.

He had to admit, it felt good to move around without that damn fake leg propping him up. He'd started the job with it strapped in place, same as always, but after a certain depth, the dead weight had become too unwieldy. He'd heard that some amputees nowadays had something called a flexible prosthesis, hard plastic molded around steel rods and rigged with sprung hinges at the ankle and knee. A fellow might walk almost normally on a leg like that, Herb imagined. His was nothing so fancy, just a carved wooden block of hickory Doc McKinney

8

had supplied him with back in '32. It was a discontinued model, the Doc had told him, so he didn't even have to pay for it. The foot on the wooden leg was too small for his natural shoe size, so sometimes he had a problem keeping his work-boot in place. But a free leg was a free leg, and overall the thing had been serviceable enough for most of his odd jobs through the years.

Not this time, though, not working in this hole. He had no bend in his ankle or his knee, so the rope ladder proved too tricky to navigate. Stooping was another problem. Far better, he discovered, just to leave the leg topside.

Even so, the job was still tough, since it generally took two legs to work a shovel properly. The hole was just broad enough that he could balance himself on the back of the shovel-blade and work it down, inch by inch, rocking sideways between the walls. But the space was too narrow for him to gain much leverage against the scattered chunks of granite and limestone he encountered along the way. He had cut the shovel handle short, which gave him some slight room to maneuver, but still every ill-placed stone had to be pried loose in the smallest of increments, then plucked up from the tight clay by hand.

After seven days of awkward stooping and straining, hauling bucket after bucket up to the surface, he was only fifteen feet into the well. The walls were dank in a way that crept through his bones and stiffened his joints, making him relive every hard fall from his horse-breaking days. He didn't mind that so much—those times had been the best, when he could read a horse like a McGuffy's Primer and turn even the most ill-tempered stallion into something useful—something reliable and safe. It didn't matter that he broke a few things of his own along the way. Herb believed that if he still carried a few old aches, still felt a few sharp twinges, then maybe those days weren't altogether gone.

And so what if he couldn't break horses anymore? There weren't that many left to break. When Herb was a kid, not one family in five had an automobile; now everybody did. Horses used to be a necessity, and now they were just exotic family pets.

Hitching posts still lined the town square, but those were mostly for the produce wagons that came to town Saturday mornings for the farmers' market. Of course, Herb still kept a horse—an old swayback mare he'd found starving at the south end of the county a few years back. The last time he'd ridden it into town the sheriff had given him a ticket for dropping road-apples in front of the courthouse. Times had changed.

But Herb had changed, too, so that was all right. He'd once been the most gifted horseman in middle Tennessee, but that had ended when he lost his leg. When Doc McKinney took it from him.

He'd held a few jobs since—teamster, carpenter, gravedigger, handyman. He'd dug a few fallout shelters for wealthy folks who got panicky over the Communists. A couple of weeks back, Doc McKinney's brother-in-law, Tom Parsons, had hired him to build a regulation-size boxing ring out at the Starlight Drive-In. He'd put a lot of care into that job. Mr. Tom was an old friend who'd once been his boss at the newspaper, the one time Herb had tried his hand at working indoors, typesetting the weekly edition. Mr. Tom had been patient, and Herb had showed an aptitude, but in the end the smallness of the activity had defeated him; and anyway, he couldn't stand being cooped up all day. If he'd kept that job and steered clear of rodeos, he might have kept Ellen. But that's not how the dominoes fell. No sense complaining. Still, it was always good to see Mr. Tom around and about, and Herb was glad to be thought of for the boxing ring.

Build it like it matters, Mr. Tom had told him. So he'd sunk the corner posts in concrete and leveled the ring so precisely a marble wouldn't roll off. Jersey Joe Walcott, the world's heavyweight champ, was coming to town to put on an exhibition, and Herb was proud to be a part of it. Mr. Tom had paid him a buck an hour for the work and had given him a ten-dollar bonus when the ring was finished.

The Doc had picked this spot himself—the rockiest stretch of the yard, just beneath the black walnut tree that loomed out over the clearing—and told him to dig until the job was done, however long it took. The entire project would be his alone—that's how the Doc had hooked him. Herb didn't care if the hole might be bottomless, as long as he could be his own foreman. Too many times he'd run afoul of assholes with no idea how to handle a work crew, and too many times he'd been asked to leave a job before it was finished.

But now, a full week into the hole, he was having second thoughts. This undertaking was starting to look too much like permanent employment, which was more than he'd bargained for, especially when every new shovelful took more effort than the last. If he ran into shelf-rock, he might even have to fill the hole back in and start over somewhere else on the property.

He stared again at the thick swirl of greenish-gray clouds above him, wondering if a serious storm might be blowing in. If so, he'd have to cover the hole to keep it dry. The digging was hard enough already—he didn't need rainwater to squat in.

As he studied the clouds, a sudden spray of dirt showered down on him from the crumbling edge of the hole. He turned his head away, but too late—his right eye caught a piece of grit. He blinked at the dark bottom of the well and tried to force out a few tears. The wind was kicking up, it seemed. He tugged loose his shirttail and carefully wiped the mote from his eye.

"That you down there, Mr. Gatlin?"

Mary Jean's voice startled him. He squinted up toward the surface, but his vision was blurred.

"Last time I checked," he answered.

"I believe I might have kicked some dirt down on you," she said. "Sorry about that. I was trying to be careful around the edge of this hole."

He blinked a few more times until he could see her standing above him, her blonde head peering down over the curve of her belly, her hands holding the front of her blue maternity dress modestly against her legs as the wind rippled around her from behind.

"No harm done," he said. He smiled up at her. This was an unlooked-for gift. He knew Mary Jean came around the property from time to time, checking the progress of her house, but he never imagined she might speak to him. That was something Doc McKinney would have frowned on.

"Looks like you're making real progress," she said. "That's a long way down."

"Might look like progress," he said, "but it's still just a dry hole."

As a rule, Herb tried not to be judgmental. He could turn a blind eye to most circumstances, because he knew what it was like to commit a transgression and what a burden that was to haul around. But the more he thought about Mary Jean's well, the more it bothered him. He didn't mind hard work, that was how he'd lived his life for nearly half a century. Fortitude, his mother had called it—his lone cardinal virtue. But what he couldn't abide was wasted effort. There were seven deadly sins, he recollected, and even though he couldn't call to mind what they were exactly, he felt certain wasted effort must be somewhere on the list. And that was the problem here. He didn't feel right sweating for no good reason, and there was no good reason for this well. The house Doc McKinney was building for his daughter would have indoor plumbing, so this thing Herb was digging was pure folly. It was supposed to be a wishing well, for cripe's sake, with a rock wall around it and a little shingle roof and a hand crank to lower a wooden bucket. Maybe even some goldfish flopping around. An overblown lawn ornament, that's all it amounted to, with nothing real to offer but a brief stopover in idle conversation and one more place for cats to drown. It was the kind of well no one built anymore, not since drills had been invented, the kind of well that showed up in storybooks for little kids, with Jack breaking his crown and Jill tumbling after. A quaint gesture to the past, that's how Doc McKinney talked about it, and certainly he could afford that kind of extravagance. But affording it didn't make it right.

Besides, Herb knew there was more than nostalgia involved, more than giving young Mary Jean a useless decoration for her yard. Guilt and revenge were two weights on the scale, that much he was sure of, though after twenty years anybody's motives might be difficult to sort out. Maybe the Doc himself had lost track and hired him now more from habit than from a need to balance out old debts. In any case, Herb was in no position to gripe about it. A man with his limitations had to take what work he could get.

"How long you been down there?" Mary Jean asked. A sudden gust brought her ponytail tumbling around the side of her face, but she flipped it back over her shoulder with a quick toss of her head. Her mother had a ponytail once, Herb remembered. Back when she delivered papers for *The Observer*.

"Hour and a half, I reckon." He pulled his damp handkerchief from his back pocket again and blotted his forehead. "There's a rock down here won't cooperate. Thinks he's got squatters' rights."

She shook her head. "You ought to come up," she told him. There's a big storm coming. Radio says we're in for it." She glanced over her shoulder toward the half-built house. "Everybody else has gone home already."

Herb didn't doubt it. That was a lazy bunch the Doc had hired to build Mary Jean's house, always looking for an excuse to lay off work, always taking breaks for whiskey or cigarettes. If Herb had been in charge, she'd have herself a home by now instead of just that sorry skeleton of two-by-fours.

The branches of the black walnut swayed wildly above her, the wind hissing and rattling through the leaves. Herb felt oddly out of step with the moment. Where had his mind been? It wasn't like him to lose touch with the weather, yet this shifting sky had caught him unawares.

"Then maybe you ought to head home, too, Mary Jean." Mary Jean. He'd always balked at that name. It was far too plain for a bright flower like her. He'd have called her Lilly or maybe Iris. Or Rosemary—was that a flower? He couldn't remember. He began to pull himself awkwardly up the ladder.

"Think I'll stay a while," she said, raising her voice slightly over the wind. "I want to see what happens."

Herb laughed. "You'll get wet, that's what'll happen."

"I want to do something special for Leap Day."

"Is that today?" he asked.

"February 29th," she announced happily. "We all get an extra day."

Once his head and shoulders were above ground, he gripped the wooden stakes anchoring the ladder and hoisted himself up over the lip of the well, then rolled sideways onto his rump and propped himself upright. He perched there on the edge with his leg dangling into the hole and tried to draw breath as evenly as he could. He didn't want to appear winded in front of her.

A chilly gust buffeted his back. Now he understood the deep pain in his joints. If his bones had it right, there was a hard blow coming.

She stepped around the well toward him and paused beside the low stool where Herb took his lunch breaks. Herb's artificial leg stood there, leaning obscenely against the stool, preventing her from sitting down, but she seemed to make a point of not looking at it. Herb felt a wave of humiliation. He grabbed the leg by the ankle and tossed it aside, as if it were nothing more than clutter at his work site with no connection to who he was.

"You can sit if you need to," Herb said.

She nodded her thanks and eased herself onto the stool. "I've been studying Chinese philosophy," she said, planting her legs against the base of the dirt pile to steady herself. "That's why I want to see the storm up close."

Herb stared past the gnarled branches of the black walnut. The sky looked entirely untrustworthy now, darkening toward early night. The bottom might fall out any minute. He needed to get a tarp in place fast.

"Don't the Chinese know to come in out of the rain?" he asked.

"They know more than you think," she said. "Lao Tzu said that water benefits all things and does not compete with them."

"I guess he didn't know many farmers. Too much rain at the wrong time can wash out a whole season of work."

Mary Jean ignored him. "I started learning about the Chinese last fall, over at Mary Baldwin." She lowered her eyes. "I was in college there."

Herb had never heard of Mary Baldwin, but he thought it best not to say so. "I bet you were the smartest of the bunch," he offered, and she smiled.

"That's just what Bobby said. But you're both wrong."

"Who's Bobby?"

"Bobby Malone," she said, and her face seemed to brighten and cloud over at the same time. "You might have seen him down at the hardware store. He used to work in the back."

"Oh, sure, I know who you mean. Skinny dark-haired kid. Pitched last summer for the Masons."

"That's him." She smoothed a few strands of hair from her face, but the wind blew them instantly back into disarray. "Bobby's in Korea now, but we're getting married as soon as he gets home."

"I'm happy for you," Herb said, although in truth he felt sorry for them both, and for whatever half-baked plans they had. Bobby had always been a good boy, as far as he could tell. But if he did come back from Korea, he'd come back a different person. Not necessarily better or worse, but different. That could be a tall hurdle for any couple starting out.

"What I really wanted was to read up on Korean philosophy, so I could understand how people think over there. I wanted to know what Bobby was up against. But there was nothing about Korean philosophy in the county library. Chinese was as close as I could come."

"I imagine that'll do," he said. Herb wasn't clear on his own philosophy, much less anybody else's, but he knew people were pretty much the same all over. They all wished for better than they had. And when times got hard, they all wanted somebody to give them the benefit of the doubt.

"The Chinese came up with answers for everything," Mary Jean said.

"So did the Baptists."

She frowned. "But the Chinese did it by paying attention to nature. So that's what I'm fixing to do."

"You think sitting in a thunderstorm is liable to teach you something?"

"It's bound to. If I'm in the storm, I'll be part of it. I'll know what the storm knows." The wind died suddenly, and a quiet fell across the hillside. "Real knowledge comes from experience, not from a classroom." A note of defiance had crept into her voice, and Herb sensed the leftovers of some unresolved argument, either with Doc McKinney or with Ellen.

"Well, Mary Jean, I've been caught in more than my share of downpours, and I can tell you what the lesson is: Take an umbrella."

He hoped this might bring another smile, but she was dug in.

"You don't understand," she said. A fresh wind rose, sifting noisily through the leaves. The hem of her dress snapped like a flag in battle, and she reached down to gather it close. "It's about learning how everything fits together. It's about contemplating the sound of one hand clapping."

Herb had nothing to say to that. He didn't believe things fit together at all, and he was pretty sure nobody could clap with one hand anymore than he could click his heels together with just one leg. Of course, he'd never tell Mary Jean that. She was right about experience—she'd have to learn some things for herself.

"What about the baby? You get soaked, you might catch a chill." A chill wasn't really what he was concerned about. Mary Jean was bigger than a prize pumpkin, so that baby was probably set to come out any time now. Even a close thunderclap might get her jump-started, and Herb would have no idea what to do.

She frowned and slapped a twig away from the folds of her lap, releasing her dress to billow again at her knees. "This baby'll have its say soon enough. But for now I'm still calling the shots."

He'd had run-ins with pregnant women before, so Herb knew better than to argue. Mary Jean's own mother had been testy like that, years ago, before she was Doc McKinney's wife, back when she was still Ellen Parsons. Herb sighed. He couldn't leave Mary Jean out here in bad weather all alone.

He took up the slack in the twine he'd tied to the top rung of the ladder and began to haul the rock-filled tin bucket up from the floor of the well. This was the heaviest load yet, and the rough twine bit into his fingers. He feared for a second the line might break, but no, it held, and he lifted the bucket from the well and settled it securely in the soft dirt beside him.

"How about you help me get a canvas over this hole," he said, pointing to the folded green tarp beyond the dirt pile. "Then maybe I'll sit out the storm with you. See if I cain't learn something new myself for a change."

"I guarantee you will," she said, her voice again light as a hummingbird. Herb could tell she was glad, and maybe even relieved, to have some company. "We can learn tons from the Chinese," she continued. "They got more wise sayings than you can shake a stick at. All about nature and stuff."

Mary Jean pushed herself up from the stool and squatted awkwardly beside the tarp. She gripped it along an edge and stood up, giving it a single shake as she rose. The wind unfurled it like a sail, then ripped it from her grasp and carried it, tumbling and twisting, down the long hillside.

"Oh my gosh, Mr. Gatlin," she said. Her face filled with child-like dismay, and for a moment Herb was reminded of what she had been like as a little girl. She spread her arms to the side and looked down helplessly at her huge belly. "I can't run after it."

Herb took a long breath and looked at Mary Jean. "Me neither," he said. He wasn't sure why this struck him as funny, but it did, and he started to laugh. The tarp continued to cascade over itself, rolling in chaotic fits toward Mulberry Avenue at the bottom of the slope. "Don't worry about it, Mary Jean," he told her. "It'll catch on a bush or a fire hydrant before it hits the town square. I'll get it back later."

"I couldn't hold onto it," she apologized.

Herb smiled. "Maybe the Chinese got a saying for a situation like that."

"They probably do. Only I haven't read that far yet."

"I had me a fortune cookie once," he said, "from a Chinese restaurant over in Lewisburg. Told me I was headed for a lucky break." He watched as his tarp took a right turn on Mulberry and continued on its way downtown. Herb sighed again. "But that never really panned out."

"That's not the kind of wise sayings I mean," she told him. "I mean real wisdom. Things like Ben Franklin might have said."

He brushed a dried clod from the front of his shirt. "Okay, let me hear one."

She leaned toward him and got a serious look on her face. "The town may be changed, but the well may not be changed."

He waited for the rest of it, but she was finished. She held him in a steady gaze, her eyes wide. He could see she expected some kind of response.

"That's it?"

She straightened back up and stared out across the treetops at the bottom of the hill. "You have to think about it."

He bit the inside of his cheek and tried to look like he was thinking, but it was no use. "I don't know, Mary Jean. Seems to me, if you have to think about it, maybe it's not all that wise."

"It's from the *Book of Changes*," she said, a little defensively. "People have been quoting from it for thousands of years."

Herb nodded his head, as if that information made some kind of difference. But the quote still made no sense. He knew for a fact that people changed their wells all the time. One hole went dry, you drilled another, simple as that. If this was the best the Chinese could come up with, he'd stick with whatever he could put together on his own.

"How about the Romans?" he asked. Herb didn't know beans about the Chinese, but he could talk about the Romans. He'd read all about their empire way back in Mrs. Moore's Latin class thirty years before, and the gist of it had stayed with him. Ellen Parsons had been in that class, and he'd studied hard to impress her. In all his days of school, that was the only "A" he ever got. "Those Romans had a lot of smart things to say, too," Herb told her. A few large drops of rain spattered in the dirt around them.

"Like what?" Mary Jean asked, clearly skeptical.

"All roads lead to Rome," he said. A couple of cold drops hit the back of his neck and ran down under his collar.

Mary Jean shook her head and laced her hands beneath her belly. "That's not smart. It's not even accurate."

"Okay, how about this one: Beware the Ides of March." Herb expected the sky to open up on them then, but instead, the drops quit falling and the wind died away. Another deep stillness settled over the slope, and it seemed to Herb as if everything in the world around them had suddenly stopped to listen.

"What's the Ides of March?" she asked.

Herb paused to count up in his head. "I think it's two weeks from Saturday."

Mary Jean snorted and looked away. "No, I mean I don't know what it is."

"Oh—it's what the Romans called March fifteenth. That's the day Julius Caesar got himself stabbed to death on the steps of the Roman senate. Didn't you ever study Latin?"

She resettled herself onto the stool and blotted away a few raindrops from her face with her sleeve. "Daddy said Latin was a wrong direction for me. He made me take typing instead."

That figured. The Doc hadn't fared too well in Latin class, as Herb recalled. Of course, he wasn't the Doc back then, he was just plain old Wally McKinney, who never got picked first in gym class and who always sat by himself in the lunchroom. Herb had it all over Wally in those days, or so he'd thought at the time. Funny that Wally would go on to medical school, where Latin actually mattered.

But Wally got his degree, and that changed everything. When he came home as Dr. Wallace McKinney and hung out a shingle, everybody saw him in a different light, Ellen included. Herb couldn't blame her for that—Wally was an altogether different fellow with a bright career ahead of him. Even so, Herb still had the edge on him, right up until the accident. He couldn't blame Ellen for the way things had gone thereafter. Though her timing had been bad.

"In my day, we didn't have a choice," Herb told her. "Latin was it for everybody."

"Anyway," Mary Jean went on, "you're batting zero in the wise saying category."

"Beware the Ides of March was good advice," Herb objected.

"Only if you're Julius Caesar. And I gather even he didn't put much stock in it."

An old regret flared up, and suddenly Herb wanted to offer Mary Jean something she could hold on to. He ransacked his brain for some worthwhile nugget, and then there it was— the phrase he'd first translated for Ellen that day he'd helped her with her homework on a bench on the courthouse lawn. She'd kissed him, right there where anybody could see, and for the first time in his life he believed he was worth something, that his days might unfold happily from that bright moment on.

Lord, why hadn't he married her when he had the chance? What made him think he had to make something of himself first? Pride, that must have been it. Foolish pride. For pride goeth before destruction—and destruction was pretty much the hallmark of his life.

"*Ab uno disce omnes*," he said. "From one, learn to know all."

Mary Jean furrowed her brow, and after a moment, she nodded. "Now that's more like it," she said. "That one's good enough to be Chinese."

Herb felt strangely elated, as if it were a rodeo day and he had stayed the full eight seconds in the saddle. He looked up at the black walnut's broad canopy stretching across the upper end of the clearing. Not a leaf trembled. The lengthening stillness made conversation easier, at least, and Herb was grateful for that. But there was something untrustworthy in this lull. It was a false calm; he could feel it in the air.

He glanced over at Mary Jean and saw that she'd followed his gaze to the webwork of dark branches spreading above them. "That's my very favorite tree," she said. "Mother thinks it's over three hundred years old."

"I hate it," Herb said flatly.

"How can you hate it? It's beautiful."

Herb knew she was right—it was a picture-book tree, with massive shaggy limbs arching out over the well site. That tree was probably the reason the Doc wanted the well here in the first place. But sometimes beauty was the least important thing.

"Black walnut," he said. "That's poisonous to horses."

"Horses can't eat walnuts?"

"Not the green casings, they cain't. But that's not the real problem. There's an acid in the wood that horses don't tolerate. You bed a stall with black walnut shavings, the horse'll soak up the acid through his hooves. Once the acid gets hold of him, he'll founder in three days."

"What's founder?"

"The bones in his foot die. If a horse founders, you have to put him down."

"Then why would anybody use black walnut in the first place?"

"Nobody would on purpose. Not horse people, anyway. But when you pick up a load of shavings or sawdust from a mill, they don't always give you the straight dope on what kind of wood it came from. That's why you've got to watch a horse real close when you put down fresh bedding. If he gets a fever in his feet, you've got to get him out of the stall, stand him in a cold stream all day. Maybe feed him some wheat germ, that can help. But it all depends on how toxic he is. Sometimes if you catch it quick enough, the horse'll survive."

"Did you used to be a rancher?" she asked.

"Nothing so grand as that," he answered. "But I used to be a horseman."

He could tell she was struggling not to look at his empty pant leg, rolled tightly against his stump and safety-pinned in place.

"I wanted a horse, growing up," she said. "But Mother and Daddy never would let me have one. They said horses were dangerous."

"They can be," he said.

"Is that what happened to your leg?"

"No, ma'am, that was something else entirely. I got myself stomped by a bull." He paused. "Your daddy had to cut the leg off. Said it was the only way to save my life." In a different place and time, Herb would have told a more bitter version of what Doc McKinney had done to him. But for here and now, that was the best way to say it.

"Why were you messing with a bull?"

"Rodeo nonsense."

"For prize money?"

"There was some of that," he admitted. "Fifty dollars, I think it was. Lot of money back then. Thought it might set me up with my girl." *Your mother*, he wanted to say. But not every truth needed to show its full face.

Thunder echoed in from the far side of the hill, rumbling steady and slow, like wagon wheels on a wooden bridge. The wind pitched itself forward again, spreading through the trees in a shrill whine. Herb looked behind them, toward the unfinished house, where small whirlwinds were kicking up twigs and dust. The pressure was still dropping. Something difficult was coming.

"Mary Jean," he said, raising his voice above the growing clamor, "I think we ought to take cover." There were finished houses over on the extension of Elk Avenue, maybe two hundred yards across the slope. He could send her on ahead while he strapped on his leg.

She said something, but the wind gusted in his ear and he missed it. But the look on her face told him enough. She was enjoying this sudden upsurge. Her ponytail whipped around her face more violently than ever, but she didn't seem to care. She sat there smiling, chin up and eyes closed, like it was a balmy summer night and she was listening to band music on the courthouse lawn.

He tugged the hem of her dress and gestured toward the Williams' house over on Elk. She shook her head no.

"It's something I can tell Bobby," she shouted, then let out a joyful yelp against the rising howl of the wind, and Herb saw once again how useless it was to argue with the young, to tell them what was stupid and dangerous, to warn them about what sometimes hid behind the face of things, because all they saw was what they wanted to see: a benevolent world overstocked with grand gestures and romantic notions, no deadly crossroads, no rats gnawing through the bedsheets, no dark force of nature hiding in the alleyway, waiting to brain them with a two-by-four. "Mary Jean—" he started, then froze. The clouds beyond the pumping station had dipped nearly to the ground, as if someone had pulled a plug and now darkness itself was pouring through a gaping hole in the sky. Herb knew what it was. He'd seen twisters before, sweeping through the high tablelands down near the Alabama line. But he'd never been this close. He called her name again, but she was lost in the thrill of the storm. There was no chance to take cover, not anymore. The boiling black mass of wind and debris crested the hill and swung wildly down the rocky slope in a path maybe fifty yards across, shredding the landscape as if the whole world were nothing more than scraps of tissue. And there he was, stuck in harm's way with Mary Jean, watching for the wind to shift right or wrong, good or bad, for fortune to make up its fickle mind. Old tires and mattresses tumbled upwards from the weeds, Coke bottles and tin cans rose like birds, scrub trees flattened, then sprang, uprooted, into the air—all vanishing into the dark wall of the funnel. The roar was louder now, more all-consuming than any sound he'd heard, so loud it drove the thoughts from his head, a million sounds at once, nature screaming for its life. Mary Jean turned, finally, just as it swept back toward them. She raised a hand to her mouth, but made no effort to get away, and they both watched, transfixed, as the full force of the twister scoured away the framework of her house in an instant. It hovered there on the devastated foundation, as if mustering its strength, and then plowed forward into the black walnut. The thunderous crack of the trunk splitting away from itself brought the din to a new height, and the larger half of the massive tree began a slow, dreamlike descent upon them.

Herb grabbed Mary Jean by the left wrist and jerked her backwards off the stool. If she cried out, he didn't hear it, but pain didn't count for much at this point anyway. As the groaning canopy of the black walnut came toppling towards them, he pulled Mary Jean past him and into the mouth of the well. Herb swung his leg up from the hole and pivoted onto his stomach, still gripping her wrist. He'd wrenched his shoulder out of joint, he knew, but that was unavoidable, and dangling her into the hole was the only protection he could offer. A familiar fear flashed through him, the one he used to feel when he'd been thrown by too stout a horse—that long and helpless moment in the dirt before the hooves came down.

He braced himself as best he could as the upper limbs of the black walnut crashed hard across his legs and back, pinning him in place. His breath left him in a rush, and a new, raw pain jolted his body. He strained to raise himself, but there was no squirming free, and he knew he would soon suffocate beneath the weight. But then the wind roiled up through the broken canopy, lifting the tree slightly and dragging it a few feet to the side, where it rammed the mound of earth Herb had piled beside the hole. The stub of a branch knifed through his shirt and gouged a trail along his rib cage, but at least he could gulp another breath. The fallen tree rocked sideways as the wind whirled back into the sky, giving him a precious moment of grace, but the weight was too much for the sky to hold, and the limbs came crashing down again amid a furious hissing of leaves. His vision clouded. Sounds became distant, and everything pulled away, like a tide heading out to sea. A soft haze encircled his mind. He was passing out, he knew—maybe for the last time—and there was nothing he could do to stop it; his will was too weak. And even as his last conscious thought cried against it, his fingers loosened, and he dropped his pregnant daughter into the darkness of the well.

Doc McKinney

Even after it became clear that his office wasn't about to collapse into rubble, Dr. Wallace McKinney was slow to crawl out from under his desk. He'd taken cover when the storm had first begun to shake the small brick building where he'd practiced medicine for the past twenty-two years, and to his surprise, he found that he liked the cool, dark safety of the desk's cubbyhole. The smell of the varnished mahogany was a pleasant relief from the stringent odor of alcohol that usually dominated the room, and even the polished feel of the wood against his cheek was somehow comforting. But what appealed to him most was the sheer novelty of it, of hiding under furniture in the middle of the day. He'd never been beneath his desk before, except to retrieve a pencil or a paper clip. Lately, he'd begun to feel stale—that every examination, every diagnosis, every course of treatment was a tedious re-enactment of work he'd already done. Not déjà vu—at least that would have been interesting. This was more a feeling of numbness, a weary disinterest in the drab routine of his life. Every meal, every conversation, every thought in his head seemed a bland repetition brought forward from the day before, or the day before that. Against such stagnation, even the underside of his desk was a welcome change.

He uncurled himself carefully and eased out into the light, which was far brighter than it had been just minutes earlier. All six panes of his office window were broken, and his wooden blinds, hopelessly tangled and twisted, stretched along the ox-blood cushions of his tufted leather sofa. The sky had cleared almost as soon as the tornado had passed, and now a cheerful sun shone down on whatever damage and clutter had been left behind. The deflated remains of a child's blue wading pool lay draped across the window sill. One end of his red Persian rug was soaked from the driven rain, while papers, broken glass, and even small clumps of municipal shrubbery—boxwoods planted only recently by the Rotary Club around the town square—lay strewn about the room. He had covered his face even before the window had exploded, so he'd witnessed none of what had happened. But the sheer cataclysmic sound of it, together with the knowledge that danger—real, honest-to-God danger—had barged into his placid world, had triggered his excitement in a way he hadn't felt in years, maybe not since the early days with Ellen, when love—or at least desire—had sometimes led him to ridiculous or terrible extremes. But this was different even from that.

He opened the door to his waiting room to check on Mildred. He knew there were no patients to be concerned about. His practice had dwindled over the past couple of years—many of his older patients were dying off and the younger crowd often opted to take their coughs and rashes straight to the new hospital on the west side of town. He'd begun to cut back on his work schedule as a result, and now he no longer saw patients on Fridays at all. Instead, he used the time to read or catch up on his paperwork. For Mildred it was inventory day, and she worked at her desk by the front window cataloging their ample supply of tongue depressors and hypodermics.

The window was shattered in here, too, and the room was awash in soggy, wind-torn back issues of *Life* and *Look* and *Reader's Digest*. His lithographs of waterfowl hung crooked on the paneled walls, but none had fallen. The oak planking of the floor was spotted with puddles in the low spots, the largest one just inside the opened front door, where Mildred now stood silhouetted, her palms pressed to the side of her face, surveying the scene outside.

"Everything all right?" he asked.

She turned toward him, but the glare from the street kept her face in shadow. "The Lord warned us about this," she said, her voice as grim as he'd ever heard it. "Upon the wicked He will rain snares, and fire and brimstone, and a horrible tempest."

He forced a smile, the kind he used when he wasn't sure he understood an ailment. "Surely it's not as bad as all that," he said. He stepped up beside her and stared out across the town square. But for once she was right.

The entire north side lay in ruins. Becker's Jewelry Store had collapsed into rubble, as had the Please-U Beauty Parlor, Sir's Sporting Goods, and Red Goose Shoes. Margie's Dress Shop on the northeast corner had been reduced to a gutted hole. The cannon from the courthouse lawn now protruded from the second floor of the Union National Bank, and, at the center of the square, the courthouse itself had lost both its roof and its clock tower. Smoke billowed from the broken windows above Rexall Drug. Several cars lay overturned on the sidewalks, and others sat buried in their parking spaces beneath uneven piles of debris. Fallen branches covered much of the pavement, and what appeared to be an entire elm tree hung precariously from the roof of the newspaper office. The marquee of the Capitol Theatre now obstructed the intersection of Elk and College, half a block away.

"Look at Church Street," Mildred said. At first he didn't know what she meant, because Church Street was one block over from the square and obscured from view. Then he realized: the steeples. First Episcopal, First Baptist, First Methodist, and First Presbyterian had all lost their steeples. The entire skyline of the town had been wiped away. He turned to Mildred, trying to read her face. Her husband was the minister at First Baptist.

"Do you need to go?" he asked.

She pursed her lips and stared hard toward the empty piece of sky that had once held the First Baptist steeple. "No," she said finally. "The Lord preserveth the faithful."

Dr. McKinney had his doubts about that—a loose brick could fall on good or bad alike, and Reverend Tyree's odds were no better than anybody else's. But he was glad to have Mildred stay, whatever her rationale.

A storm this brutal would mean injuries, perhaps unlike any he had seen before, and he felt a guilty excitement at the prospect. The whole community would turn to him for help. He could make a difference here, a contribution. Ellen and Mary Jean would have no choice but to be proud. For once he could even upstage his brother-in-law, Tom Parsons.

Tom had been basking in public approval for more than a month now, ever since he'd finalized the arrangements for Jersey Joe Walcott to come to town for a boxing exhibition. Boxing was a sordid and barbaric pursuit as far as Dr. McKinney was concerned, and it depressed him to see so much excitement generated over so squalid an event. Now he felt a smug satisfaction when he realized that, in the wake of the tornado, the exhibition would almost certainly have to be cancelled.

As he and Mildred watched, the streets around the square began to fill with people. They emerged slowly at first, disheveled store clerks and bank tellers, bedraggled ladies still clutching their shopping bags, professional men in their water-stained linen suit coats, slack-jawed stock boys and disoriented shop owners, all picking their way carefully between fallen timbers and around heaps of bricks and splintered lumber. A few people coughed in the dust that now drifted down from the exposed rafters of partially toppled buildings, but no one seemed able to speak. The devastation was enough to stun everyone into momentary silence.

"I'd better go see what I can do to help," he said. "You stay here and start putting the office back together. Then get hold of Jimmy Vann—we'll have to file an insurance claim." It felt good to be taking charge again.

28

"Jimmy's got his hands full," Mildred said, and pointed to the northwest corner the square. Dr. McKinney squinted through the afternoon light to where young Jimmy Vann was now shinnying down the drainpipe from his second-floor insurance office above Willard's Barber Shop. It appeared that a substantial portion of his office—several green filing cabinets and a fluttering mass of papers—had made it to the sidewalk ahead of him.

Dr. McKinney sighed and blotted his brow with his handkerchief. "Then just clean up what you can for now, and make a list of everything that got broken." He took off his suit coat and handed it to Mildred.

"We might get some walk-ins," she pointed out.

"Tell them I'll be back directly." He removed his gold cuff links and slipped them into his pants pocket, then rolled his white shirtsleeves to the elbow. "If they're sound enough to get here, they're sound enough to wait."

"Do you want me to call your wife?"

His wife. Of course someone should try to contact his wife. Why hadn't that occurred to him? His own home may have been hit by the storm. He felt himself turning red.

"I'm sure the phone lines are down," he said. "But I guess it's worth a try. If you get through, tell her I might be late for supper."

As if it mattered. Ellen barely spoke to him anymore, and their housekeeper, Grace, prepared all the meals. In the beginning, Ellen's distance had bothered him, but he'd learned to accept it. In some ways, he was grateful for it. When he had to be around her for any length of time, he always felt she was searching him out for clues, as if she suspected him of something. He had to keep his guard up.

He patted Mildred's arm dismissively, then hurried through the cluttered intersection and headed toward the crowd that had begun to gather across from the Rexall. Black plumes of smoke streamed from the old building's tar-covered roof, and flames leapt outward from the window casements on the upper floor.

"You all need to move back," he called out. "That brick façade could come down any minute."

In truth, no one was near enough to the building to be in any danger, even if the walls did somehow come crashing forward. But that wasn't the point. He needed to announce himself, to let them know there was a prudent voice among them. A few people took a half step back, possibly out of politeness, but most simply ignored him, as he'd expected they would. A couple of the younger ones tried to muster up a look of annoyance, but that didn't bother him either. He'd seen that look on his daughter's face at least a thousand times.

His daughter. Didn't she say she might come into town today? He'd told her to stop traveling alone—her due date was barely a fortnight away—but she'd grown too headstrong lately to listen to common sense. Like mother, like daughter, in so many ways.

He'd been patient, nobody could claim otherwise, not even Ellen. How many fathers would build a new home for a daughter who brought such open disgrace to the family? And he'd sure as hell have a thing or two to say to that snot-nosed Malone kid when the boy got back from Korea.

Mary Jean could have done so much better than a stock boy. Four years at Mary Baldwin College could have opened the door for her to be anything she wanted. She could have been a senator's wife. Instead, she'd swollen like a watermelon from her sinful indulgence with Bobby Malone and hadn't lasted even a single semester.

She was probably at home with her mother, writing letters to that son of a bitch right now. But he had drawn the line on that—he had put Mary Jean on notice that she could write her precious boyfriend all the letters she wanted, but no money of his would pay for postage.

"Somebody ought to get hold of Andy Yearwood," said an old man in bib overalls.

That was good advice, and Dr. McKinney wished he'd thought to say it. Andy had recently been named head of the volunteer fire department.

"Andy's right here," said a freckle-faced woman Dr. Mc-Kinney didn't recognize, and all eyes turned toward the slender young fire chief standing at the rear of the crowd, head down, hands shoved deep in his jeans pockets.

Dr. McKinney felt an immediate wave of misgiving. He'd known Andy all his life—had delivered him in fact—and while Andy had always been genial and well-behaved, and had made it all the way to Eagle Scout, there was another issue only Dr. McKinney knew about. The birth had been difficult, the first one for which he'd ever used forceps, and though he'd been able to reshape the boy's tiny head somewhat before presenting him to his mother, he always feared that some damage had been done, that Andy Yearwood was a slow fuse burning toward some frightful detonation.

Andy glanced toward the fire hall just off the square, where the town's fire engine stood ready in the open garage bay door. The storm had skipped over that section of Main Street, leaving the buildings undamaged and the roadway clear, and already a few of the volunteer firemen stood by the front of the truck, waiting. Andy turned back toward the crowd, a pained expression on his face.

"I left the keys in my other pants," he said, and Dr. McKinney felt the boy's embarrassment as if it were his own.

"The keys to the fire truck?" the farmer in the overalls asked.

Andy nodded.

"Maybe you should go home and get them," Dr. McKinney suggested, as gently as he could.

"My car's in the shop," Andy said.

"What shop?" the old farmer demanded.

"That one over there." Andy pointed to Williard's Barber Shop on the north side of the square, where Jimmy Vann was now hopping down from the wheel well of a Nash convertible that was wedged upside down in the double-doorway.

"Good Lord, Andy," said Dr. McKinney. "Are you all right?"

"Yes sir, I'm fine," he said. "I was in the Rexall when it got snatched up."

Dr. McKinney turned to the crowd. "Can anybody here give Andy a ride out to his house so he can get the keys to the fire truck?" A series of popping noises came from somewhere deep inside the drug store.

"I'd be afraid to drive anywhere," said the freckle-faced woman. "There might be power lines down."

The woman was right, and now everyone, including Dr. McKinney, scanned the ground around their feet for potential sources of electrocution. But the utility poles on the square had survived intact, and though all kinds of debris dangled from the wires, none of the lines seemed to have broken loose.

"I'll take him," said the farmer. "My tractor's just two blocks over. It's slow, but it'll climb right through this mess."

"Thank you," said Dr. McKinney. A loud and prolonged cracking sound, maybe from an interior timber giving way, erupted from the burning building. As Andy and the farmer headed down Green Avenue past the funeral home, Dr. McKinney raised his arms to try to regain the attention of the crowd. "Maybe the rest of us can get some of this debris out of the street, clear a path for the fire truck."

"Shouldn't we look around to see if anybody needs help?" asked Miss Lois Brock, a seamstress with chronic indigestion. "There might still be people in some of these buildings."

"First things first, Miss Lois," said Dr. McKinney. He pointed toward the drug store. "Fire spreads. That makes it our most immediate concern. Besides, none of you ladies should be poking around through these damaged buildings. They aren't safe. The best thing we can do right now is make these streets passable."

People looked at one another, probably hoping someone would expose this plan as a bad idea. But no one spoke, and one by one they all moved grudgingly toward the piles of brush and wreckage.

Dr. McKinney tried to set a good example by heading for a large fallen hickory limb that had been torn from one of the commemorative trees planted seventy-five years earlier by the Daughters of the Confederacy on the courthouse lawn.

The limb looked almost airy, with its broad and twisting fan of branches, but it turned out to be much heavier than he anticipated, and he found he could do little more than rustle its leaves. The others had parceled themselves into groups of two or three and were now busy hauling limbs, car fenders, store signs, and other large pieces of wreckage from the street to the courthouse sidewalk. No one moved to pair up with him, so he decided to forget the hickory limb and focus instead on salvage—separating out the various housewares and articles of clothing that might still be returned to the store owners. A gesture like that, he imagined, could have a powerful impact on someone who had just lost everything. Right away he found a pair of Keds—inexplicably, still in their shoebox—and a nightgown from Margie's Dress Shop. He was just in the process of examining a waffle-iron from Malone's Hardware when one of the women in the crowd let out a scream.

It was Mrs. Reese, who played golf with his wife every Tuesday afternoon at the country club. She'd always been an outdoorswoman, perfectly at ease cleaning fish or game, not skittish at all, so whatever she'd found was bound to be interesting. The two men beside her—Dan Massey, who worked for Avalon Dairy, and a beefy plaid-shirted fellow Dr. McKinney didn't know—both stood staring openmouthed at the flattened remnants of what once might have been a large wooden packing crate, the kind an electric cook-stove or an overstuffed armchair might come in.

"You'd better take a gander at this, Doc," Dan Massey said, and everyone dropped whatever trash they were hauling and moved tentatively toward the splintered crate. Dr. McKinney shouldered past a couple of teenagers and made his way up beside Mrs. Reese, who was now mumbling what he took to be fragments of Scripture, her hands knotted together at her chin. He eased her away from the crate.

"You go sit down, Ailene. We'll handle this." He turned her toward one of the stone benches at the edge of the courthouse lawn and gave her a gentle shove, as if she were a toy boat he was launching across a pond. Then he shifted his attention to the crate, which was now completely surrounded by wide-eyed gawkers.

"Holy Jesus," someone said.

Dr. McKinney maneuvered his way back up to the edge of the crate. Even after Ailene Reese's reaction, he wasn't prepared for what he saw.

Tangled inside the frame of the crate lay the naked body of a young white man. His nakedness was disconcerting enough, but even more appalling was the condition of the body. In all Dr. McKinney's years of practicing medicine, he'd never seen a human corpse so badly battered. The storm had shaken this poor man like a rag doll until his bones had turned to paste. Not that the body was particularly bloody, although there was some of that. But every appendage seemed to have been twisted into an unnatural pose, and every joint had been wrenched backward in its socket. The scarred head lolled from the torso on an elongated neck. The man's jaw had been pulled or jarred loose from his skull, distorting his face into so ghoulish an expression that he barely seemed human anymore. Worst of all was the gaping wound in his abdomen.

More than a wound, really.

The man had an extra leg sticking out of his rib cage.

The extra leg wasn't naked. It was dressed in a work-boot and a long black cotton sock.

"Keep the women and young back," ordered Dr. McKinney.

"Keep me back too, Doc," said Dan Massey. "I didn't need to see this shit at all."

Dr. McKinney frowned. He wanted to tell Dan to watch his language, to remind him that there were tender ears present, to scold him for making a bad situation worse. But he held his tongue. Given the circumstance, he knew he'd lose credibility if he sounded like a prig.

Everyone crowded closer to the crate.

"Is he dead?" asked one of the teenaged boys.

"At the very least," said the beefy plaid-shirted man.

Dr. McKinney leaned over the edge to get a better look. How could a tornado drive a leg into someone's chest? He'd heard stories of broom straws piercing telephone poles, but this was a different thing entirely.

"Does anybody know who this man is?" asked Dr. McKinney.

"I've sure never seen him before," Miss Lois offered, and the rest murmured their agreement. The man was a stranger.

"There must be another body," said the plaid-shirted man. "That spare leg came from somewhere." He glanced uneasily over his shoulder.

Dr. McKinney reached out and gripped the heel of the brown work-boot. He shook the leg, to see if it were truly lodged in place. It was definitely stuck, but something about the feel of it didn't seem right. He circled to the other side of the shattered crate for a better view. Most of the exposed portion of the leg—the few inches between the sock and the rib cage—was obscured by blood and disfigurements from the storm, but he could still make out a small section of the leg itself.

What he saw was wood grain. Hickory, it looked like. He carefully poked a spot on the upper calf with his index finger to verify his diagnosis, then straightened and turned to the crowd.

"It's an artificial leg," he announced.

Everyone seemed to take this as good news—but there was still the matter of the dead man.

"Shouldn't we . . . do something?" Miss Lois asked.

"We should get the sheriff," said the plaid-shirted man.

Miss Lois clenched her teeth and sucked in a breath of air as if she were in pain. "But shouldn't we . . ." She indicated the leg. "I mean, it doesn't seem decent to leave the poor man in this condition, even if we don't know who he is."

Dan Massey waved his hands in protest. "Ma'am, you can count me out on that one. I made me a list of things to do today, and I guarantee you, yanking a wooden leg out of a dead man sure as hell wasn't on it."

"If it was me," said the freckle-faced woman, "I sure wouldn't want my family to see some strange leg sticking out of me like that. It's bad enough just being dead."

"The thing's got to come out sometime," said the teenaged boy. "They cain't bury anybody like that."

"I think it's illegal to tamper with a body," said the plaid-shirted man. "This might be a crime scene."

"I don't think that's likely," said Dr. McKinncy. "I'd be surprised if that leg was even the cause of death." He pushed his shirtsleeves further up his arms and grabbed the wooden ankle with both hands. He heaved upward and unplugged the leg from the dead man's chest. It came loose with a wet, sucking noise, and a groan of sympathetic disgust rippled through the crowd. He held the leg low beside the crate so no one would have to see the drippings.

"There still might be another body," said the plaid-shirted man. "That leg didn't come off no showroom floor."

The plaid-shirted man was right, Dr. McKinney realized. Anyone who'd been caught up in the storm so violently as to lose his prosthesis would almost certainly have perished, just like the man in the crate.

And then a second revelation hit him, one that he hardly knew how to process. He stared intently at the leg, the sock, the boot. He examined the wood grain more closely, the time-worn coloration of the clear varnish, the outdated design, the bloody hooks and straps. A flood of hope washed through him. A sinister and degenerate hope, one born of the worst elements of his nature, but one he seized upon completely. This leg might be the herald of his salvation, of his long-awaited delivery.

Not delivery from evil, exactly—no piece of wood could bring him that much grace—yet a delivery from something that had ravaged his family from the very beginning and strangled every chance of happiness he'd ever known. But now that chapter of his life might finally be coming to a close.

God, how he hoped so. For two decades he'd been haunted by the walking ghost of Herb Gatlin. First, do no harm, that was the oath he had sworn to live by. But what oath could bind him when Herb Gatlin was the man lying on the table in his office? Herb had mocked him all through school—for his clumsiness at sports, for his thick glasses, for his awkwardness around girls. For everything, in fact. And while pitiful Wally McKinney had spent years pining for Ellen Parsons, Herb was the one she'd always wanted, the one she'd shamelessly chased after for almost a decade before finally getting him to take the bait. But what kind of life could Ellen have hoped for with Herb Gatlin? He was a cowboy, for God's sake, a rodeo bum, with nothing real to offer. Ellen deserved more than that—she deserved someone with a brain, someone stable and respectable, someone who could give her a big house and a better life. She was halfway to ruin already, the baby just beginning to show. Someone had to save her, someone had to sort out the awful mess, and suddenly there was Herb Gatlin on his operating table, unconscious from the morphine, with a badly broken leg, and suddenly pitiful Wally McKinney wasn't so pitiful anymore, he was Dr. Wallace McKinney, and he had the upper hand for once, and not just the upper hand, but absolute control over how their lives would go from that moment forward. He knew what he had to do, not so much for his own sake, but for Ellen's, and even for her unborn child's. So he'd cut off the leg, cleanly, with cold precision and a clinical detachment, knowing there was no medical reason to do it, but knowing, too, that Ellen was not the sort of woman who'd spend her life caring for a cripple, even if that cripple was her baby's father.

Besides, the leg had a truly nasty break, one of the worst he'd seen, so who's to say there wouldn't have been complications somewhere down the line—an infection, maybe, or a blood clot? Who's to say the leg wouldn't have had to come off eventually anyway? It was a possibility, at least. Maybe the story he'd later told Herb and Ellen was true—that Herb would have died if the leg hadn't come off. Doctors weren't fortune-tellers. They couldn't always know how things might turn out. Maybe he'd saved Herb Gatlin's life. Maybe he had no real reason to feel guilty at all.

But either way, he could put it all behind him at last. It was as if the storm had miraculously washed the past clean. He could start fresh, with no more secrets to guard, no more phony charitable handouts to the man he hated most in the world, no more constant reminder of the darkest failing of his life. The curse was finally being lifted. Half a lifetime's worth of feelings surged wildly through his veins.

He raised the artificial leg from the crate and held it out before him, a torch lighting his clear path into the future. The crowd gasped at this new escalation of gore and impropriety. Blood dribbled onto Dr. McKinney's wrist and trickled along his forearm, but he didn't care. His hand began to shake, causing strands of fresh gore to drool from the stump of the prosthesis to the top of the crate, but that was all right, too, nothing could dampen the spreading joy of this moment he'd waited so long to experience. The entire gruesome spectacle was a glorious baptism, his escape from a final day of reckoning, his holy reintroduction to the world.

"Doc, are you okay?" asked Miss Lois. She rested a tentative hand on his shoulder.

All eyes were now on him, he realized. He felt transparent, his guilt revealed, as if every dark thought burned bright as neon, telling everyone what had happened between him and Herb Gatlin. He flushed with embarrassment.

"I know this leg," he said quietly, and lowered it to his side. His pathetic soul was altogether lost, that much was clear. He knew it from his tight grip on the hickory. He knew it from the joy that bore him up.

Mary Jean McKinney

As her mind bobbed gently to the surface and her eyelids fluttered open to the absolute darkness surrounding her, Mary Jean's first conscious thought was the worst: She was already dead and buried. Then she remembered the string of moments that had brought her here—Mr. Gatlin dangling her into the well as the twister bore down on them, her flailing about for a handhold and finding the rope ladder just as Mr. Gatlin released his grip, the clumsy descent, rung by rung, while the air howled overhead, and, finally, the collapse onto the rocky floor of the well. She wasn't sure whether some trick of her pregnancy had diverted too much blood from her brain, or whether she had simply been overcome by fear, but whatever the case, a lightheadedness had swirled through her thoughts like water circling a drain, and she had fainted.

Apparently, she'd been unconscious for hours. The rainwater had nearly dried from the front of her dress, even in the chilly dank of the well-bottom. Night had fallen, leaving her in the most complete darkness she'd ever known. A stiffness had settled into her neck and back, probably from lying so long in a single, awkward position, and a chill ached through her bones. Her hip throbbed against a partly buried rock. Her left shoulder burned when she tried to lift her arm—she must have pulled a muscle when she'd first tumbled backwards into the hole. The rear of her dress was soaked through, as if she'd sat in a puddle, though the ground around her felt only slightly damp beneath her fingers. She shifted her weight and began to grope with her right hand along the curve of the dirt wall, feeling for the ladder. When she found a rung, she pulled herself to her feet and stood there for a minute, fighting a wave of dizziness and nausea. She had to hook her arm through the ladder to keep from sinking back to the floor of the well. The baby had never felt so heavy inside her.

Why had Mr. Gatlin left her here alone?

She took a deep breath and let it out slowly. The last of her grogginess was lifting, and she felt certain she could scale the ladder in the dark, even in her present condition. But before her foot could find the first rung, a sudden cramping flared through her lower abdomen, and, with a quick gasp, she doubled over, scraping her cheekbone on the jagged wall. It occurred to her that her face was probably bleeding, but she didn't care, not now, not while this other thing was happening. She wrapped her arms around her stomach and tried to take a breath, but a sob erupted in its place, followed by a long, low moan. Somewhere inside her a bare fist was squeezing a white-hot coal, and her whole being seemed to knot itself around that core. She must have hurt herself more seriously than she'd realized. She moaned again, louder this time, as the wave continued through her, battering whatever got in its way. She heard herself wail in the darkness.

And then, as abruptly as it had arrived, the wave subsided. The knot released itself, and all she felt was a cold, fresh layering of sweat.

"Mr. Gatlin!" she cried out. "I need some help!" She listened for a response, but none came. In fact, beyond the halting whisper of her own ragged breath, she heard no noises at all—no crickets, no wind, no pattering rain, no katydids buzzing in the leaves, no night owl sounding out its prey. For a second time, she wondered if she might be dead, wondered if her spirit might be lingering in some empty, silent limbo. Nothing in this world was familiar, nothing but the chill and the dark.

But something in the brittle stillness finally broke, and sound began to filter through from somewhere—faint and fragmented at first, but growing louder and more clear. Voices. She heard voices floating in the night air. She couldn't pick out any words, but someone was talking, she was sure of it. Two people, coming closer.

"I'm here," she called. "I'm in the well."

The voices stopped.

"I'm here!" she cried again.

She grabbed the rough rope and began to pull herself up the ladder. The climb was difficult without the use of her left arm, but, little by little, she managed it. She was nearly halfway to the surface when twin beams of light crested the edge of the hole and found her clinging to the crumbling dirt wall. A warm relief surged through her as the beams settled on her upturned face. The glare was blinding, but she didn't mind. She opened her mouth to speak, but before she could utter a syllable, someone screamed—a child maybe—and one of the lights blinked out.

The other light held steady.

"Miss Mary Jean? That you down there?" The woman's voice was deep and lilting, and Mary Jean had known it all her life.

"Nolla Rae!" A small laugh bubbled from her throat. She struggled up another rung.

"What in the world are you doing in that hole?" Nolla Rae asked.

"Right now I'm trying to get out," she answered, pulling herself further up the ladder.

"Can you make it all right?" Nolla Rae repositioned her flashlight to illuminate the remaining rungs.

"I'm okay on this part," Mary Jean said. "But I think I'll need a hand when I get to the top."

"You scared the bejeezus out of little Jerry Lee. He thought you was some kinda haint." She let out a low chuckle. "Cain't say as I blame him, neither. You quite a sight, coming up out of the ground like that."

"I think something's wrong," Mary Jean said. Her head and shoulders emerged from the hole, but with no more rungs to pull herself up by, she'd run out of leverage. She gripped the ladder stake with her right hand and tried to heave her stomach up past the lip of the well, but it was no use. She was stuck.

"Sugar, there's all kind of things wrong," Nolla Rae told her. "The whole town's changed like you wouldn't believe." She shone the beam on Mary Jean's face again. "And you still bleeding, looks like." Nolla Rae set the flashlight aside, its beam now disappearing into the ruined canopy of the fallen black walnut tree. "But first things first," she said, and abruptly grabbed Mary Jean by her bad arm and dragged her up out of the well. Mary Jean cried out as her shoulder popped loudly.

Nolla Rae released her arm and picked up the flashlight. "Lord, girl, what did I just do?" she asked, scanning Mary Jean with the light.

Mary Jean lay still and braced herself for more pain, but none came, not like she expected. She sat up in the dirt and tentatively moved her arm. It felt better.

"I don't know," she said. "There was something wrong with my shoulder, but I think it's fixed now."

Nolla Rae touched the shoulder gently. "Well, don't say nothing to your daddy," she laughed. "He'll say I'm practicing without a license."

Mary Jean looked at the darkness around her. The landscape here wasn't much brighter than the bottom of the well. The black walnut lay shattered only a few feet away, but she couldn't even distinguish the trunk from the branches. Low clouds obscured the moon and stars, and no lights came from town or any of the neighborhoods nearby. The only other light she saw was the bouncing beam from Jerry Lee's flashlight, seventy yards further up the gravel road. He was probably heading for the swing on his mother's porch—assuming the swing and the porch were still there.

"Is your house . . ." she began, and stopped.

"The twister passed us by," said Nolla Rae, "which is more than most folks can say tonight."

Nolla Rae's house was old and small—a three-room tar paper shack with no electricity or plumbing, and no heat but a cook-stove in the kitchen. But it had the advantage of being tucked below a sheer outcropping of rock near the top of the hill, so it was always protected from any severe weather that came in from the north. Mary Jean had played at that house as a child, climbing on the mountain of tires in the front yard and on the tin roof of the chicken coop in the back. Nolla Rae had been her babysitter, the one who'd watched after her when her mother had gone off to shop or play bridge or golf. It seemed she had spent half her childhood on the rickety porch where Jerry Lee might now be waiting, and when her father had asked where she wanted her own house built, she'd chosen this spot simply because it was close to Nolla Rae's.

She never told her father that, of course, because he'd have found her reasons too sentimental. Besides, he was happy with her choice for reasons of his own—the land was cheap, for one thing, and it was only four blocks from the town square, which meant she wouldn't need an automobile.

"I'm sorry for what happened to your place," Nolla Rae offered. "But at least you didn't lose the foundation. I bet it won't take but a week for those boys to get that frame back up again."

Mary Jean got carefully to her feet and steadied herself against one of the arching limbs of the black walnut.

"Mr. Gatlin?" she called. "Are you here?"

"Nobody here but us," said Nolla Rae, but there was an uncertainty in her words.

"He was with me when the tornado hit," said Mary Jean. "He's the one put me in the well."

Nolla Rae lowered her voice to a whisper. "You mean Mr. Gatlin with the bad leg?"

"Yes ma'am. I'm worried he might be hurt." She took the flashlight from Nolla Rae and began to shine it through the tangle of broken branches. "He could be caught up under some of these tree limbs," she said. She bent a fan-shaped branch aside and ran the flashlight beam along the length of the split trunk. But there was no sign of Mr. Gatlin.

Nolla Rae put an arm around Mary Jean's shoulder and pulled her gently away from the fallen tree, away from the well. "Oh, sugar," she said. "They was talking about Mr. Gatlin in town this evening. They say the twister got him."

Mary Jean felt the flashlight slip through her fingers, watched the beam dance across her ravaged yard and then wink out. Her stomach dropped, and for a moment she thought she might faint again. Nolla Rae kept a firm grip on her shoulder, holding her upright, but the dizziness from the floor of the well returned, swamping her in nausea.

Nolla Rae spoke again, but Mary Jean's mind was too far away now. Though the words reached her, they arrived empty of meaning, a jumble of useless sounds, with nothing to offer beyond the single cold reminder that, even with Nolla Rae's kind hands keeping her steady, she was alone on a narrow and thorny path. She began to shiver uncontrollably.

She felt herself being led away, up the long dark hill toward Nolla Rae's house, but that was no comfort anymore, not if a man were dead because of her. Poor Mr. Gatlin, who had told her they shouldn't be out in the storm. So why hadn't she listened? Why did she always stiffen inside when anyone told her what she ought to do? What was wrong with her that having her own way meant more than doing what was smart or safe or right?

It was a part of her she despised, and yet she seemed unable to change it. Nolla Rae had told her once that she'd dug in her heels the day she was born, and Mary Jean knew it was true, that she had lived her life with her head lowered, ready to ram forward under almost any circumstance, ignoring every warning. But why? What had made her such a misfit, permanently at odds with the world around her? Why had she grown up so resentful of her father's rules, of his attitudes, of his smothering attention to her life? And where was her mother in all this, other than passed out in the bedroom from her fifth gin and tonic?

And why did she resent this baby inside her, whose very existence, she knew, was her own willful doing? Why did she resent her teachers from high school and everyone at Mary Baldwin and the workmen hammering on her house and poor Mr. Gatlin, for whom she felt an inexpressible sorrow, and even Bobby, God help her, whom she'd manipulated so easily into impregnating her before he shipped out, and why, why on earth would she have done that, why trap herself into a life of changing diapers and waiting silently, angrily, for her husband to come home, as her mother had done, merely to find fault, as she knew she would, when he arrived each evening from the hardware store, tired and inattentive, and to argue with him over which movies to see, or what brand of toothpaste or cereal to buy, or what color of paint belonged on the living room walls—things that should carry no weight for people in love, but things they would succumb to anyway—and now she saw that even if Bobby did come safely home from the war, he would soon tire of the selfishness she'd inherited from her parents, he would stop loving her, which would crack her heart into more pieces than she could put together again, and they'd both be miserable, locked in a life of petty bickering, and the baby screaming in its bassinet, and laundry piling on the floor, and dishes stinking in the sink, and yet this marriage, this union she was plummeting toward, as bleak and strangled as it might turn out to be, was still what she prayed for, night and day, because even a lifetime of small disappointments would be better than the alternative, if the alternative kept Bobby from ever coming home at all, which was a possibility that grew larger each day—she understood that now—even though she'd hidden from it for weeks, from the paralyzing fear that he was already dead, telling herself the flimsiest of lies, that there could be problems with the post office, that his daily letters home had stopped because of some unforeseeable breakdown in the army's delivery system, that sacks of mail had somehow tumbled from the boat or plane and drifted now in the aimless currents of the ocean's dark bottom.

The pain in her abdomen began to build again.

"Watch your step now, sugar," Nolla Rae said softly as she helped her up onto the porch. "Mr. Statten's asleep inside—he's got an early day tomorrow—so you best stay out here."

Mary Jean looked around. Jerry Lee sat with his flashlight on the slatted porch swing, his knees drawn up to his chest, watching her intently. He focused the beam on her face.

"I'll fetch you out a blanket for that chill," Nolla Rae went on.

Mary Jean realized her teeth were chattering. Goosebumps had risen along the backs of her arms.

"Thank you," she said. She squinted into the light and tried to smile. "Jerry Lee, I think I need to sit down. You mind if I join you on that swing?"

She couldn't make out his face, but she could see that he wasn't moving.

"Boy, I'll jerk a knot in you," Nolla Rae hissed, and he scooted sideways to make room. "Now, Jerry Lee, you be nice to Miss McKinney. There's nothing to be afraid of. And quit shining that light in her face. That's not polite."

"She got blood," he said, his voice small and wavering.

"That's 'cause she hurt herself. Now you hush."

Nolla Rae stared at the boy until he sighed and switched off the light. Then she stepped quietly into the house, taking care not to let the screen door clack shut behind her. Mary Jean settled herself carefully onto the swing. The cramp was knotting more tightly now, but the pain was still manageable. She knew if she moaned or cried out it would frighten Jerry Lee, so she tried to shift her mind to something else.

"How old are you now?" she asked.

"Seven," he told her.

"I remember when you were just a baby," she said. "I used to visit your mama a lot when I was younger."

He had nothing to say to that, so she tried again.

"I'm not a haint," she said. But she heard the strain in her voice.

"Daddy says we don't believe in haints," he told her. He shifted away from her, cramming himself against the armrest, and the swing wobbled on its chains.

"You don't sound convinced," she teased him. "What's your mama say?"

"She says she knows what she knows."

Mary Jean touched her hand to her face. Her cheek and her forehead were crusted with blood or dirt, or maybe both. "I must look a sight," she said.

Then the cramp hit her in earnest. She gritted her teeth and shut her eyes tight, but the pain was too much for her. She snorted out a few short, wheezing breaths.

"You breathe like Rufus," Jerry Lee said.

She almost laughed. Rufus was an old stray in the neighborhood who'd been ransacking Nolla Rae's garbage cans for as long as she could remember. She'd once come close enough to touch his tail. She opened her eyes again.

Nolla Rae emerged quietly from the house with a blanket folded over one arm and her hands cupped around a small mixing bowl. She set the bowl carefully on the swing and then wrapped Mary Jean's shoulders in the blanket. The wool felt scratchy on her skin, but she was glad for the kindness.

"I'm sorry we got no hot water," Nolla Rae said as she drew a white washrag from the bowl and wrung it out. "But cold's better anyway if you're bleeding." She blotted the rag against the side of Mary Jean's face.

"Hurts," Mary Jean managed to say.

"I know it, sugar, but we cain't leave a scrape this dirty."

"No, my stomach." She clenched her jaw and clutched the wooden arm of the swing. "Oh, God, it hurts," she said, her voice tightening to a whine. Jerry Lee scrambled to the porch and ran inside the house. Water sloshed from the bowl as the swing bounced in its chains.

"What kind of pain?" Nolla Rae asked, but the wave was cresting now and Mary Jean couldn't sort out an answer. Nolla Rae put her hand on Mary Jean's brow. "Is it cramps, or something else?"

"Worse," Mary Jean said, and a sob escaped her. "Like I ate poison."

Nolla Rae let out a sigh. She draped the washrag over the arm of the swing, then moved the water bowl to the porch floor and eased herself down beside Mary Jean. "Just ride it out," she said. "We'll talk when it passes."

Mary Jean wanted to argue. What if it didn't pass? She'd had egg and olive sandwiches for lunch—maybe the mayonnaise had been bad. Or what if she'd somehow got into rat poison, like strychnine or arsenic? Or drain cleaner? Most people kept that stuff around, and accidents did happen. But in the half second it took for these fears to form, the pain somersaulted forward through every nerve in her body, and all she could do was wail hoarsely across the darkened porch. She dug her fingernails into her palms to try to distract herself, but it was no use; the pain now swallowed her whole—it was a wolf, a giant snake, a whale—and she was caught inside it.

And then it eased up. Calmed down. Melted away into the soft, cool corners of the yard. Her breath came more evenly, and she was herself again. She pulled the blanket close around her and cried quietly with relief.

"You still poisoned?" Nolla Rae asked.

Mary Jean shook her head.

"I didn't think so." She folded her arms across her breasts and tapped her foot methodically on a loose board. "Was this the first time?"

Mary Jean sniffed and wiped her nose on her sleeve. "No, ma'am. The first was a little while ago, when I was down in the well."

"You know what it is, don't you?"

Mary Jean shook her head again, more vigorously this time. "It can't be that. Daddy says I'm not due for another two weeks."

Nolla Rae snorted and rocked back in the swing. "Yeah, doctors like timetables. But sometimes a woman's body got plans of its own."

Mary Jean didn't know what to say to that. They sat in silence for a full minute, Nolla Rae easing the swing back and forth with her foot while Mary Jean picked up the washrag and gingerly dabbed at the remaining blood on her face.

"It'll come back, won't it?" Mary Jean finally asked.

"Like a railroad train," Nolla Rae said. "And you tied to the tracks."

"What should I do?"

"Pick yourself a spot to have it," she said. "That's about all the choice you got left."

"Then I need to go to the hospital," Mary Jean told her.

"That's a spot," Nolla Rae agreed.

"Can you drive me there?"

Nolla Rae shrugged. "Got no automobile."

"Can't we call an ambulance?"

"Storm took out the phone lines," she said. "But it wouldn't matter anyway. Every street in town's tore up. Cain't get half a block without finding somebody's roof in the road."

"Then I'll walk," she said, abruptly pushing herself up from the swing. She dropped the washrag into the bowl and walked, unsteadily, to the front of the porch. If she really were about to have her baby, she wanted to be somewhere safe, somewhere with bright lights and wide, clean hallways. A place with doctors and nurses to take care of anything that might go wrong. And ether for the pain. She pulled the blanket from her shoulders and tried to hang it across the porch rail, but it slid to the floor.

"You in no condition," said Nolla Rae. She rose from the swing and pulled open the screen door. "Jerry Lee," she said softly, "come out here."

The boy emerged from the doorway and stood silently before his mother. She leaned over and touched her head to his. "I want you to run around back of the house and fetch me Daddy's wheelbarrow."

The boy stepped away from her. "There's . . . things back there," he said. "I hear 'em sometimes."

"Just clap your hands," she told him. "That'll scare all the bad things away. You can sing, too, if you want. Now hurry up and do what I said."

Jerry Lee walked past Mary Jean with his head down and then disappeared quickly around the side of the house, furiously clapping his hands. "Jesus loves the little children," he sang, his reedy voice fading into the night air. "All the children of the world . . ."

Mary Jean gripped the support post and leaned her weight against it. Nolla Rae was right—she'd never make it to the hospital on her own. But she wasn't crazy, either.

"Nolla Rae, I don't think a wheelbarrow is such a good idea," she said. "Besides, I couldn't ask Mr. Statten to do a thing like that."

"Mr. Statten's not available," Nolla Rae said curtly. "I'll be taking you myself."

A loud clatter came from somewhere behind the house.

Mary Jean hardly knew what to say. A wheelbarrow? How was that even possible? The hospital was out by the fairgrounds, clear on the other side of town—nine or ten blocks away. She'd never used a wheelbarrow herself, so she wasn't too clear on how easily they operated, but surely Nolla Rae couldn't haul her all the way there without help.

Nolla Rae seemed to read her thoughts. "It's all downhill," she said. "Won't be a problem at all."

Jerry Lee rounded the corner of the house, awkwardly guiding the wheelbarrow ahead of him.

"It had bricks," he said. "I had to tump it over."

"That's a good boy," Nolla Rae told him. "I'll give you a penny when I get home."

"I scared the bad things away," he said.

The screen door banged open and Mr. Statten stepped out onto the porch. Mary Jean couldn't make out his face in the darkness, but from his movements she guessed he was pulling his suspenders up over his shoulders.

"What's all the racket out here?" he demanded. "Nolla Rae, you know I got to go to Huntsville in the morning."

"Mary Jean McKinney's done gone into labor," Nolla Rae explained. "I'm borrowing your wheelbarrow to take her to the hospital."

Mr. Statten took a step toward Mary Jean and looked into her face, then at her swollen belly, then at the wheelbarrow, which Jerry Lee had propped beside the porch step.

"Awright, then," he said, "but this young'un ought to be in bed." He turned and went back into the house.

"You heard your daddy," said Nolla Rae, and Jerry Lee followed his father into the house. "Now you," she said, turning to Mary Jean, "get in the wheelbarrow. We need to cover some ground before the next contraction."

Mary Jane stepped down into the yard. "How . . . ?"

"I'll tip it forward," she said. "You just cradle into it, and lean back."

Mary Jean did as she was told, and Nolla Rae wheeled her from the yard to the street. Gravel popped beneath the tire as they wobbled their way ridiculously down the slope. On any other day of her childhood, she would have thought it fun to ride like this through the night. But childhood was over now. Her new house had vanished in a puff of wind. Mr. Gatlin was dead. The baby was coming too soon, tearing her body apart. And Bobby was missing in Korea.

She started to say something to Nolla Rae, something trivial, about Rufus the dog, or haints, or bricks in the back-yard—anything to keep a conversation going, anything to keep herself distracted.

But she changed her mind. Sometimes it was better not to talk. Bobby was lost somewhere in the war, and talking was a waste of breath.

But he'd come home soon, he had to. She needed him, she saw that now, really needed him, clear down to her bones. She'd never told him that, but she would, first thing, and then he'd smile and scoop her up and pull this rusty knife blade from her heart.

For now, though, she needed to focus. She needed to pre-pare herself. She needed to greet the next pain differently, whenever it arrived.

Ellen Parsons McKinney

Ellen McKinney woke to a glaring sun and a throbbing headache. Both were her fault. She'd forgotten to pull the shades before she got into bed the night before, which accounted for the sun, and she'd forgotten to stop drinking after her third Manhattan, which accounted for the headache.

At first she thought she'd overslept. Not that she had to be up at any particular time, but still, it seemed wrong to have completely missed both her husband's return from work and his departure again the next morning. It wasn't until she wandered into her daughter's room looking for headache powder and found the bed still freshly made that she realized neither Wallace nor Mary Jean had come home last night at all.

She tried to telephone his office, but apparently the previous day's storm had knocked a limb onto the lines somewhere, and the call wouldn't go through. At first she thought she should just sit and wait for them both to return, bringing with them the explanations and comic anecdotes that no doubt accompanied whatever missteps had stranded them in town overnight. *All things come to those who wait*, she reminded herself, and waiting, after all, was what she did best, was the thing she'd practiced to perfection over the past twenty years, day after day, guarding the home front, keeping the dogs out, keeping the air conditioner running, keeping her lipstick straight, keeping her doorbell polished for the Avon lady and the Fuller Brush man and the little Cub Scouts, in their blue uniforms and yellow neckerchiefs, selling jars of brightly colored candy. She was the patient queen of the castle—and it was a castle, really, she could still take comfort in that, two stories of fine gray stone with a parapet for sunbathing above the garage. From her earliest days she had taken the story of the Three Little Pigs to heart, and when Wallace had asked her to marry him oh-so-long-ago, she had told him yes—if he would promise to build her a house of brick or stone. She would not spend her life in a house of sticks, waiting for the walls to come down.

But she soon realized, as her head cleared enough for worry to take hold, that waiting wasn't good enough. She would get dressed and drive the new Packard Sedan into town to find out what had happened.

The dress she chose was modest—a flowing floral print with a scooped neckline to accentuate her string of pearls. She'd bought it down in Huntsville at Newberry's, part of their new spring line. But she wouldn't wear her gloves today, she decided. A warm March morning called for a more casual approach. She might not even wear a hat.

As she sat at her vanity putting on her makeup, she noticed an unflattering darkness around her eyes. She could cover it up for now, of course, but she might have to start taking better care of herself. Get more sleep, perhaps. She wasn't yet fifty, but that landmark was looming on the horizon. She was thin enough, thank God—or thanks, rather, to her drawing the line after only one child. But if she wanted to keep herself pretty enough for a man to come home to, she would have to start buying more creams.

The drive in from the ridge was uneventful. She had thought she might stop off at the fruit stand by the cotton gin on her way into town, but it was closed for some reason. So was the driving range and the roller rink, she noticed, which was odd for a Saturday. Then as she approached the single-lane bridge at the south end of town, she realized that hers was virtually the only car on the road. Was it a holiday she had somehow lost track of?

But then she saw the line of sawhorses that stretched across the highway at the entrance to the iron-girdered bridge. A hand-painted sign reading "Bridge Out" was tacked to the center sawhorse.

But that was ridiculous, the bridge wasn't out at all. It looked perfectly fine—or at least as fine as a monstrosity like that could look. God, she hated that bridge. The people who designed it, the engineers or whoever they were, must have thought this was one of those Communist countries in Eastern Europe, where everything was supposed to look hideous. This bridge was nothing but a claustrophobic crisscrossing of massive rust-colored beams studded with knobby bolts, and it ruined anyone's first impression of the town. Lincoln was a decent, God-fearing community, and it deserved better. Someday she'd get herself on the right committee and have the eyesore torn down and replaced with something more aesthetically appealing, something more airy, with graceful, swooping cables like she'd seen on bridges in California. And maybe now was the time to look into it, if the sign on the bridge were correct.

Then she realized: If the bridge had been closed, that might explain why her husband hadn't driven home last night. He'd have had to go halfway to Winchester just to get across the river. Detours were always tedious; she understood that perfectly well. He and Mary Jean might have chosen to avoid the drive and stay the night in his office. She knew his couches were perfectly comfortable—she'd picked them out herself.

So maybe she had her answer already. Maybe she didn't need to go into town after all. She turned left into the empty parking lot at the Skate Haven roller rink, thinking that would be a roomy enough place to turn around. Surely there were things she had to do this morning back at the house, craft projects she'd postponed from other days. Or maybe she could start a garden of some sort. Besides, she didn't like to drive on sunny days. The glare through the windshield made the air hot, so she inevitably had to roll down the windows to keep from sweating. Then her hairdo would get mussed from the wind.

But an odd misgiving nagged at the back of her brain, and instead of turning the Packard around, she drove it to the far end of the lot, to a guardrail above the riverbank, and shut off the motor. The Stone Bridge, a relic from the previous century, was just fifty yards farther downstream, and though it had become too unstable to support automobiles or horses, it was still open to foot traffic. She could cross the river there and be at her husband's office in a matter of minutes. Of course, that route meant walking by the jailhouse, a three-story brick embarrassment that loomed above the opposite bank. She knew she'd be safe enough, but still, just walking past the place struck her as an unsavory prospect—she had no desire to be watched by strange men from behind barred windows. But sometimes people had to do things they didn't like.

She hadn't set foot on the Stone Bridge in nearly a quarter of a century, and she was shocked by its state of disrepair. It had once been a beautiful landmark—a majestic arch atop five stately columns of stacked white stone. Now the mortar was crumbling and parts of the columns had disappeared into the river. From a distance the bridge still appeared charming—she would have been the first to say so—and it had always been the perfect choice for a souvenir postcard of the town. But the way it had been allowed to disintegrate was an absolute shame. How could the city fathers have let this happen? Why hadn't anyone started a fund to restore it? The Stone Bridge had stood for nearly a hundred years—it was a part of the town's heritage. Such blatant disregard for their history was inexcusable. The past was a treasure to be acknowledged and preserved. She resolved to write a letter to the editor.

The archway itself was overgrown with grass, so that her alligator high heels became an immediate handicap. She removed her shoes and walked as delicately up the slope of the span as she could, hoping not to snag her new nylons.

She had just crossed over the peak of the arch when she felt a stinging in her foot. A childhood memory flashed through her mind, and she knew at once she'd stepped on a prickly pear hidden in the long grass.

"Sugar!" she hissed, and hobbled to the rock wall at the side of the bridge. She sat as carefully as she could to avoid dirtying her dress and snapped open her pocketbook to rummage for her eyebrow tweezers. She found them tucked inside her leather cigarette case, right alongside her Viceroys, though she couldn't imagine how they got there. Funny where things ended up sometimes.

As she quickly discovered, there was no lady-like way to get a good look at the bottom of her foot. She turned her back to the jailhouse to gain as much privacy as she could, tugged her dress up well past her knees, and propped her injured foot across her thigh. She'd left her reading glasses at home, so she had to lean in close to locate the needles. It was an awkward and unflattering position, she realized, and she smiled at the thought of how absurd she must look.

She found only two needles and plucked them out easily. But as she rubbed her instep to soothe away the sensitivity, she thought she glimpsed a slight movement further along the wall, something skittering, perhaps. She turned quickly to look, but it was gone. It may have been only the shadow of a bird, or even a bird itself returning to its nest. There were gaps and crevices all along the wall where stones had broken loose, and she knew that barn swallows loved to nest in such places. She'd always been fascinated by barn swallows. As a girl she had spent long hours watching the activity around the nests above her porch. Once the eggs had hatched, the parent birds worked tirelessly, from dawn until dark, scavenging insects to feed their chicks. But the chicks complained constantly, chirped without ceasing whenever their mouths were empty, and fought over the food when it arrived. Inevitably, one of the chicks would miss a feeding and grow weak. Then the others would push it from the nest. The contrast had always amazed her—the selfless parents and the ungrateful, murderous young.

She picked up her shoes and her pocketbook and moved quietly toward the first crevice, a gap maybe two feet wide in the center of the wall. She held her breath and leaned out over the hole. The chicks weren't chirping, so they might not have hatched yet. That meant the mother would still be sitting on the nest, and she didn't want to startle her. But she did want to see her, the beautiful bright blue highlighting the brown fork at the tail. It was rare to see a barn swallow from above.

She peered into the shadowy hole, but could make out nothing. Again, she wished she'd brought her glasses. She leaned her face closer.

"Hello, little birdie," she whispered.

In a rush of small shrieks and hisses, water rats poured from the hole.

Ellen straightened up screaming, and began to dance wildly around as the fleeing creatures scurried over her bare feet and between her legs. She dropped her shoes and her pocketbook and ran, still screaming, the rest of the way across the bridge. From there she kept going, down the lush, green approach, then onto the freshly tarred roadway that led up the hill into town. By the time she came parallel to the jailhouse, her lungs were bursting and her throat had tightened into a painful knot. But even as she stumbled to a stop, too stricken to go on, she couldn't set aside the terror. Something had split open inside her, and she shuddered uncontrollably at the thought of vermin touching her skin. She could still feel them. Their tiny claws and their black, hairy bodies. It was just too awful. She stood there in the middle of the oily street, shaking and gasping for breath.

"Ma'am, are you all right?"

She spun to face this new assault, and would have shrieked, but her voice was too shredded to muster more than a raspy gurgle.

"You look like you seen a ghost," he said, stepping toward her. He was a pleasant looking man, round and ruddy-cheeked, somehow familiar, and she quickly realized that her state of panic was no longer appropriate.

"Rats," she said, struggling to compose herself. "On the bridge." She smoothed her dress and touched her palm to the side of her hair, which was still sprayed firmly in place.

He squinted toward the river and ran his pudgy fingers through his thinning blond hair.

"There's a lot of them down there," he said. "Not just rats, neither. Snakes, frogs, muskrats, possum, coons, you name it." He shrugged. "All critters like water, I guess." He wiped his hand on his pants and held it out to her. "I'm Marshall Raby, by the way."

She forced a tight smile and reluctantly accepted his hand. "I'm pleased to meet you, Marshall," she said, her voice a hoarse whisper. "I'm Ellen McKinney." She looked at her feet, which were sticky with road tar, and cleared her throat. "I apologize for my unkempt appearance."

"Ran right out of your shoes, did you?" He chuckled in a way that set her teeth on edge. "Ma'am, that's nothing to apologize for. We get rats here at the jail sometimes. They come right up through the toilets." He shook his head and grunted. "We all leave dents in the ceiling when that happens."

He seemed rather informal for a marshal, but she supposed her shoelessness invited that sort of thing.

"I hate to impose," she said, "but would it be possible for you to go down there and get my pocketbook and shoes for me? I'm afraid I just dropped everything in the fever of the moment."

His eyebrows narrowed, and a frown crept over his face. "I'm sorry, ma'am, but that wouldn't be possible at all. I can't leave the premises."

"But my wallet is down there," she protested, "and the key to the Packard. I can't just leave them."

He chewed the inside of his cheek and nodded. "That could be a problem," he admitted.

"Then surely you can do me this one favor," she said. "And after all," she added, her voice growing more insistent, "I'm a taxpayer. Isn't part of your job to help people like me?"

He looked confused. "Not that I know of," he said. "Besides, the sheriff would skin me alive."

That made no sense. Wallace had taken her to see plenty of Western movies. She'd followed the exploits of Roy Rogers and Gene Autry and Tim Holt and Tex Ritter. She knew what kind of authority a marshal had.

"But doesn't a marshal outrank a sheriff?" she asked, playing her trump card.

He opened his mouth and stared at her blankly. Then his face gradually reshaped itself into a broad, toothy smile.

"I think I see the confusion," he said. "I'm not *the* marshal. My *name* is Marshall." He chuckled again. "That's a good one. I'll have to tell that to the fellows."

"Then . . . what are you?" she asked, her level of uneasiness beginning to rise.

"I'm a trustee here at the jail," he told her.

She took a slow step backward.

"And you're . . . loose?"

"Oh, we're all loose today," he said, "all except Bryce Hatton. He's locked up for shooting his cousin." He looked up toward one of the windows on the third floor. "The sheriff didn't want Bryce on cleanup detail. Afraid he might turn rabbit."

The world whirled around her, and her face and neck felt suddenly clammy.

Marshall raised his palms as if she were holding him at gunpoint. "But don't get nervous on my account," he assured her. "I'm no criminal. Well, technically, I guess I am, but not the way most people think of criminals. I just had me some errors in judgment. Misunderstandings, really, is all they were. Even the sheriff would tell you, Marty Raby's a good egg. That's why he left me in charge."

Marty Raby. Oh, dear Lord. She remembered that name from grammar school. But there was no conceivable way she could ask this convict if he were the boy who had sat behind her in Miss Goodman's class, the boy who'd taken her to the seventh grade dance. Her first date, ever. He was the first boy she'd held hands with. Not her first love, thank God, she felt certain of that, but at least her first distraction. True, that boy hadn't been quite so rotund, so balding. So imprisoned. But it truly was him, she saw that now. She remembered the bulging blue eyes, the too-wide smile, the grating laugh.

For a moment she was terrified of being recognized.

Then she began to wonder why he didn't recognize her. Had she changed that much? Had she lost all of whatever it was that had once made Marty Raby send her notes in study hall and wait by her locker and give her candy on Valentine's Day?

"I have to go now," she said, though she didn't know where. The bridge was unthinkable, but so was walking barefooted downtown.

"Don't step on any live wires," he said cheerfully.

What live wires was he talking about? Was this some current expression, like *don't take any wooden nickels*, or *don't let the bedbugs bite*? Somehow she didn't seem to understand anything Marty Raby said anymore, and that annoyed her.

"I have business downtown," she said by way of excusing herself. "I'm meeting my husband, Dr. Wallace McKinney."

Marty Raby raised his eyebrows. "Oh, I know who he is. Dr. McKinney's the one identified the leg."

Was the man brain damaged? Did he not know how to carry on a coherent conversation? She was on the verge of setting him straight about her husband when a loud banging noise from a third floor window interrupted her. Marty Raby scowled up toward the source of the racket.

"Bryce, I told you to cut that out," he hollered. "Don't make me tell the sheriff on you." The banging continued. He shook his head and sighed. "Another error in judgment on my part," he said. "Bryce asked for a hammer so he could hang a picture on his cell wall. Now he's trying to knock out the bars on his window."

"Oh, my word," she said.

"The sheriff ought to be back from cleanup detail before too long. That'll put a stop to it."

"I don't understand," she said. "What cleanup detail?"

He glanced briefly toward Bryce Hatton's window and leaned in toward her. "Truth be told," he said, his voice low and confidential, "it's really more of a search-and-recovery detail. The sheriff didn't want regular citizens finding any more corpses in public places. That naked man on the square was plenty. So he deputized the inmates and took everybody out on a sort of scavenger hunt."

"What in God's name are you talking about?" she demanded.

Bryce Hatton ceased pounding on his window bars and began instead to hammer at the surrounding casement. Small chips of mortar and brick rained down into the grassy strip between the jailhouse wall and the curb, and some smaller chunks sailed all the way to the street.

"I know," Marty Raby apologized, "it's all pretty gruesome. I probably shouldn't have said anything. But when half the town gets sucked up by a tornado, it's hard to know what belongs in polite conversation anymore."

A tornado. So that's what this was all about. And Wallace must have stayed to help with the injured. It all made sense now. But still, a new uneasiness began to take hold.

"And people were killed?" she asked.

"Two, that I know of," he told her. "One used to be a pal of mine—old boy I went to school with. Sad thing is, I bet he saw it coming and just couldn't get out of the way. Poor fellow only had one leg."

She sat down hard in the street.

Herb Gatlin. Of all the people she had preferred not to think about in her adult life, Herb Gatlin headed the list. For years she had avoided him, sidestepping every chance of an encounter, even when her husband had kept throwing him in her path, hiring him—perversely, it seemed to her—for odd jobs around their property: digging post holes in the yard, tilling the garden, painting the house, waxing their automobiles. She'd always pretended she had other places to be, other people to share her time with, just so she would never find herself alone with him, never have to speak to him, never have to hear a single sentence come out of his mouth.

And as if all that hadn't been difficult enough, only last week Wallace had hired him to dig a well for Mary Jean on Reservoir Hill, which had raised new nightmares. Their daughter was no longer a child—she might notice things she'd overlooked before. What would happen if Mary Jean allowed herself to chat with the handyman she'd known from a distance for most of her life? What if they ever looked hard at each other, face to face?

But now he was dead. There was nothing to worry about anymore. Herb Gatlin could never confront her or her daughter, never cause a scene by dropping a loose remark or asking an indiscrete question.

Of course, he would never have asked the question she feared most. Herb already knew why she left him, she was certain of that. But she'd made the right choice, obviously, so she had nothing to apologize for. Wallace had been the only answer that had made any sense, even back then.

So why did she feel now like the life had just gone out of her?

She'd had feelings for Herb once, childish feelings, back when she was still fool enough to mistake attraction for love. He'd been a dashing figure, that was all, a carefree horseman like all those heroes in the movies. When she'd kissed him there on the courthouse lawn, it was her first real kiss, and yes, that counted for something. The other boys she'd gone out with—the Marty Rabys and the Wally McKinneys—had been sweet but callow, and she'd never taken them seriously. Herb was a rough-edged cowboy brave enough to ride wild bulls, and for years she believed he was everything she wanted. The accident had brought her back to earth. Even if he hadn't lost his leg, she would have outgrown him soon enough, surely that had to be the truth. Weren't all those rodeo boys just riff-raff at heart? Weren't all of them headed toward disaster of some sort, a lost leg or worse, followed by a life of menial labor among a host of low-class friends? Herb Gatlin would have been the wrong man to stake her future on.

Still, there was Mary Jean. Maybe Herb would have straightened out for her sake. Maybe he would have outgrown the need to risk his neck riding wild animals. He'd begun to change already, taking a job at the newspaper with her father and her brother. That had been such a good sign.

But then it was too late. Nothing could put back a lost leg. She hated to admit it, even to herself, but she couldn't bear the thought of being with a man so damaged, so incomplete. She'd have been ashamed to go out of the house with him—they'd have been stared at on the streets, and people would have made cruel jokes behind her back. She couldn't have stood it. She just couldn't have stood it.

No, if Herb Gatlin had wanted a life with Ellen Parsons, he never should have entered that rodeo. They could have gotten by without the prize money.

"Mrs. McKinney?" Marty Raby squatted beside her and placed a solicitous hand at her elbow. "Is there something wrong?"

"Oh, Marty," she said.

The hammering stopped. A crumbling cascade of cement chips and dust showered down the side of the building. A moment later an iron bar clanked loudly against the curb and bounced end over end into the street beside them.

She and Marty both looked up as Bryce Hatton poked his leg and shoulder between the remaining bars. It was a tight squeeze, but he forced himself the rest of the way through and perched like a child on the window ledge.

"Dammit, Bryce!" Marty yelled. "Don't you even think about it!"

What in the world was there to think about, Ellen wondered as Bryce Hatton hesitated above them. He was outside his cell, but there was nowhere to go. He was still three stories from the ground. No one would make a leap like that. No one could be that desperate.

But even as this certainty formed itself in her mind, Bryce Hatton sprang away from the building and dropped like a sack of rocks to the rain-soaked yard.

Marty Raby stood up quickly. "Oh, geez," he said. He put his palms on the top of his head, as if he were trying to hold it in place. Bryce Hatton lay face down in the grass not fifteen feet away, groaning.

"I'm in trouble now," Marty said softly. He lowered his hands to his sides and turned to Ellen. His face seemed suddenly shiny with sweat, and she could see the panic in his eyes. "You have to go," he told her.

He looked like he wanted to cry. She couldn't be sure, but she thought she remembered that look from years ago, from the end of seventh grade, maybe, when she'd told him she didn't like him anymore. Poor Marty. And poor Herb and poor Ellen and poor Wally. All just children who didn't know what they were doing to each other.

As she rose from the dark macadam, she turned her gaze to the crumpled figure in the jail yard. He groaned louder now, and one of his arms moved slightly. She took a breath to steady herself. Her husband and daughter were somewhere in Lincoln, and she needed to find them. She hurried away toward the center of town, and never once looked back.

Jerry Lee Statten

His mama said anything he found, he could keep.

It was like a big treasure hunt. God had sent a strong wind to take things from the stores and hide them all over the countryside. Some things might be broken, but other things might be good as new. If Jerry Lee found something he liked, he could put it in his wagon and bring it home with him.

The idea of it amazed him. He might find all the toys he'd ever wanted. Red rubber balls or toy hammers or slide whistles or tops or cat's-eye marbles. There might be toy soldiers that he could send out on patrol and pretend that one of them was his brother, Web. He might even find his favorite, the wooden gliders that cost a nickel at the Rea & Derrick.

But his mama also told him to remember his family. He should leave room in his wagon for gifts, because God's blessings should always be shared. So if he found clothes that weren't his size, or things for the kitchen, or ashtrays, or anything else good for grown-ups, he should gather those up, too, for his cousins and his aunts and uncles and his grandma. Maybe he could even find something to give his daddy for his birthday, she had told him.

He'd only been searching for a little while, and already he'd found a lamp that was broken in half but that still had good wires in it. He'd also found a broken picture frame with a color picture of a collie in it, and a bed sheet that was heavier than it looked because it came out of the creek. If his mama didn't want the bed sheet, he'd use it for his costume next Halloween.

He found a tire that his daddy might like, but it was too big to put in the wagon. Maybe Jerry Lee could come back for it later. But he also found a brand new fancy shoe like his daddy wore sometimes when he and Mama went out in the evenings. *Wing Tips*, his daddy called them, even though they didn't have any wings. This one looked real nice—shiny and black with stitches sewn all over it. Maybe he'd even find the other shoe that went with it. But it would still be a good gift, even if he didn't. One shoe was better than no shoe; Jerry Lee had learned that much already.

There were also plenty of boards with good nails in them, but the ones that weren't broken were too long to carry. Besides, these boards probably came from the new house Miss Mary Jean was building down the street from his mama and daddy's place, and it wasn't right to take things that belonged to a neighbor.

The toys were harder to find than he thought they would be. In his mind, he'd seen them hanging from tree branches like it was Christmas morning, low enough that he could walk right up and pick them, easy as crabapples. He did see some things in the trees, but they were too high up, and anyway he couldn't tell for sure what they were. They might have been parts of houses, and he didn't think his mama needed anything like that.

Still, he would keep looking. There might be grand surprises in the tall grass further along the creek bank toward the river, and today was finders-keepers day.

He stood at the crest of the higher bank beside his half-full wagon and scanned the creek bed for more presents. Something caught his eye downstream, something lodged in the mud at the mouth of a culvert. He left his wagon and walked a few steps closer, squinting hard to make out what it was. When it finally came into focus, his heart leapt and he broke into a run along the rocky bank.

It was a catcher's mitt, the kind he'd seen in the window at Malone Hardware. Maybe it was the very same one. And there was no one else around to call dibs. The mitt was his alone.

He knelt in the rocky mud at the outer rim of the concrete tunnel that ran under the roadway and pulled the mitt from the tangle of mud and weeds. Even dirty, it still smelled brand new, and it was so stiff he could hardly bend it, even with both hands. Neatsfoot oil, that's what he needed to loosen it up. Web had told him that was how to make a baseball glove soft—soak it in neatsfoot oil and tie it shut overnight with a baseball tucked in the pocket. He didn't know what neatsfoot oil was, but he knew his daddy could find him some.

Jerry Lee scraped most of the mud off with his finger and slid his hand into the opening. His fingers were too short to reach all the way inside, but that was all right, he was growing every day, that's what his mama told him. He pounded his fist into the pocket, the way he had seen Web do when Web and his daddy had thrown the hard ball around in the chicken yard. It stung his fingers, but that was all right, too. Big boys didn't mind if something hurt a little bit.

Web had taken their ball with him to the army, so Jerry Lee would have to get himself another one. But maybe he'd find a ball today, too. Then he could take Web's place with his daddy in the chicken yard, and his daddy could cheer up again.

He tucked the mitt under his arm and began to look around for other windfalls. Almost right away he spotted something. Not four feet away, just inside the edge of the concrete tunnel, partly hidden by weeds and a chunk of concrete, was another shoe. He could only see part of it, but he could tell it didn't match the Wing Tip he'd already collected. This one was a dark brown instead of black, and it didn't look very new at all. Still, two shoes were better than one, no matter what they looked like.

He clapped his hands loudly to scare away any snakes or rats that might be waiting in the dark crevices beneath the tunnel and scooted down the bank to the lower edge of the culvert. He couldn't climb inside the tunnel very easily without stepping in the creek, and he didn't want to do that. He was barefooted, and there were crawfish under the rocks, sometimes big as his hand, with pinchers strong enough to make him bleed. Besides, this early in the year the water was still too cold for wading.

He set the mitt carefully on the curve of dry cement at the top of the arch, then he gripped the side of the tunnel and leaned out across the dark opening. He felt a little uneasy, because he didn't know what kinds of things lived in tunnels under the road. Maybe bears. Or bobcats. Maybe wild dogs, like Rufus. His mother had told him to stay away from wild dogs because they might have rabies. Rabies meant you foamed at the mouth and went crazy and were afraid of water. If Rufus lived here, though, he couldn't have rabies, because there was water all around. And Rufus wasn't as bad as his mother thought, anyway. Jerry Lee told her he had walked right up and patted his head once, and Rufus hadn't minded. His daddy had laughed when he said that, but told him he was brave.

He needed to be brave now, too. He reached out as far as he could and hooked the heel of the shoe with his fingertips. He tried to pull it toward him, but it seemed to be caught on something. He tugged harder to try to break the snag, but the shoe still wouldn't budge, so he edged closer and reached across the shoe-top for a better grip. But as he closed his fingers over the tightly strung laces, he suddenly understood something, and a terrible fear squeezed him from inside. He froze. The shoe was hard to move because it wasn't empty. There was a foot in it, and probably a leg beyond that, stretching off into the darkness of the tunnel. Jerry Lee had grabbed hold of something straight from his worst nightmares, the ones where Jesus didn't save him from the Enemy. And now he was too afraid to let go.

But he didn't have to let go. The shoe pulled away from him all by itself, and a sorrowful moan rose up inside the tunnel, echoing louder than what any normal person ever sounded like, more like a monster waking up. Jerry Lee sprang backward and scrambled up over the top of the culvert to the gravel surface of the road. Whatever it was, it was now directly beneath him.

It moaned again. Jerry Lee crept back to the edge of the culvert and snatched up his new catcher's mitt and held it to his heart. He didn't know what to do next. If he ran for his wagon, he'd have to go back along the creek bank, and the thing in the tunnel could see him. Maybe if he just stayed where he was, he'd be safe.

But what kind of monster moaned so much and wore brown shoes?

In the story of the Three Billy Goats Gruff, the billy goats had a bad troll under their road. He didn't know exactly what a troll was, but in the picture book it didn't wear shoes. Maybe that didn't mean anything, though. He remembered that all the goats were smarter than the bad troll, and so it hadn't been able to win. And Jerry Lee was even smarter than goats, he knew that for a fact. They were dumb enough to eat tin cans. So maybe he didn't have as much to be afraid of as he thought.

Still.

His mama had promised him there was no such thing as trolls, and his daddy had said he shouldn't believe in any of that kind of stuff—not in trolls or fairies or goblins or Paul Bunyan or the Wolf Man or even haints.

But the Tooth Fairy had already brought him a nickel three times. Every year the Easter Bunny left candy eggs out in the yard, and that was sure no regular bunny. Reverend Johnson warned them every Sunday about the Devil, and all the magic tricks he used to catch their souls. Santa Claus had to be some kind of haint, floating up and down chimneys the way he did. And Jesus was definitely a haint, because he was the Holy Ghost.

Maybe some people didn't believe in things like that unless they saw it for themselves. Daddy said Web was gone, that the Enemy got him. But Mama still talked to Web at night some-times, and to Jesus, too. So he knew his mama believed in haints, no matter what his daddy had to say about it. And if Web was a haint now, then Jerry Lee believed in them, too.

So there was no telling what this thing under the road might be.

It moaned again, and then Jerry Lee thought he heard it call out something in a nearly normal voice, though he couldn't make out the words. Somehow the thing didn't sound as scary now. It didn't sound mad, it sounded more like it was hurt, like it needed help. He remembered a story about a little boy who pulled a thorn out of a lion's paw, and then the lion was his friend forever. Maybe he could do something like that, too.

He got down on his hands and knees and crawled quietly to the edge of the culvert. He leaned his head out far enough to see the brown shoe near the mouth of the tunnel. The shoe was right where he'd left it, but now the tunnel was filled with a groaning noise that went up and down, like the way his grandma breathed.

"Who's there?" Jerry Lee asked. The groaning noise stopped.

"Who's there yourself?" The voice was deep and ragged, and after it finished the question, it went into a harsh cough.

Jerry Lee didn't want to say who he was, so he tried to think of a way around it.

"I believe in Jesus," Jerry Lee answered.

There was a silence, followed by a shifting around inside the tunnel. Maybe Jerry Lee had found the Enemy, and it was about to come after him. The Enemy didn't like Jesus. His daddy had said so.

"Me, too, I reckon," said the voice. "Washed in the blood of the lamb," it added, which was the same thing Reverend Johnson said sometimes. Jerry Lee didn't know what it meant, exactly. But he knew it was supposed to be a good thing, even though it sounded awful.

Jerry Lee decided to take a risk.

"I'm Jerry Lee Statten," he announced, as boldly as he could speak it.

There was another silence.

"I know some Stattens," the voice said at last. "You any kin to Sammy Statten, up on Reservoir Hill?"

This caught him off guard.

"That's my daddy," Jerry Lee said.

"Well, your daddy's a good man," said the voice. "He's had a tough row to hoe here lately. I guess you all have."

Jerry Lee climbed down the side of the culvert and peered around into the tunnel. It took a little while for his eyes to see in the darkness, but what he finally saw made him somehow happy and frightened at the same time. Leaning back against the curve of the concrete wall was a man with only one leg.

"You're Mr. Gatlin," he whispered.

"Reckon that's right," said Mr. Gatlin. He looked around and scooted further up the wall, dragging his leg out of the trickle of water in the bottom of the tunnel. "Where exactly are we right now?" he asked.

"Under Mulberry Avenue," Jerry Lee told him. "In the creek."

"Norris Creek? Down by Roy Hopkins' filling station?"

"I don't know," said Jerry Lee. "There's an Esso station."

"That's the one," said Mr. Gatlin. He wiped his shirt sleeve across his brow. "I don't guess you'd happen to know how I got here," he said.

Jerry Lee didn't want to answer, because Mr. Gatlin might take it as bad news. But it was too big a thing to lie about.

"You got killed by the tornado," he said.

Another silence.

Mr. Gatlin cleared his throat and spit something out onto the tunnel floor. "No wonder I'm feeling poorly," he said, and he started to cough in a way that sounded like laughing.

"You was digging Miss Mary Jean's well," Jerry Lee went on.

"I remember that part," said Mr. Gatlin. "And I seem to recall being mashed by a tree. But the rest is all God's mystery."

"My mama took Miss Mary Jean to the hospital in my daddy's wheelbarrow," Jerry Lee said.

"Miss Mary Jean? She didn't get hurt, did she?"

Jerry Lee heard something that sounded like fear in Mr. Gatlin's voice, but he knew that couldn't be right. Haints had nothing to be afraid of.

"No, sir. I think she was just having a baby."

Mr. Gatlin let out a raspy sigh. "Well, glory be," he said, and settled into another silence.

Jerry Lee stepped carefully into the mouth of the tunnel and squatted against the wall across from Mr. Gatlin. He waited there in the quiet, with his baseball mitt clutched to his chest, listening to Mr. Gatlin breathe. After a little while, he saw Mr. Gatlin's eyes shining in the shadows.

"I see you're a ball player," Mr. Gatlin said.

"Yes, sir. When I get big I'm gonna play for the Brooklyn Dodgers."

"Like Jackie Robinson," said Mr. Gatlin. "I hear he's the highest-paid player on the team."

"He's the best," Jerry Lee told him.

"Well, your brother was mighty good," said Mr. Gatlin. "No reason you can't be, too."

"I don't have a ball," he said.

"That's not a problem. I never had me a ball neither. Used to play catch with hedge apples. You ever try that?"

"I roll them down the hill sometimes," said Jerry Lee.

"That's fun, too," Mr. Gatlin agreed. He winced as he shifted his weight onto his side. Then he leaned his head forward into the light and spit something dark into the creek. Jerry Lee felt bad seeing what shape he was in. He looked like he had rust spots all over him, on his face, down his neck, even in his hair. His shirt collar had rust spots, too, and his sleeves were crusty with mud and with the chalky white dust from the cement walls. Mr. Gatlin looked at Jerry Lee like he could tell what he was thinking.

"I guess I must look pretty stove up," he said.

"Yes, sir."

"I'll tell you the truth, Jerry Lee," he said propping himself on his forearm. "I feel stove up, too. That twister was rough as a cob."

"Rough as Jersey Joe Walcott," Jerry Lee said.

Mr. Gatlin nodded and smiled. "You know about Jersey Joe, do you?"

"He's the champ. That means he can knock down anybody he wants." Jerry Lee pretended to scowl and swung his right arm in a small circle, delivering an uppercut to some invisible foe. "Jersey Joe's not afraid of anything."

Mr. Gatlin turned his face to the trickle of water and coughed hard. "That gives him a leg up on me," he said, wheezing out his words like there was a fishbone in his throat.

"I could get you an aspirin," Jerry Lee told him. "My mama keeps some in the medicine chest."

"That's a kind offer," said Mr. Gatlin. "But I've got my own aspirin at home. I just need to get there."

"Where do you live?" Jerry Lee asked.

"Not far." He reached down past the cement lip of the culvert and dipped his cupped hand into the creek. "You know where the stockyards are?" he asked, and splashed his face with water.

"I can hear the cows sometimes," Jerry Lee said.

"I've got me a little place back of the holding pens," he said, wiping the drips from his stubbly chin. "On a normal day, I could just walk right on over there. But today's not a normal day for me."

"No, sir."

"You know why?"

Jerry Lee pointed to the place where Mr. Gatlin's right leg came to a sudden stop. "You missing your wooden leg today," he said.

Mr. Gatlin chuckled and nodded his head. "That's exactly the problem, Jerry Lee. But you could help me out, if you wanted to."

"You need my daddy's wheelbarrow?"

"Thank you, but I don't think that would do it." Mr. Gatlin squinted out at the creek bank. "Do you know what crutches are?"

"My Aunt Nelda got crutches when she stepped in a gopher hole."

"Well, that's what I need."

"But she lives in Skinum," Jerry Lee told him.

"That's all right, son, it doesn't have to be those particular crutches." He waved his hand at the opening of the tunnel. "I suspect there's a whole mess of fallen tree branches out there. Is that right?"

"Yes, sir."

"Well, I need you to drag one down here. The biggest you can handle. One with a fork in it about yay-high." He held his hand up to the concrete ceiling, taller than Jerry Lee's head. "You understand?"

"Yes, sir." This was the part he'd been waiting for. The favor. He would do Mr. Gatlin this favor, and then Mr. Gatlin would always be on his side, always protect him from the Enemy. He stood on the lip of the culvert. "I'll get you a good one," he said, and jumped to the near bank. He didn't know why a haint needed a crutch to get home, but that part didn't matter. Maybe haints could only fly after dark. Or maybe this was just a test, something Mr. Gatlin made up so Jerry Lee could prove himself. He climbed quickly to the crest and ran to his wagon, where he tucked his catcher's mitt inside the wet bedsheet.

Mr. Gatlin was right, there were broken limbs everywhere. He ran from one to another, searching for the very best crutch. Most were too small, just spindly twigs with bunches of leaves. A few were too large, thicker than fence posts, and fanning out so wide that he knew he could never drag them down to the culvert. Some looked good at first, stout and dark with no leaves at all, but those all ended up being rotten.

It was like the story of the Three Bears, where everything was either too much or too little, until something in-between showed up and turned out to be just right. That's what he needed now, the one that was in-between, and he knew it would be here somewhere because that was the lesson of the story. He could always find the exact thing he needed if he looked hard enough. Just like he had found Mr. Gatlin.

He ran a little farther up the hill and climbed up onto the rock wall that ran along the back of the Crabtrees' yard, where he wasn't supposed to go. The Crabtrees had a little black and white dog with pointy ears and a flat nose that always barked and tried to snap at him when he came too close. But today it wasn't there. Maybe the tornado had got the Crabtrees' dog the same as it had got Mr. Gatlin.

From the top of the wall he could see all the fallen branches on the hillside. He cupped his hands around his eyes to block the sun, and stared hard at the piles of brush dotting the slope. None of the limbs looked right. He took a few steps along the wall and was about to hop back to the ground when he noticed a thick, forked branch poking from a bush beside the Crabtrees' back stoop. He couldn't be sure until he'd pulled it out, but it looked like the size Mr. Gatlin needed—thick as the neck of a baseball bat, but twice as long, with all the little branches broken off already. If it wasn't rotten, it would be just right for a crutch.

He jumped into the soft dirt of the flower bed and ran to the thick row of bushes along the back of the house. As he tugged at the stick, which was caught up somehow in the heart of the bush, he was startled by a sudden rapping at the kitchen window. It was unfriendly rapping, the kind that said, *Get out of my yard*.

Jerry Lee jerked hard at the stick, and as it broke free of the snag, he stumbled backward and tripped over the edge of one of the Crabtrees' sidewalk stones. He fell onto his backside just as the person who rapped on the window—Mrs. Crabtree, most likely, or maybe her maid—opened the back door halfway. The little black and white dog burst through the opening and leapt from the concrete stoop toward Jerry Lee, snarling all the way. He tried to fend off the dog with his bare feet, kicking at its muzzle, but it was too quick for him, and before Jerry Lee could squirm away, the dog had bitten his foot and sunk its teeth in his leg, shaking its head back and forth and ripping the blue jeans that his cousin Arthur had just recently outgrown.

Jerry Lee grabbed up the perfect crutch and slammed it down on the dog's head. It let go of his leg and jumped sideways, yelping, and Jerry Lee hoped this was his chance to get away. He scrambled to his feet and hobbled backward toward the rock wall, still holding the crutch and keeping his eye on the dog, which was already shaking off its injury and growling louder than before.

"Sic him, Chester!" came a woman's voice from inside the darkness of the house, and the dog ran at him again. But this time Jerry Lee was better prepared, he had Mr. Gatlin's crutch to keep the dog away instead of just his bare feet, and he aimed the pointy end, the end where the branch had broken unevenly from the tree, at the dog's face to make it stop. But the dog didn't stop at all—it sprang forward like all it wanted in the world was to tear Jerry Lee to pieces and if it first had to eat a stick to get there, then that was just fine. But the moment the dog leapt was also the moment Jerry Lee jabbed the stick forward, and the blade-like end of the branch disappeared into the dog's open mouth. Jerry Lee could feel the jolt all the way up to his shoulders, and he knew he'd poked through something inside the dog's throat.

The dog thudded to the ground and frantically scooted backward from Jerry Lee toward the safety of the house while blood spurted from its mouth onto the sidewalk stones. It turned and clawed its way back onto the stoop, spraying blood across the concrete and even up along the white siding of the house before it disappeared at last through the open doorway. The woman inside the house screamed.

Jerry Lee crossed to the rock wall and hoisted himself up using Mr. Gatlin's crutch. The woman, probably Mrs. Crabtree, was still screaming as he jumped from the wall. He limped as fast as he could manage across the littered hillside. His mama would spank him for tearing his new jeans, but that couldn't be helped. His leg was beginning to feel like fire, and on any other day he would have cried. But there was no time for that now. The Crabtrees might come after him for killing their dog, and if they did, he'd have to lead them far away. He would circle up through the woods above Mulberry Avenue, then sneak down past the Esso station and come up the creek from the other end.

He couldn't let anyone follow him back to the tunnel. Mr. Gatlin might be skittish in the daylight, and if the Crabtrees came around, Mr. Gatlin might disappear. Then the bargain would be broken.

He wondered if dogs could be haints. Maybe Chester's spirit would track Jerry Lee down, like any dog could, and get back at him in the night.

No. He would bring Mr. Gatlin the perfect crutch, and Mr. Gatlin would protect him from Chester and from everything else, even the Enemy. Jerry Lee had made friends with a haint. He'd never have to be afraid of the dark again.

Tom Parsons

Tom Parsons had more headlines than he knew what to do with.

"Lincoln Devastated by Tornado" had to be the lead, of course. But there was also "East Side of Square Destroyed by Fire," which on any other day would have been the story of the decade. Now it was just a sidebar to the tornado.

"Naked Man Found Dead in Square" was a big story, especially with Herb Gatlin's artificial leg to factor in. That story might get even bigger, depending on who the dead man turned out to be and what actually became of Herb Gatlin. In any case, he'd have to tone down the details so as not to offend people's sensibilities.

"Local Woman Gives Birth in Wheelbarrow" was probably his favorite, since the woman in question was his niece, but with everything else going on, that one might even get bumped off the first page.

The uprooted tree that still dangled from *The Observer*'s office roof thirty feet above the sidewalk would have deserved twenty column inches only a week before, and now it was barely worth a mention.

Of course, he needed to run something about Jersey Joe Walcott. People needed to know the champ was still coming to town.

This was a great time to be a newspaperman.

The tree worried him though. *The Observer* building was a hundred years old, and the wood frame had been sagging for decades, ever since his grandfather's days at the paper. When Kate was alive she used to nag him about preventive maintenance, arguing that it was cheaper to fix a problem before it got started. Maybe she had been right. Now the roof was riddled with rotten planking. It couldn't support a full-grown hackberry tree for very long. But who could have guessed it would ever have to?

Every strategy had a weakness, he supposed. His strategy had always been to expand, rather than maintain. Money that might have gone into a new roof for *The Observer* went instead to new projects, new acquisitions. Besides the newspaper office, he now owned three buildings on the undamaged side of the square, an orchard out on the Huntsville Highway, a hundred acres next to the golf course, and the Starlight Drive-In. All his properties were scraggly and run-down, but at least he held the deeds. And the Starlight was sure to generate some extra income when Jersey Joe Walcott came to town. Jersey Joe's fee for the exhibition had been steep, but Tom expected the gate receipts to more than cover it. Not that the money really mattered. Some things were worth doing just to give people something to read about in the paper. Maybe now what he should do is make the boxing exhibition a fundraiser for folks who lost their homes in the tornado.

The tree on the roof was an unexpected wrinkle, but he refused to let a thing like that stop the presses—or, rather, the press, since he had only one, also a hundred years old, operated with a hand crank and capable of inking just one double-sheet at a time. His grandfather had used that very same press to spread news of General Sherman's advance on the town in September of 1863. He couldn't let it sit idle now, in an even bigger crisis.

Dickie Bagley had an old crane that he used for building barns. Maybe Dickie would get the tree off the roof in exchange for a few months of free advertising. It was worth a shot. Most people he'd talked to seemed eager to help out in the rebuilding effort, so Dickie might go along. The tornado seemed to have brought a lot of new community spirit into town. Even the inmates at the jail had volunteered for the cleanup and had gone into some neighborhoods ahead of the power company crews, when there were still hot cables on the ground. He might run an editorial about reducing their sentences, lobby to get them a little time off for their conspicuously good behavior. Kate would have liked that idea.

Of course, poor Bryce Hatton wouldn't make the list. That had been another story with lead potential: "Local Inmate Injured in Daring Escape Attempt." Maybe he would stop by the hospital later and try to get a statement.

Or maybe that was the worst idea in the world. Bryce wasn't too happy about being on trial for killing his own cousin. He would never agree to give an interview to Tom Parsons, since Tom was the one he'd actually been trying to shoot in the first place.

Right now, though, he needed to walk over to Fred's Five-and-Dime and check the status of the naked dead man. Tom was curious to know if anyone had identified the body, but he was also curious to see how the store was working out as a part-time mortuary. The previous evening at the Elks Lodge, they'd all met to discuss the town's state of emergency, and Charlie Monahan had told them his funeral home had lost most of its roof in the storm. He'd have to shut down operations for at least a few weeks. That's when Fred Gallant volunteered part of his dime store. Fred's place was right next door to Charlie's, so it was the perfect venue for any funerals or viewings that came up in the meantime. People could still use Charlie's parking lot.

He was surprised that no friends or relatives had yet come forward to claim the dead man. Even in a war zone, with machine guns strafing the fields and trench mortars exploding left and right, people still managed to keep a clear tally of their own. What kind of man could leave the world anonymously, unencumbered by even the simplest facts of his life, without a single soul to say who he was? Sheriff Tune had checked the nearby towns and found that, with the exception of Herb Gatlin, no one anywhere had been reported missing.

Maybe the dead man had just been passing through from someplace else, some other state, maybe. He might have been a tourist, or a hobo. Or a salesman whose sample case went one way while his body went another. Maybe the dead man had people waiting for him, wondering about his progress, worried for his safety, annoyed at his delay. Or maybe he was local after all, some hick or bumpkin from one of the deep hollows up in the north end of the county, where nobody but revivalist preachers ever came or went.

Or maybe he was nobody at all, a mystery sent by God, a dark visitation, a ghost of the whirlwind. Anything was possible.

The newspaper should offer a reward. That might even help with circulation.

Tom stepped carefully down his two gray wooden steps into the alien shadow of the dangling hackberry. He would definitely have to get that taken care of—such precarious disarray might frighten away advertisers. The streets were open again, which was a major accomplishment, but the square was still a mess. All the oversized debris—the theater marquee, the clock tower, and a few large sections of roofs—had been dragged up onto the courthouse lawn and piled around the monument to the Confederate dead. Mayor Strong had already contacted Carter Construction about removing the bulk of it, since they were the only local company with large earthmoving equipment. Tom would probably write an op-ed piece praising the mayor for his quick action. An early start on removing wreckage was essential, since there would be plenty more of it in the days to come. Smoke still rose from the fire-gutted remains of the entire east side of the square. Once those charred timbers and bricks had cooled, bulldozers would have to be brought in to scrape the rubble clean.

As he rounded the corner of the burned-out drug store and came in sight of the funeral home, he understood why Charlie was temporarily closed for business. The roof was shredded, one of the side walls had collapsed, and three of the five white columns from the front of the mortuary had been knocked into the side yard. Charlie might need to work out a longer-term deal with Fred Gallant.

Tom should have made the rounds before noon, he realized, but he'd accidentally polished off a fifth of Jack Daniels after last night's Lodge meeting and passed out at his desk again. His head was still splitting, and if he didn't get some food in his stomach soon he might start throwing up bile. He hated that.

The worst part was in knowing he'd have to confess it all at the A.A. meeting on Tuesday night. He didn't believe in A.A., but Kate had made him join after a Christmas binge one year when he'd hired a taxi to take him to St. Louis, four hundred miles away. He knew that A.A. was a valid lifeline for some people, but for him their twelve-step program was like a game of chutes and ladders, with Tom sliding back to the start on every fresh roll of the dice. Politically, it was a good group to belong to because there was loyalty among members—a sacred bond, in fact—and many of his A.A. buddies were among the more prominent lights of the community. They were all obligated to watch out for each other, and in Tom's case that meant he could count on certain alcoholic bankers and business owners to buy regular advertising space in *The Observer* and thus keep his struggling newspaper afloat.

But Tom didn't look for A.A. to cure him of his ills. Drinking was the least of his problems. If Doc McKinney had it right, Tom was already halfway out the door. The night sweats, headaches, weight loss, and all the other things he'd thought were part of grieving over Kate turned out to be something a little more complicated: leukemia. No way to sidestep that one. So why torment himself with relentless sobriety when alcohol wasn't the real culprit anymore? If a man falls out of an airplane, there's no point fretting about a toothache on the way down.

The dime store looked packed. Fred's wrap-around row of parking spaces, Charlie's freshly paved parking lot, and even the farm-implement yard across the street from the mortuary were all overflowing with automobiles. People were bunched in front of the building, jockeying for position to see something in Fred's full-length display window. Because of the midday glare on the glass, Tom couldn't see what they were staring at until he'd made his way up to the front of the crowd.

The dead man was laid out in a coffin in the dime store window. A scrawled cardboard sign was propped against the lower end of the casket asking, "Do You Know Me?"

Tom sure didn't know him, nor would he have wanted to—the man looked like a tasteless Halloween prank. Charlie had obviously tried to reshape the head to make it presentable, stitching it together along the jaw-line and popping out some of the dents in the skull. But the head was still too lumpy and lopsided to look fully human. Tom hadn't seen a body that abused in more than thirty years, not since his final days in France. Kate would have cried if she had seen it. But Tom wasn't moved by tragedy anymore. Kate's death had bankrupted him in that department.

To the left of the casket, near the dead man's battered scalp, was a pyramid stack of electric razors fronted by a more neatly lettered sign: "In our country, it's you, Mr. John Q. Public, who determines popular choice! Only Shavemaster has the powerful 16-bar armature self-starting real motor!"

To the right of the casket was another display, this one featuring an assortment of folded shirts, pants, and overalls. The sign propped behind the stacks of clothing bore a colorful illustration of four men—a bus driver, a gas station attendant, a farmer, and a cowboy—all engaged in a smiling conversation. The text above them proclaimed, "No Question About It—LEE is your best value in work clothes!"

The dead man's new outfit had been assembled from clothes in the display. He was dressed like the cowboy in the picture, with the same red bandana around his neck and the same big chromium buckle holding his belt in place. His yellow checkered shirt still had a price tag on the collar.

Tom pulled open the glass door and entered the store. Six large black ceiling fans spun noisily overhead, keeping the place cool even with so much sunlight pouring in through the front window. That was a good thing, it seemed to Tom, considering how quickly dead things could start to turn in the heat. The product bins and shelving units had been brought forward to make room for a funeral and viewing area, which was sectioned off by a row of free-standing hospital curtains near the rear of the store. There were gaps between the white muslin curtain segments, and Tom could see that Charlie had set up several rows of metal folding chairs in front of an empty bier.

The store was mobbed, which was about what he expected. Tom understood people, and he knew that in spite of how pious they might act on Sundays, most reverted to their natural state the rest of the week. A deformed dead man was an irresistible freak show, especially with no grief attached.

Fred Gallant waved to him as he entered, and wove his way over through the crowd, all smiles.

"I can't believe what this has done for my business." He gestured to the front counter, where Fred's daughters, April and Ida May, worked furiously to make headway on their growing checkout lines. "I had to put in a second cash register. They're buying out the store."

"That's so their neighbors won't think they're just gawkers," Tom told him.

Fred wrinkled his nose and leaned in close. "Damn, Tom," he said, lowering his voice. "I can smell it all over you."

"We'll talk about it Tuesday night," Tom answered. He clapped Fred on the shoulder and ambled off through the crowd.

He spotted Andy Yearwood standing by a clearance bin at the head of the housewares aisle, writing in his reporter's notebook. The boy was the best hire he'd ever made. He worked cheap, for one thing, because in a town like Lincoln there weren't many jobs for local graduates that didn't involve axle grease or a spatula. Andy had enthusiasm, which Tom knew would burn out in a couple of years, but in the meantime it meant Andy would cover his beat without complaint. His beat, of course, was everything.

Tom had paved the way for him as best he could. He had made sure Andy got invited to join the Rotary, the Lions, the Elks, the Moose, the Kiwanis, the Masons, the Jay-Cees, the Civitans—everything, in fact, but the American Legion and the VFW, for which Andy wasn't eligible.

Tom was eligible for both, but he had enough nightmares to contend with already. He didn't need a weekly reminder of the worst moments of his life. Besides, what was there to say? The 305th Machine Gun Battalion was irrelevant now, and everything he'd learned as a soldier was useless. It didn't matter that the Vicker machine gun was inferior to the French-made Hotchkiss, which was lighter and easier to reassemble. Or that mustard gas smelled like crushed onions. Or that he had seen four of his friends die in the Argonne Forest just ten days before the Armistice. Certainly none of it made him feel like joining a club.

Tom had also convinced the mayor to appoint Andy as the volunteer fire chief, figuring that would give the boy a front-row seat for any fire and rescue stories. The appointment wasn't working out as well as he'd hoped, but at least Tom could make sure nothing overly embarrassing to Andy showed up in the paper. Anyone could misplace a set of truck keys. That was part of the human condition.

"What's the story?" Tom asked, and Andy looked up from his pad.

"Hey, Mr. Tom. I'm just about done with it." He returned his attention to his notes, biting his lip in concentration. Tom watched as the boy finished his careful lettering and tore three pages from his notebook. "Here you go," he said, smiling and handing Tom the sheets. "It's about Casey Tibbs over there." Andy nodded in the direction of the dead man.

"You got his name?"

"Naw, that's just what I call him." Andy furrowed his brow. "You never heard of Casey Tibbs? He won the national rodeo finals out in Oklahoma last month. Got crowned World's Champion Cowboy. He's famous now."

"I guess I don't keep up."

"Him and the dead man wear the exact same outfit."

"That's not what we'd call newsworthy, Andy. Those aren't the clothes he arrived in."

"Oh, that's not the story." He pointed to the foot of the casket. A clear liquid dripped from the bottom of the bier into a galvanized bucket on the floor. "It's a race against time."

"He's melting?"

"They put ice in the bottom of the casket to keep him fresh. There's public health issues."

"The ice was my idea," announced Morgan Motlow, who had crept up on him from behind. Morgan was a health inspector with the state—big and burly, with a tendency to brag. Morgan was a pup compared to Tom, maybe twenty-six, but the year he'd spent fighting the Japanese had aged him in other ways, and he carried his war experiences with him like an overstuffed knapsack. He claimed to like his job because it got him free meals and left him plenty of time to hang around the VFW hall. But his real interest was poker, and he and Tom had been in a regular game for seven years now, ever since Morgan came back from the service.

Morgan had been there the night Bryce Hatton shot his cousin, so he and Tom were both witnesses, along with Jimmy Vann and Sheriff Tune.

"I figure the cooler we keep the body," Morgan added, "the more time we'll have for a positive identification."

"Look who's thinking ahead for a change," said Tom, shaking Morgan's hand. Morgan wasn't a bad sort, sober, though he did have a habit of saying the wrong thing at the wrong time. Bryce Hatton could attest to that. Morgan had dealt the hand that pushed Bryce over the edge, and if Morgan had just kept his mouth shut, they might all have gone home peacefully that night.

"I saw plenty of bodies on Guadalcanal," Morgan told them. "Once that death stink sets in, there's no way in hell to turn it off. It'll seep into everything in the store, especially fabrics. Fred ain't figured out that part yet. Three more days and all his beach towels and nightgowns are gonna smell like bad meat."

"So how long you plan to let the freak show go on?"

"This damn heat spell ain't helping," he said. "I'll probably have to shut things down by tomorrow morning, no matter what Fred says. If nobody claims the body before then, we'll just have to go ahead and bury him. Charge it to the county."

Tom turned to Andy, who was taking more notes. "Go get me a coke."

"They don't sell cokes here," Andy told him. "Only dry goods."

"Thanks for the update," Tom said. "Now get me a coke." He fished a nickel from his pocket and flipped it toward him, but Andy's hands were full and he bobbled the catch. The coin tumbled into the clearance bin, vanishing into a mound of cut-rate cosmetics and colognes. Andy looked confused, then flustered, then panicky. He reached into the bin and pretended to retrieve the nickel. "Yes, sir," he said, dropping the imaginary coin into his shirt pocket. "What kind you want?"

"Doesn't matter. Grape, if you can find it. Or root beer. Just something to settle my stomach."

Andy hustled away through the crowd, and Morgan sat back against the lip of the clearance bin, watching him go.

"Nice kid," he said, "but he could sure use a tour in Korea."

"Nobody needs Korea," Tom corrected him. "Anyway, the boy was 4-F."

"I just hope to hell my house never catches fire." Morgan folded his arms and let out a low belch. "Say, you still bringing in Jersey Joe?"

"Sure. Why not?"

"Town's tore all to hell," Morgan said. "You won't get much of a crowd."

"We've got six days. Folks ought to have their messes cleaned up by then. Probably be ready for a big night out."

"I hope you're right," Morgan said. "I'm hoping for a wagering opportunity."

"You're always hoping for a wagering opportunity."

"Optimism's my gift," he said. He lowered his head and frowned. "I guess you heard about Bryce."

"I run the newspaper, Morgan—what do you think?"

Morgan shrugged. "I think sometimes you miss big chunks of the action."

Tom settled against the bin beside him. "Andy stays on top of things. He fills me in."

Morgan tilted his head toward Tom and spoke in a soft, gravelly rumble. "You figure Bryce was just trying to get away, or trying to come after somebody?"

Tom couldn't help but laugh. "I think we're safe, Morgan. Bryce knows we're not the enemy."

That was one advantage Tom had over these young fools he played cards with: He understood the way emotions could skew things temporarily. But that kind of craziness never lasted. Storms always blew over, and just because a man tried to kill you didn't mean there had to be hard feelings afterward.

"Somebody must be the enemy," Morgan insisted, "or Patty wouldn't be divorcing him."

Morgan was probably right. Patty Hatton was a bright, hard-working girl, prettier than most, but she did have a few shadows to get clear of, and it wasn't difficult to believe she might have been stepping out on Bryce. Patty's father was a moonshiner who sometimes sold wood alcohol to people he didn't like, and her mother had once gone to jail for six months for beating a Bible salesman with a shovel. So Patty came from hard stock. But she had put herself through typing school, and now she was a stenographer at the courthouse, which, by local standards, constituted a success story. After Bryce lost his job at the cotton gin, most people figured she'd leave him.

That was why Tom hadn't been surprised when he came across the court filing. And that was also why he hadn't wanted Bryce in their poker game—he knew better than to gamble with a man whose home life was in the crapper. But Bryce's cousin, Walter, had vouched for him.

"You shouldn't have said anything about the divorce," Tom said.

Morgan threw up his arms. "How the hell was I supposed to know Patty never told him? A wife files for divorce, you figure the husband must have a clue. Christ, it was in the goddamn newspaper. You printed the article."

"And you figured Bryce Hatton for a reader?" Tom asked.

"I figured Bryce Hatton for a moron. But news is news."

"Anyway, it wasn't an article," Tom corrected him. "It was a list of official notices and court filings. Nobody reads that stuff—it's just there for the public record."

"Well, I read it." Morgan shook his head. "If a thing's in the newspaper, it's fair game for conversation, that's what I say."

"Then you're as dim a bulb as Bryce."

Morgan smiled. "I'm not the guy who had to dive under the table."

Some of the details were still hazy in Tom's mind, because he'd had a lot of bourbon that night. He remembered Bryce going all-in on the last hand, trying to buy the pot. Tom had known he was bluffing—Bryce had a pitiful poker face, and all night long every crease in his forehead had been a roadmap to his wallet. When Tom laid down his three queens to take the hand, Morgan laughed and made a crack about Bryce being broke and Patty leaving even sooner than she'd planned. As Tom raked the cash toward him, Bryce stood up and drew his gun from the pocket of his baggy work pants.

Tom remembered realizing that Bryce was about to shoot him, and he also remembered thinking how unfair that was, since Morgan had been the one who mouthed off about Patty. Maybe Bryce meant to shoot them all, and Tom was merely first in line. But whatever the case, none of it was debatable at that point, so Tom just shoved himself backward and plunged head-first beneath the tabletop. He pulled a muscle by his rib on the way down.

Two shots came through the table. One went straight into the knotty-pine floor, and the other into Walter Hatton's cowboy boot just above the ankle.

There was a scuffle, Tom recalled, though he hadn't seen it from beneath the table. But suddenly Walter Hatton was on the floor beside him, holding his foot and swearing. Then Walter gritted his teeth and pointed a finger at his cousin.

"Bryce, you better not shoot me again," he said.

Bryce didn't shoot him again, partly because he hadn't meant to shoot Walter in the first place, and partly because he'd already been wrestled to the floor himself by Jimmy Vann and Sheriff Tune.

Then Morgan called the ambulance—for both Tom and Walter. Tom was certain he'd only pulled a rib, but Morgan was convinced it was a heart attack, so Tom agreed to ride along, just to keep Walter company.

Once Bryce had calmed down, they all talked it over and decided a low-key approach might be best. Walter said he knew his getting shot was just an accident and was willing to overlook it if Bryce would pay the medical bills and buy him a new pair of boots. Tom offered to overlook the attempted murder part, and Jimmy Vann said he didn't really mind that Bryce had shot holes in his table and his floor. For his part, Sheriff Tune, who was as reasonable a man as Tom had ever known, said he'd figure out the least possible thing Bryce could be charged with and let it go at that. He didn't even bother to arrest him at the time.

So while Bryce, Jimmy Vann, and Sheriff Tune straightened up the mess they'd all made wrestling around in Jimmy's living room, Walter and Tom went outside to wait for the ambulance, where Walter could pull off his boot and bleed into the flower bed.

"I like nights like this," Walter had said, sitting there with his foot dangling over the brickwork of Jimmy's porch.

Tom looked out at the clear night sky. "You talking about the stars or the gunfire?"

Walter smiled. "Stars never impressed me all that much."

The hospital was less than two miles away, and the soft whine of a siren rose in the distance.

"Mighty nice of you to let Bryce off the hook," Tom said.

Walter shrugged. "I owe him things."

The ambulance arrived shortly, blaring the neighborhood awake, and Tom realized they should have driven Walter to the hospital themselves, without all the fanfare.

"Don't make this look too embarrassing in the newspaper," Walter warned him as the two of them climbed into the back of the ambulance together.

That was the last thing Walter Hatton ever said. The attendant gave him a shot of pain medicine so he'd be more comfortable on the ride, but Walter had a severe allergic reaction and died before they got him to the hospital.

As a matter of law, Bryce Hatton had to be charged with murder because the shooting was what had started it all.

Now Charlie Monahan, dressed in his black funeral director's finest, solemnly pushed open the front door of Fred's Five-and-Dime and paused there at the threshold with some kind of ledger book tucked under his arm.

"Clear a path, please," he announced, and strode forward into the store. Behind him four men in dark blue suits carried a small child-sized coffin, and everyone fell silent.

"Oh no," a woman said quietly.

The pallbearers moved solemnly through the crowd, first down the center cosmetics aisle, then on past laundry supplies, floor mops, and Fred's newly arrived collection of ceramic woodland figurines. As they came to the dividing curtain at the rear half of the store, Charlie drew a section of the white muslin aside and the procession entered the makeshift funeral space. Tom, behind Morgan and a cluster of curious shoppers, followed Charlie's crew through the gap.

The men rested the coffin on the bier and moved aside, taking up positions by the stockroom door like soldiers on sentry duty. Charlie opened the ledger book and placed it on an old brown card table next to the bier.

"Please sign the visitation book before you leave," Charlie said, gesturing to the ledger. Then he stepped to the coffin and propped open the lid. "The viewing will run through six o'clock this evening. Interment will be at two o'clock tomorrow at Rose Hill Cemetery, following a short graveside service."

Tom and Morgan both shouldered their way to the front of the crowd. There in the coffin lay Herb Gatlin's cleaned and polished wooden leg. A thin navy-blue dress sock stretched to mid-calf. Herb's work-boot, sporting new black laces, had been shined to a gloss it had never known in life.

"What the hell is this?" Morgan demanded, far louder than necessary.

"The earthly remains of Herbert Gatlin," Charlie told him.

"It's a wooden leg," Morgan pointed out. "That's no more Herb Gatlin than a set of encyclopedias."

"Nevertheless," said Charlie, his undertaker's calm in full force, "it's what we have to work with."

Morgan turned away in disgust and shoved his way back toward the woodland figurine display.

Tom stared at the artificial leg. He'd known Herb Gatlin since grade school. Smart boy, when he wanted to be, with an overwhelming love of horses. Maybe Herb would have been a World's Champion Cowboy himself, if things had gone differently, and kids like Andy Yearwood would have looked up to him. Or maybe after his cowboy days, Herb would have come back to work at the newspaper, and he and Ellen would have returned to the path they'd started on together. Yes, that would have been a nice alternative to what happened. But life didn't unfold like a movie romance, and Herb's true story wouldn't sell many tickets. Boy meets girl. Boy loses leg. Boy loses girl. They didn't write them like that in Hollywood.

Kate's story, too, had fallen far short of a Hollywood ending. The breast cancer had eaten her up, and by the end she'd weighed no more than sixty pounds. In some ways she'd been terribly transformed, and her own brother, Moody, said if he'd met her on the street he might not have recognized her. But

Tom had seen past those corruptions of the body—no disease could cover up the light of who she was, not from him. Kate's was the spirit he had bound himself to. She was his guide, his mirror, his measure of all things. That would hold true until Judgment Day.

He had wrestled with her obituary for days before discovering the one she had written for herself and left in his files. Bare facts, and nothing more, about her family and her general circumstance. Typical of her, really. Still keeping the low profile. No word at all about who she really was. No mention of her patience with him after the war, when for ten years he hadn't been able to sleep through the night. No mention of their miscarriages. No final comment on his drinking. No insights, no proclamations, no catalog of all the things that had made her laugh.

But what did Tom know? As far as he could tell, every life ended sadly, and nobody's true story ever got told. Maybe he should take his cue from Kate and write his own obituary ahead of time, to help whoever had to sort out the mess after he was gone.

But what could he say? That he'd been a damaged soldier? A difficult husband? A drunk? A man too weak to get over the loss of his wife? Nobody wanted that kind of truth.

Big dreams, that's all his life amounted to. And for two years now, he'd had nobody to share them with.

He understood finally why Kate had written her own obituary. She knew he'd have written something too sentimental, something that would have embarrassed them both. Newspapermen were supposed to be unbiased.

But how could he be unbiased about Kate's wasting away, cell by cell, until every rasping breath swamped her in agony?

And now it was his turn: the body turning against him, rotting from the inside out. God, for a quick and simple death like Walter Hatton's. That, he supposed, was the last blessing anyone could hope for in this world—though he couldn't say whether Walter might have shared that point of view or not.

He'd been right there when Walter died, had watched his blue-gray eyes as the lights quietly flickered out. Tom had tried to read something in their expression, to ferret out some twist of the story that would make sense of things. But it was no use. Death offered no comment one way or the other. Walter kept his poker face on.

Patty Hatton

After consulting with Reverend Tyree, Patty Hatton felt less inclined to kill her husband. She hadn't told the reverend outright what she wanted to do, hiding her intentions behind a series of clever what-ifs, but she still got the sense that he was discouraging her. Most of what he told her was aimed at shoring up her righteousness—platitudes she'd heard before about forgiveness and love and not killing people.

But that had been on Thursday, with Bryce in jail and the town still a town. A lot had happened since then. For one thing, the wrath of God had come down hard on First Baptist, rebuking it clear to its foundation. If Reverend Tyree had possessed any real understanding of God's ways, he should have seen that coming. But no, he'd been blindsided right along with everyone else. So the reverend was probably no more plugged in than Madame Zubu the Mysterious.

Then there was Bryce's ridiculous escape attempt that had put him in the hospital, which was a hopeful sign. People died in hospitals all the time.

She considered waiting to see if that might happen. If Walter could die from a painkiller, surely Bryce could die from a three-story fall. But in the end she lacked the patience for that kind of vigil.

Still, killing Bryce would be a big step, and she didn't want to make a mistake, so she opened up her New Testament, figuring if anybody could offer guidance, it would be Jesus. She was right.

A man's foes shall be they of his own household, Jesus told his disciples. *I came not to send peace, but a sword.*

Clearly, Jesus understood her situation. It was entirely possible that Jesus wanted Bryce dead, too.

She put their wedding photo into her handbag and set out for the hospital. She wasn't sure why she wanted the photo with her. There was nothing special about it—just the wedding party posed before the altar at First Baptist.

Then it occurred to her that everything in the picture was now gone from her life. Not just the sanctuary, which the tornado had destroyed, but the people. Bryce, smiling and holding her hands. Walter, the best man, leering impishly over Bryce's shoulder. Mary Jean McKinney, her maid of honor whom she hadn't seen since that day, grinning stupidly by her side. Even the altar itself, where she and Bryce had consecrated their vows, had become a casualty.

The more she thought about it, the more she realized that her wedding photo had evolved into a summary of the worst failures of her life. She imagined pinning it to Bryce's chest with a steak knife.

As she walked up Green Street toward the hospital, she was surprised at how normal everything looked. The twister had missed this part of town, so there was no storm damage at all, no clutter in the yards, no debris on the sidewalks. Here the daffodils were coming into bloom. Lawns were cropped short, hedges were trimmed, trees stood leafy and unbroken. The day was unseasonably warm, and the air had a spring-like freshness that reminded her of Easter. On any other afternoon, she might have mistaken the world for an orderly place.

The hospital parking lot was packed with automobiles. A lot of people had been hurt, she realized, though she'd heard there had been only one or two fatalities, which was miraculous.

Miraculous, but also infuriating. If God could save so many people from so powerful a tornado, why couldn't He have saved Walter from the ambulance?

As she pushed her way through the front door to the admitting desk, the sharp, sour smell of the place nearly stopped her cold. The hallways reeked of the same pungent odor that had cloaked her father those days when he had visited his stills. She had learned to despise that alcoholic stink in all its forms, and even though she understood the smell here to be medicinal and antiseptic, that didn't keep the queasiness from churning through her stomach.

The memory of her father bothered her as much as the smell itself. She hadn't seen him in months, and didn't want to. His contribution to her life had ended on her wedding day, as far as she was concerned. He hadn't even shown up to walk her down the aisle, but had gone on a three-day bender instead.

Not that her mother was much better. When she drank, her mind narrowed to a brick alleyway, with no room to turn around. That had been the case when the Bible salesman had come nosing up onto their porch. Her mother had mistaken him for a revenuer because of his dark suit, and, in spite of Patty's pleas to the contrary, she had attacked him with a shovel.

The receptionist at the admitting desk looked haggard in the waning afternoon light. Patty knew she must have had a long day, probably her busiest ever, preparing paperwork for the injured and answering the fearful questions of relatives and well-wishers.

She wondered who her own well-wishers might be, if she ever wound up here. Her relatives had all slunk back into the woods for now, and might not emerge again for generations. Her friends had moved away or gone to college or gotten drafted. Reverend Tyree might stop by, but his reasons would be strictly professional, a shepherd keeping track of a wayward sheep, and a visit from him would only depress her.

She took a handkerchief from her pocketbook and held it over her nose as she looked around the crowded lobby. All the chairs were occupied by tired-looking women, and men in wrinkled suit coats slouched against the walls smoking cigarettes. Patty stepped up to the admitting desk and stood there, waiting to be acknowledged, but the haggard woman was absorbed in a chart and didn't look up.

"Excuse me, ma'am," Patty said. "I'm looking for Bryce Hatton. I understand he's a patient here."

The woman raised her eyes and studied Patty carefully over the top of her glasses. "He's a patient, all right." She took a cigarette from a pack on her desk and lit it with a tarnished silver lighter. Then she picked up a clipboard and scanned down a row of names. "Maternity ward," she said. "Two floors up. Go left when you get off the elevator."

"He's in the maternity ward?"

She blew a cloud of smoke toward the ceiling. "We're crowded," she said. "He was lucky to get that."

"Thank you," Patty said, and headed toward the elevator.

"You'll have to check in with a deputy when you get there," the woman called after her. Patty felt the blood rise to her face. All eyes, she knew, would be staring at her now.

After an excruciatingly long wait, the metal door slid open and the elevator operator unlatched the brass accordion gate and ushered her inside. His red uniform jacket seemed too bright for the cramped space, and the gold braid on his cap had started to fray. He was elderly, with bristles growing from his ears and a thin trail of dried tobacco juice streaking his chin, and she wondered how he managed to endure his life, riding up and down in a cage all day. The county jail would be better than this, she imagined. He didn't even have a place to sit down.

But maybe this was what he had coming to him, maybe this was God's punishment for crimes of his youth. Yes, she could see it in his withered frame, and in the scaly features of his face and the rheumy distance in his eyes. He had probably been reckless and cruel, committing unspeakable acts of violence or depravity, surviving this long only through selfishness and luck. Maybe there was a woman somewhere who would rejoice to know the world had closed in so tightly around him, reserving only this bleak mechanical box for him to wait out his days.

People were a disappointment; she had to remember that. Pity was a wasteful indulgence. Old men were pathetic because they deserved to be, because they had all once been young and smug and full of snakelike charm.

"Have a nice day, Miss," he said hoarsely, pulling the gate aside to let her off at the third floor.

She stepped off the elevator and looked around. The floor seemed quiet, nearly deserted except for three people perched on a wooden bench at the far end of the hallway. One of them was a sheriff's deputy. He sat with his hands clasped in his lap and his head tilted back against the wall. His mouth hung open, and she guessed him to be asleep. The two women sitting next to him both looked vaguely familiar. They stared at her in silence.

Across from the elevator was the viewing window to the nursery, so Patty strolled over to pretend an interest in the newborns. All the bassinets were empty. There was only one baby on display—a girl, judging from the tiny pink cap and blanket—and she was in some kind of glass box with a heat lamp beaming down on her.

Get used to it, kid, she thought.

Funny that Bryce would be the one to make it to the maternity ward, and not her. Maybe if she had gotten pregnant, things would have gone differently between them.

She shuddered at the thought. Bryce didn't drink, but in other ways he was even more insufferable than her father, always staying out late to play pool or cards, skipping work whenever he felt like it, and, after he got fired, spending money on a bass boat when they hadn't even paid the electric bill. Bryce was infantile at best, a terrible role model, and any child of his would have been further cursed with freakishly good looks and a crippling capacity for snide self-satisfaction. The spawn of Bryce Hatton would have bullied other children on the playground, cheated on tests, chalked obscenities on the blackboard, stolen lunch money from the cloakroom, spat on the cafeteria floor, lied to the principal, and vandalized the boys' and girls' bathrooms.

Perhaps she should start with castration.

Patty turned toward the women, who were now whispering together, and the deputy, whose mouth was now closed, and strode down the hall. But before she'd covered half the distance, one of the women rose from the bench and hurried forward to greet her.

"Patty, it's wonderful to see you again," the woman said, wrapping her in a warm hug. Then she gripped Patty by both shoulders and looked her up and down. "Look at you, all grown up," she said. "I might not have recognized you if Rose hadn't told me who you were."

Rose. Lord God in heaven. The other woman on the bench was Rose Hatton, her mother-in-law, who now sat stiffly in place, clutching her handbag in her lap, staring vacantly ahead. She didn't expect Rose to be civil—after all, Patty was the devil who had led her boy astray and then betrayed him. She probably blamed Patty for all of Bryce's failings, including the ones he had before he met her.

Rose had always looked out of place, no matter where she was, but today she appeared particularly uprooted. Her make-up was caked on the way a child might have applied it, and she had dyed her hair an unnatural strawberry blonde that resembled cotton candy. Her black, magnolia-patterned dress hung on her like a flour sack, and she looked ready for a long, uncomfortable bus ride. She and Patty always tended to avoid each other except at official family gatherings, and even then they staked out opposite ends of the yard. Still, Patty should have recognized her.

But who was this other woman? She was far better dressed and better made-up than Rose, a different class altogether. Her fixed smile showed a mouth full of even white teeth, which put her well outside her parents' social circle. Maybe Patty had met her at the courthouse. A lawyer's wife.

"I'm here to see Bryce," Patty said, glancing past the woman to the deputy, whose eyes were still closed.

"My son does not want to see you," said Rose, and the deputy opened his eyes.

He got to his feet and adjusted his belt and holster. He was a large man, the kind who would have played football in high school, with a round, flat face and a bristle-cut of blond hair. "We have to keep a pretty tight rein on visitation, ma'am," he said. "Family members only."

"I'm his wife," she said.

Rose snorted, but didn't say anything.

The deputy glanced uneasily at Rose. "That counts," he told her.

"Try not to wake up Mary Jean," said the other woman, lowering her voice to a stage whisper. "I know she'd love to see you, but right now she's exhausted."

Of course. The woman was Mrs. McKinney. Patty had met her a couple of times in high school, back when Mary Jean and Patty had been co-editors of the school newspaper. Mrs. McKinney had served them lemonade once while they worked on layout at the McKinney's dining room table and had warned them not to drip glue on the glossy veneer. Then Patty had seen her again at the wedding.

"What's wrong with Mary Jean?" Patty asked.

"Poor judgment," she said, rolling her eyes, and Patty remembered why Mary Jean used to complain so much about her mother. "Her baby might have died."

"What baby?"

Mrs. McKinney gestured toward the nursery. "That little girl in the incubator," she said. "She doesn't have a name yet. My granddaughter."

Mary Jean was a full year younger than Patty. How could she have had a baby already? And when had she come home from college? Patty felt the color rise in her neck. The world was excluding her, bit by bit, carrying on its business in secret, changing the landscape every time she looked away. Well, she was sick of it, sick of this string of pop quizzes she hadn't known to study for. She needed to regain control.

"I'll only be a minute," she said.

The deputy held the door for her, and Patty entered the hospital room alone. She was surprised he didn't search her for weapons or hacksaws. Wasn't that what wives did for their jailbird husbands, bring them the tools to make good their escape? Not that the deputy would have found anything to confiscate. For all her anger and her plans to cause Bryce harm, she'd forgotten to pack any useful hardware. The most dangerous thing she carried was an emery board.

The room was bright with afternoon sun. Mary Jean lay sleeping in the first bed, and even unconscious she looked like a wrung-out washrag. Her face was pink and blotchy, with scabbed-over scrapes and scratches covering her right cheek and temple. Her eyes had sunken into dark hollows, making her look years older. Her hair was matted to her forehead in a slick tangle of knots, and the side of her head was crusted with what appeared to be clods of dried mud.

So that was motherhood.

Bryce looked far worse, rigged into his bed near the window with straps and pulleys. He wore a cast on each leg and on his left arm, while his right wrist was handcuffed to the bedrail. But his face was what she couldn't help staring at. All the delicately chiseled features of his face had been semi-obliterated, and stitches now held shut the gashes that had opened on his chin and cheekbones from the impact of his fall. His skin was purple, for the most part, and swollen so that his eyes were no more than slits. His nose was spread extravagantly across his face, as if the cartilage had been flattened out with a ball-peen hammer. His jaw seemed to fit crookedly in his skull. He looked more like a circus freak than he did her husband.

She felt elated. Bryce had given himself the pounding he deserved and in the process had left himself disfigured. True, the swelling would go down and his coloring would return to normal, but he'd never look like his old self again. From here on out, Bryce Hatton would be scarred. Less attractive. Maybe even ugly. The boy who thought he could coast through life on nothing but his looks would have to change his plans.

She leaned over his face and peered into the purple slits, hoping for some flicker of recognition.

"I could do anything to you right now that I wanted," she hissed.

"He's not much fun," said Mary Jean.

Patty straightened and eased away toward the foot of the bed. Mary Jean stared at her with half-closed eyes and a feeble smile on her lips.

"They've got him all doped up," she added.

Patty put her hand on Bryce's leg cast and shook it, but he didn't respond. Then she shoved the cast hard, clacking it against the other leg. Bryce still lay undisturbed, breathing peacefully.

"You don't seem glad to see him," Mary Jean slurred.

"Go back to sleep," Patty told her. "You've got a baby to rest up for."

"I don't remember," she said. "They gave me ether for the bad parts. Then something else later on." She laughed softly. "I feel pretty good now."

"I can tell," said Patty. "Now go back to sleep."

"Did you see the baby?"

Patty sighed. "Yes."

"What's her name?"

Mary Jean hadn't been drinking, but she might as well have been, and Patty felt her annoyance building. She had long ago tired of coping with drunks or crazies or anyone else who couldn't keep a clear head. People were bad enough without shuffling wild cards into the deck.

"You haven't given her a name," Patty told her.

"Good," Mary Jean said. "Names limit a person."

Patty couldn't argue with that. *Mrs. Bryce Hatton* had been the sorriest limitation she'd ever known.

"The tao that can be named is not the eternal tao," Mary Jean declared. She stretched her arms over her head and yawned. "That's Chinese."

This was not the scene Patty had envisioned. Bryce was sup-posed to be awake, begging for his life. Mary Jean was supposed to be away at college—or anywhere else in the world, for that matter. Anywhere but here.

Mary Jean sat up in bed and picked at the mud in her hair. "You don't like me anymore," she said.

"No, Mary Jean, I don't."

"We were friends in typing class," she said. "I was in your wedding."

"You were also at the rehearsal."

Mary Jean narrowed her eyes and nodded. "I shouldn't have let Bryce kiss me," she said. "I know it looked bad. I was just trying to be polite."

That had been the moment, there in the alcove by the baptismal font, with Mary Jean backed into the corner and Bryce hunched over her, his hand edging up the side of the ugly bridesmaid's dress like he was about to cop a feel, that was when Patty had known she should call it off, that she should go tell Reverend Tyree that she'd changed her mind. She could have used her father as an excuse, told them all she couldn't get married without the old man there to give her away. But Bryce had snaked his way out of it, telling her she had it all wrong, that he was just celebrating with their friends. And maybe that's all it had been—maybe she had exaggerated everything in her mind because, deep down, she was afraid of what she was do-ing, afraid she didn't know how to be a wife. But still, the sight of Bryce pressing himself against another woman, even if the woman was just mousy little Mary Jean, had tripped an alarm in her brain, and she realized that this was a boy she would never fully trust, not if they lived to be a hundred.

She had wrestled with her doubts right up to the ceremony, beyond the ceremony, in fact, because the instant Reverend Tyree had pronounced them man and wife, her first thought was to beg for a do-over, another shot at getting the answer right. *Do you take this man?* the reverend would ask again, and this time she would say *No, no, I don't, I suspect he's a no-good son of a bitch.* But it was too late. In the blink of an eye, organ music was sweeping them down the aisle, everyone was smiling and throwing rice, and her married life was already underway.

"Your ceremony was so beautiful," Mary Jean said. "That's when Bobby and I decided to get serious."

"Good for you."

"He drove me home afterward and I let him take off my bra. Things went pretty fast after that. I got pregnant the next weekend in the back seat of his dad's Studebaker."

So that was the story. Bobby Malone and Mary Jean McKinney, high school sweethearts with a baby. They didn't stand a chance.

"Would you be my maid of honor?" asked Mary Jean. "If Bobby's not dead, I mean."

He might indeed be dead, Patty realized. Korea was taking a heavy toll, and at this point they all knew boys who had died there. Harlan Simms, Hank Moffitt, Jack Broadway, the Hatcher kid who had sat behind her in home room, Doug Pitts from the farm next to her parents' place. Bobby Malone could easily join the list.

Bryce had been one of the few who'd stayed behind, having blown out an eardrum playing with firecrackers when he was ten.

Maybe that's why she'd fallen for him—there wasn't anybody else around. The Selective Service had taken all the good ones. Nothing left but 4-Fs and old-timers.

"Bobby won't die," Patty said. But she knew the realities. Even if Bobby Malone made it home from Korea, and even if he felt guilty enough to marry Mary Jean when he got here, there would be no happy-ever-after for their situation. Patty had learned a lot typing transcripts at the courthouse, had read the trial testimony of countless couples who started out in love but ended up at each other's throats. She knew firsthand the way good intentions turned to dust. At best, Mary Jean and Bobby would pack up their belongings and move to another town. Then they could live out their downfall among strangers, which would at least be less humiliating than failing at home.

"Bryce won't die either," Mary Jean offered. She meant it as a kindness, Patty knew, but still a thick curtain came down over her heart.

"I wish he would," she said.

Mary Jean bit her lip and frowned, and Patty could see she was struggling to concentrate.

"Why?" she asked.

No point hiding anything at this late date, she figured. Besides, by the time Mary Jean came out of her cloud, she'd have forgotten Patty was ever here.

"I loved somebody else," Patty said. "Bryce killed him."

Mary Jean opened her mouth, but no sound came out. She shook her head and lay back against her pillow. "I'm confused," she said at last.

"Walter Hatton," she explained.

"But you're married to Bryce," Mary Jean said.

"Bryce doesn't know what married is," said Patty, glancing toward him on the bed. "If he ever expected things to work out between us, he needed to stay home a few nights, not roam around like some stray dog."

"Not roam around," Mary Jean repeated. "That's right. It's bad to roam."

Patty realized she had trapped herself. If infidelity was the measure, she was every bit as guilty as Bryce. All he had on her was a head start.

"Can't be helped, though," Mary Jean went on. "All roads lead to roam." She pulled the covers over her face and broke into muffled laughter.

Patty's first impulse was to slap her silly. But there was something ridiculously true in what she had said. Patty didn't know any couples her own age who had managed to stay faithful. None at all. Maybe Patty was as immature as Bryce, and Mary Jean, and Bobby, and all the rest. Maybe they were all just too young, too volatile, too full of expectations to settle into the kind of commitment marriage was meant to be.

Maybe she would have failed with Walter just as she had failed with Bryce.

"That may be the smartest thing you ever said," Patty told her.

Mary Jean stopped her giggling and sat up again, allowing the bedsheet to fall from her face. "I heard it from a dead man," she said. Then she collapsed dramatically onto her back again.

That was another thing Patty hated about drugs and alcohol. They gave people false visions—imaginary visits from all manner of haints and zombies. Her father once thought their living room rug was a sea of live rats trying to devour his legs.

But this one wasn't Mary Jean's fault. The doctors had pumped her full of their own special brand of delirium, and she had no choice but to ride it out.

She looked again at Bryce. She didn't feel like killing him anymore. The core of her malice had simply drained away. Bryce was just a haughty child—Patty, too, for that matter—and their mistakes would haunt them both for years. All she wanted now was for Bryce to live long enough to regret who he was, long enough to feel shame at how thoughtlessly he had destroyed the dreams of those around him.

"I'll be your maid of honor, Mary Jean," she said, but the girl had already drifted back to sleep. She opened her pocketbook and took out the wedding photo. Mary Jean looked good in the picture, probably better than she would ever look again, given what lay ahead. Patty propped it on the table by her bed. Times had changed. It should be Mary Jean's keepsake now.

She reached back into her pocketbook and fished out the Sheaffer fountain pen she used at the courthouse for signing legal documents. She would be the first to sign Bryce's cast. All three of his casts, in fact. When he finally woke, that would be the first thing he saw: her name written over and over on the plaster of his arm and of both legs, filling the white space with evidence of who she was.

Not Mrs. Bryce Hatton. Never again Mrs. Bryce Hatton. She would use her maiden name, and he would have no choice but to read *Patricia Elaine Hart* all day long, whenever he opened his eyes. *Patricia Elaine Hart*, until all his bones had healed.

Yes, from here on out it would be *Patricia Elaine Hart*.

That name, too, was limiting. But at least it left her room to move around.

Reverend Tyree

As Reverend Tyree settled himself onto the torn front seat of his rust-spotted DeSoto and turned the ignition, he had a brief moment of hope. The motor sputtered, coughed, and whirred without catching. He turned the key again, with the same result. The old rattletrap was trying to give him a night off, it seemed. One more failed attempt and he would be justified in staying home with Mildred and his mother and listening to the radio for a change. And why shouldn't he stay at home? The clean-up crews hadn't fully cleared the streets after the tornado, so driving could be dangerous, especially on the side of town where the county jail was located. The inmates wouldn't care if he skipped a visit. But when he turned the key a third time, the engine caught, and that was it—he was trapped for yet another Saturday night.

He dreaded the jailhouse even more than the hospital. The hospital was relatively cheerful, especially in the evenings, and he had learned that if he made his rounds about an hour after dinnertime, many of the patients he was supposed to visit would have already drifted off to sleep. Then he could sit by their beds and read magazines. He would always leave evidence of his visit—a printed card with a picture of Jesus on it and a passage from St. Luke: "Rejoice, because your names are written in heaven."

The jailhouse was a different place entirely. Everything about it made him uneasy—the dim lighting, the dirty walls, the chill that seemed to radiate from the cell bars, the creaking wooden hallways, the unidentifiable and unsanitary smell.

And the inmates. Some were from his own congregation, of course—public drunks and brawlers, mostly, whom he had come to counsel. Elmer Maddox and Jess Hawley and Tump Wood. The regulars. But there were others there, as well, strangers lurking in the shadows of their cells, men he couldn't put names to. Those were the ones who spooked him. He didn't know what they'd been locked up for, or what they might do. Sometimes they muttered things in his direction, things he didn't quite catch. But he knew they were mocking him.

He tried to remind himself that many of God's holiest servants had spent time in jail, including some of the more famous apostles, like Peter and Paul. John the Baptist had been imprisoned. Of course, none of the men in the county lockup were likely to die as Christian martyrs. These men were far too weak and insincere to let themselves be crucified upside down or have their heads served up on a platter for the glory of God. He couldn't even get them to give up dancing.

But it was his job to tend his flock, no matter how unsavory the individual sheep might be. This evening he had two inmates on his list: Bryce Hatton and Marshall Raby.

Bryce was the one who worried him. Quick tempered, surly, and disrespectful of authority. Everyone knew he'd shot his cousin. The boy's marriage was in trouble to boot, the reverend had learned that much from his counseling sessions with Patty. Their sacred union hadn't been very sacred after all, and maybe Bryce blamed the reverend for that, since he'd performed the ceremony. Who knew what craziness a mind like that might leap to?

Crazy people unnerved him. Sometimes he tried to imagine what it must be like to give in to the criminal impulse, to lose control, to take that dark plunge into chaos. But he couldn't do it. A clear head and a steady hand, those were his blessings in life. His role in this world was to respect boundaries, not violate them. He knew it might be helpful if he could empathize from time to time with church members who strayed, so that he might better comprehend their faults and offer guidance. But the power wasn't in him. People like Bryce were mysteries he would never solve.

But he had more on his plate tonight than just Bryce and Marshall. He also had business to take up with Sheriff Tune. Unpleasant business. The soul of the town was hovering over the abyss. The Beast was approaching, plain as day. He had to force Sheriff Tune to do something.

He wasn't hopeful. The reverend had brought a number of crises to Sheriff Tune's attention, and the sheriff had always advised him to take his complaints to the mayor. Herod passing him off to Pilate. Or Pilate to Herod, he wasn't sure which analogy applied. In either case, the mayor had never been any help, always thanking him for his concerns but never making the slightest effort to correct the problems. But that was hardly surprising. Both men were backsliding Presbyterians, part of Reverend Sinclair's congregation. It was a wonder they ever got anything done.

They had even ignored his warnings about Madame Zubu the Mysterious. She was corrupting the younger congregants, he knew that for a fact. The teens in his youth group talked about little else, telling lurid tales of her fortune-telling skills. They had all squandered good money to sit at her card table and watch her gaze into a crystal ball and mumble nonsense. She was a charlatan who should be run out of town. Yet the sheriff continued to allow her to practice her voodoo or hoodoo or whatever it was, right there in an upstairs front window on the south side of the square. He'd written a letter to the editor about it, attempting to alert the larger community to the problem, but Tom Parsons had never printed it. Typical. Tom Parsons owned the very building Madame Zubu had set up shop in, and from what the reverend had heard, Mr. Parsons didn't even charge her any rent.

She had no shades or curtains, so every Tuesday and Thursday night anyone passing by could see her sitting at her table, like a black widow waiting in her web. Sometimes she had a young child with her, a boy of maybe six or seven, which was disgraceful. The room was illuminated by a single string of multi-colored Christmas lights draped over a chandelier. She wore a long brightly patterned blue robe that might have been Chinese, and a shiny red turban with a wild heathen feather tucked in its folds. The walls around her were painted black. Black, for God's sake. She read palms and consulted Tarot cards and predicted the future from tea leaves and signs.

Well, he could predict things, too. He could predict that certain fools in positions of authority were treading the broad path to hell, and Madame Zubu the Mysterious was leading their parade. It was bad enough that the carnival came to town every year, dragging in perverts and derelicts from the big northern cities, but having Madame Zubu the Mysterious as a fixture on the town square was more than a decent community ought to tolerate.

And what about that prize-fighting exhibition Tom Parsons had set up? That would be a carnival, too. Drunks and gamblers and pickpockets would swarm into town from across the state line, just to watch dim-witted behemoths bash each other's brains in. He couldn't imagine why a man of Mr. Parsons' position would sponsor such violence, or why the sheriff hadn't immediately put a stop to it. Jesus had been quite specific about fighting. A good Christian turned the other cheek—he didn't trade blows until someone was unconscious. Yet Mr. Parsons had the gall to call his upcoming spectacle a sporting event. The more he thought about it, the more he realized what a dark presence Mr. Parsons was becoming in the community.

But the reverend couldn't dwell on any of that now. He had to concentrate on the matter at hand: the dead man in the window of Fred's Five-and-Dime. The one the tornado had dropped so unceremoniously onto the courthouse lawn. The stranger no one could identify.

As he pulled up alongside the jailhouse, he ran over something in the street—a piece of metal, from the sound of it—that
flipped up hard against the undercarriage and clanked back to
the pavement. He sighed. He couldn't afford any repairs right
now. He climbed out and peered underneath the DeSoto to
check for radiator leaks or broken hoses, but he couldn't make
out much in the darkness. The only light came from the dim
yellow bulb above the jailhouse door, and all it showed him was
the flaking chrome of his front bumper and what appeared to
be a crowbar lying on the pavement next to his front tire. He
reached under the automobile, careful not to soil his only suit
coat, and dragged the bar out into the light. It wasn't a crowbar, after all, but an iron rod, storm debris of some kind. He
couldn't leave it in the road where any school child might find
it—unsupervised boys could get into trouble with a bar like this.
He tossed it through his open window onto the front seat and
headed inside the jail.

On any other Saturday evening this floor of the building
would have been bristling with deputies filing paperwork and
processing drunks, and maybe a couple of trustees mopping
the halls. But tonight the place was calm, virtually empty, and
when the reverend inadvertently let the front door slam shut
behind him, the noise echoed up the stairwell like a gunshot.
All the ground-floor offices were dark except for the receiving
area, which housed the holding cell and a few old desks and
benches. Reverend Tyree eased the glass-paned door open and
stepped tentatively into the room. The sheriff sat hunched over
a deputy's desk studying a dog-eared piece of notebook paper.
Coffee mugs and crumpled Dairy Queen bags cluttered the
filing cabinets lining the walls, and thick manila folders and
mounds of mimeographed documents covered nearly every flat
surface. The holding cell at the back of the room was empty for
a change. Two men in work clothes whom the reverend didn't
recognize sat on a wooden bench in the corner playing checkers. The sheriff continued to frown over the piece of paper in
his hands, and his frown deepened when he looked up and saw

who had just come through the door. He leaned back in his chair and sighed.

"I see you're busy," the reverend said. "I'll just go on up."

The sheriff spit a wad of gum into the wastebasket by the desk. "Reverend, I believe you wasted a trip."

"Nine times out of ten," he answered, attempting a smile. "But the tenth time is what counts."

"Nothing counts this evening," the sheriff told him. "Bryce Hatton and Marshall Raby aren't available."

"You can't deny them spiritual counsel," the reverend objected, and the two men playing checkers laughed.

"All right, you two," said Sheriff Tune. "Game's over. Go back to your cells."

The two men grumbled, but they both rose from the table and ambled toward Reverend Tyree, who stepped clear of the doorway to let them pass. He kept a careful eye on them as they trudged up the stairs.

"I'm not denying anybody anything," the sheriff continued. "Bryce is in the hospital. He took a bad spill this morning."

"My Lord," said Reverend Tyree. "Is he all right?"

"I guess he'll live. Doc McKinney thinks so, anyway. But he's pretty banged up." He leaned forward and shook his head. "The real disappointment is Marshall."

If Reverend Tyree had a favorite at the jail, it was Marshall Raby. Marshall was polite and eager to please, always smiling and nodding his head. Maybe he didn't really listen to the reverend's speeches on self-improvement, but at least he didn't interrupt. Best of all, Marshall had no history of violence, he was merely a thief, and the reverend was encouraged by that. The last friend Jesus made on this earth had been a thief.

"What did Marshall do?" he asked.

"He betrayed a trust. I left him in charge here this morning. He stole a new Packard and lit out for Alabama."

"Why would he do that?"

"He got scared when Bryce hurt himself. Once the ambulance showed up, he just took off."

"How do you know all this?" the reverend asked.

Sheriff Tune raised the sheet of notepaper he'd been frowning over. "He left a letter of apology."

Reverend Tyree brightened. Maybe his counseling sessions had made an impact on Marshall after all.

"A letter of apology is a good sign," he said. "I mean, that's a Christian gesture. I think Marshall's becoming a better person."

Sheriff Tune dropped Marshall's letter onto the desk. "Reverend, yesterday he was serving six months for car theft. Today he's a fugitive in another stolen car. I don't consider that progress."

The sheriff was right, of course. The Devil had won again. The Devil always won in this town, no matter how hard the reverend tried. Sinners ignored him, or scoffed in his face, or whispered jokes behind his back. Maybe if he'd been a large man, like Sheriff Tune, he could have made people listen. But he was short, and bald, and his voice was too high, and he lived in a rented house with a barren wife, and his automobile was third-rate, and his shoes were scuffed, and no one took him seriously, even at the price of their salvation. He was as laughable now as he had been in high school, when he was shoved around routinely by every shop-class bully and every jock in a letter jacket. Sheriff Tune had probably been a bully himself, tripping the weaker, more studious kids in the hallways. But high school was over. Roland T. Tyree had made something of himself; he was a member of the clergy, and that deserved respect. He would not be put off from his greater mission.

"There's another matter we need to talk about," he said, and he could see the annoyance come over the sheriff's sunburned face.

"Like you said, Reverend, I'm kind of busy this evening." He spread his hands to indicate the pile of paperwork in front of him.

The reverend put his own hands on the desktop and leaned forward to make his point more forcefully. "There's a darkness swallowing the land," he said.

The sheriff swiveled his chair toward the window. "Yeah, I've noticed that," he said. "Happens every night about this time. I'll look into it."

"I'm talking about that thing in the dime-store window," he said.

The sheriff turned back to Reverend Tyree and nodded. "Unusual situation, I'll grant you that," he said. "But as long as the health inspector approves, there's no code violation."

"What about moral violations?" the reverend demanded. "What about standards of decency? He's turned death into a sideshow."

"All we're trying to do is find out who the poor man is," the sheriff said.

"I can tell you who he is," the reverend said, his voice rising. "He's the seven-headed beast. He's the angel of the bottomless pit. He's Abaddon and Mammon and Belial and Beelzebub and all the other minions of Satan."

The sheriff smiled. "You wouldn't have an address on that, would you?"

"I'm talking about the spiritual impact on this community," the reverend declared, and he banged his fist on the edge of the desk. He had seen a bishop do that once in seminary and had been impressed by the dramatic power of the gesture. But this was an old piece of wood, dried out by too many seasons of radiator heat. The overhanging lip of the desktop sheared away and clattered obscenely to the floor.

Even the furniture mocked him.

"You broke my desk," said Sheriff Tune, not angrily, as the reverend expected, but with mild surprise.

Why did everything always have to turn ridiculous? He was a certified man of God; he had genuine spiritual insights. Yet whenever he tried to explain himself, some grotesque absurdity always blocked his path. Jesus had talked in parables and people understood him just fine. Reverend Tyree couldn't even make a straightforward point without looking like a fool.

"That's defacing city property," Sheriff Tune said. Then he picked up the chunk of wood and held it to the fractured edge, lining up the fit as closely as possible. "Clean break, though. I might could nail it back together."

The reverend didn't know what to say. The air seemed to have gone right out of him. For a fleeting moment, he'd had the upper hand, he'd felt it, but now Sheriff Tune had the advantage again.

"I'm sorry," he said.

The sheriff put the piece of wood on Marshall Raby's letter like a paperweight. "Look, Reverend, why don't you just go on home before you break something else," he said. "This dime-store business won't last much longer, I can promise you that. The funeral's tomorrow afternoon."

The sheriff didn't understand. Reverend Tyree had been blessed with an insight. No, more than that, it was an epiphany. A life-changing vision. He had talked it all through with his wife, and though she hadn't understood him any better than the sheriff, she had at least helped him crystallize his thoughts. This abomination from the whirlwind was poisoning the town—he could feel it in his bones. The body's deformities and its na-kedness exuded a subtle and sinister power, inflaming even the weakest imaginations. People were children when it came to the unknown, and here was the boogeyman they had believed in all their lives. Mildred had filled him in on the gossip. The man was a sex fiend, an escaped killer, a Communist from the Soviet Union, even a caveman preserved by a glacier and carried south in the storm.

He knew what would come next. Before long the body would cease to be human at all, would become instead whatever best suited their collective fears—an alien from another planet, a mutated creature created by nuclear fallout, a haint born of thin air and sent by the Devil to pollute men's minds—and this last speculation wouldn't be far wrong. With every passing hour the dead man's stature would grow.

He'd seen the first signs already. Even his poor deluded Mil-dred had succumbed to the hysteria, suggesting that the naked man might be some kind of holy messenger from God. From God—as if this apparition might be a manifestation of Jesus Christ himself. She had told the reverend he should find a lesson in the man's arrival and use it in his sermon Sunday morning.

But what sermon Sunday morning? Didn't she understand that his church had just been taken away from him by the hand of the Almighty, that First Baptist was no longer a place of worship but a soggy pile of rubble? They weren't a wealthy congregation, it might take years to rebuild, and in the meantime he would lose his flock to Second Baptist, which had escaped the storm. Didn't Mildred see that her husband had just been fired? And not by the board members who paid his salary, but by God himself.

But the board members, too, would have their say. He knew they would blame him for buying the wrong insurance policy, the cheaper version that excluded Acts of God. His agent, Jimmy Vann, had advised him against cutting corners, but the reverend thought Jimmy was merely trying to pad the premium. After all, why would a church need protection from Acts of God? That contradicted everything he believed in.

"You can't bury him here," the reverend insisted. "You have to take him out of this town. Now. Tonight. He puts us all in jeopardy."

The sheriff narrowed his eyes and chewed the inside of his cheek. "I'm not sure I see it that way," he said.

The reverend took a deep breath. He felt lightheaded and needed to sit down. But he couldn't sit down, not with Sheriff Tune staring at him. A chill climbed slowly up his spine, and cold fingers tightened around his neck. He had to get out of this room. But he couldn't leave, not yet, not until he'd made the sheriff realize what was at stake. He cast about in his mind, searching for some pertinent argument that might tip the scales, but his thoughts were tumbling over one another, jumbling in his head, and before he could even begin to sort anything out, someone rapped sharply on the office doorframe behind him.

"Yes ma'am," the sheriff said, staring past him. "What can I help you with?"

A middle-aged woman in gardening clothes entered the room cradling a Boston terrier. She had blood on her pale blue blouse, and she looked stricken, as though she had already seen the fallen world that Reverend Tyree was predicting.

The reverend eased away from the desk as she approached. He didn't like Boston terriers. They were snappish dogs who couldn't be trusted. The eyes of this one followed him as he circled away toward the holding cell.

"Evening, Mrs. Crabtree," said the sheriff.

"I want someone arrested," she said, her voice shaking.

"Yes, ma'am," Sheriff Tune answered, "but I'll have to ask you to leave your dog outside. We don't allow animals in the jailhouse."

"He's dead," she said, and burst into tears. She sank down onto the bench by the door, still hugging the dead Boston terrier, whose glassy eyes remained fixed on Reverend Tyree. Sheriff Tune rose from his desk and walked quickly to her. He crouched at her feet and examined the bloody animal.

The reverend knew he could never reclaim the sheriff's attention now. This woman and her dead dog had usurped his place at the head of the line.

"We have to ensure our spiritual safety," the reverend said. "If you won't help me, I'll talk to the mayor."

The woman scowled in his direction, as if he were the one interrupting. He wanted to say something threatening and cruel, but he had no bluster left.

"I'm sure he'll be glad to see you," the sheriff said, his focus still on the dog. The implication in his tone was clear. Their conversation was over. The reverend was dismissed.

He didn't know what to do next, but he knew he couldn't stay there, not with a dead dog staring at him and the room growing smaller with every breath. He strode past the sheriff into the hallway and burst through the door into the night.

The DeSoto's motor caught on the first turn of the key—a good omen. He floored the accelerator, and by the time he crossed Green Street three blocks away, he was clipping along at nearly twenty-five miles an hour. Ten miles over the speed limit in the heart of the town. But he didn't care. Maybe a deputy would pull him over. He could get himself arrested and taken back to jail.

He swung onto Elk and entered the square, then hit his brakes and skidded to a stop against the courthouse curb. The tornado had destroyed half the businesses downtown, and the rest were closed for the night. There were no deputies, no clean-up crews, no curious prowlers. Everyone was safe at home, recuperating from their sleepless night before. He was alone in a ghost town.

He got out of his car and stood looking up at the darkened office window of Madame Zubu the Mysterious. He couldn't see her, but he knew she was there, cackling in her blackened room, conjuring up demons, casting her spells over the dozing town. The dark arts were on the rise. He shuddered and turned away. Something had to be done. He walked briskly across the street, past Dr. McKinney's office and Monahan's Funeral Home, then down the hill to the display window of Fred's Five-and-Dime.

The dead man looked pale in the moonlight, and Reverend Tyree stared at him for a long while, wondering who he might be.

The night air felt soothing on his face. An answer would come to him if he thought hard enough. If he prayed hard enough.

Never could there be a more willing servant. If God would put the weapon in his hand, he would strike. He would cleanse this town of evil and bring salvation, even to those who abused and ignored him. He might have to be stern, even severe. Sometimes a parent had to discipline a child, and this town was a child in almost every way. He would not spare the rod.

And then he saw that God, in ways more mysterious than Madame Zubu would ever know, had placed him on the proper path, had brought him here, to this storefront window, to grant him grace and set things right again. The miracle was already underway; the tool he prayed for was already in his hand. He couldn't even remember taking it from the front seat, but there it was, rough and cool in his stubby fingers, the iron bar he'd picked up from the roadway outside the jail. It was heavy, and solid, and ready for the Lord's work.

He swung it forward, like Samson wielding the jawbone of an ass, slaughtering the Philistines. The glass cracked, but didn't fall, so he swung the bar again, and this time the entire plate-glass window shattered, raining down in long shards onto the pavement and into the store. Some of it fell into the casket and onto the dead man's yellow checkered shirt. He knocked away a few jagged pieces from the lower frame and stepped through the window.

The creature was heavy, but Roland Tyree was filled with the Holy Spirit, and his normal limitations didn't apply. He hoisted the wet, cowboy-like thing over his shoulder and leapt back onto the sidewalk. The weight doubled him over, drove him to his knees on the rough pavement, and he surprised himself by growling as he straightened back up.

The eyes of the dog still followed him, even here, but that didn't frighten him, not anymore. His soul was strong again, and through this act he would strengthen others as well. God was testing him, as God always tested him, but this time he knew the answers. This time he would pass.

As he staggered up the dark hill in the empty night, the future began to form in his mind. He would put this burden in his trunk and drive across the state line, deep into Alabama, just as Marshall Raby had done. When he reached the Tennessee River he would park on the bridge, drag the body to the rail, and dump it over the side. It was the Lord's will, even Mildred could see that.

He would baptize this monster once and for all, purify it of corruption, deliver it back to the elements where it belonged. And when it had disappeared beneath the swift, black waters, the curse on his life, on all their lives, would at last be lifted.

He would kneel on the bridge and give thanks.

He would pray for the souls of the lost.

He would ask God, in his infinite wisdom and mercy, to finally give it a name.

Moody Smith

Moody Smith couldn't rouse himself enough to answer the pounding on his door. His head was too clogged with dreams. He wasn't fully drunk, not like he had been a few hours earlier, but his will was gone, and the delirium that had plagued him through the night would release him only halfway. Dead men on horses still pursued him, and the hoofbeats were closing in.

He knew how close he was to waking. His mind tottered between nightmare and the light of day, ugly propositions both, and though he might have chosen to sleep forever, even under the dark weight of the dream, the pounding was too relentless, too insistent. It broke through the stupor he had spent his final paycheck on and dragged him, thrashing and gasping, up through the chaos to the bright surface of the world, back into the squalor of his moldering front room.

He tried to speak, but his throat was raw from vomit, and he fell into a deep coughing fit that burned to the bottom of his lungs.

"No God today," he called out at last, his voice low and raspy.

He knew who was at the door. His brother-in-law, Tom Parsons. Tom always came by on Sunday mornings to wake him up for church. Not that Tom was overly religious himself, but he'd made a few promises to Kate before she died, and one of them was to try every week to get her brother, Moody, to attend services. Tom had taken things one step further, convincing the board of elders at First Baptist to hire Moody as their sexton. That way he had to show up every Sunday morning to ring the bell.

He would never admit it to Tom, but working as the church sexton was the best job he'd had in the eight years since he left the merchant marines. Ringing the bell was something he enjoyed doing, though not in some weird way, like the hunchback of Notre Dame. He just liked the sound of the bell, so strong and clear, traveling out across the rooftops of the town. He liked knowing that he was giving a signal people were listening for.

Besides ringing the bell, all he had to do was clean the sanctuary and dig graves. The cleaning was easy because people were always on their best behavior at church. He rarely had to do more than pick up the litter after services—the discarded bulletins and unused collection envelopes the children doodled on during the sermon. He would straighten up the hymnals in the backs of the pews, sweep the sidewalk out front, and lock the doors at night. Sometimes he had to clean up after socials and potluck dinners, but he didn't mind that because he always got a free meal out of it without having to bring a covered dish of his own.

Digging graves was the worst part of the job, but even that didn't bother him much as long as the weather was good—and as long as he didn't know the occupant.

Kate would have been proud of how well he was doing, especially since he was employed by the congregation they'd both belonged to as children. She'd switched to Presbyterian when she married Tom, but all the denominations were pretty much the same as far as Moody could tell. He didn't know why religion had always been so important to her. God had sure let her down, killing her with the cancer. But people had to find their own way, and her way had been as a churchgoer.

Moody had fallen away from their childhood religion long ago. He'd been to the exotic reaches of the world—Siam, Ceylon, Zanzibar, even the Arctic Circle—and for his money, being a Baptist just didn't cover it all.

But being a Baptist sexton suited him fine. He wasn't required to attend the actual services, but sometimes he played along anyway, a tip of the hat to Kate, wearing the suit coat and dark tie Tom had given him for his birthday and sitting right up front near the pulpit.

There were always open seats up front. Reverend Tyree was slightly nearsighted, so he had a tendency to focus on the people in the first pew, and whoever sat there got the full force of his bombast. Moody didn't mind that at all. He liked the feeling that the reverend was preaching only to him. It made ignoring the sermon all the more gratifying.

But not today. He couldn't face a whole hour of religious fervor. He felt vulnerable, having just fallen off the wagon after six weeks of sobriety. His confidence was low, and the last thing he needed was for Reverend Tyree to prey on his weakness. He'd seen how preachers could work their spell on a fallen man, and he had no intention of being one of those hallelujah latecomers who broke down in tears and confessed their awful sins in front of the whole congregation. Finding salvation in Jesus was all right for young people, but a man his age had no business being saved. The embarrassment alone might kill him. Besides, he carried a lot of durable grudges, and he wasn't about to trade them in on something as lightweight as forgiveness.

The banging on the door stopped, and Moody raised his head to see if Tom had decided to cut his losses and go on alone. But Tom leaned his head in through the broken front window.

"I'm not leaving, bud," he said. "Get off the couch and clean yourself up."

"Church is gone." Moody had heard about what the tornado had done, though he hadn't yet felt strong enough to go see it for himself.

"Only the building," Tom said. "Outdoor services today."

"I'm sick," Moody told him. He rolled onto his back and rubbed his good eye. There was a crack in his ceiling nearly an inch wide that he'd never seen before. More storm damage, he guessed.

"Eat some greens," Tom said. "You'll be fine."

Moody grabbed the empty Jack Daniel's bottle tucked in the cushion by his head and flung it in Tom's general direction. It hit the door, but bounced harmlessly to the floor without breaking. He was losing arm strength. Another reason not to get into the ring with Jersey Joe Walcott.

Tom took in the scene and frowned. "I see signs of a struggle," he said.

Moody sat up and looked around. The room was cluttered with empties—a couple of pint bottles of whiskey lay overturned on the wooden tomato crate that served as Moody's coffee table, and a couple more of gin lay on the seat of the ladder-backed chair by the couch. Moody counted half a dozen cola bottles mixed in with the broken window glass on the floor and spotted what looked to be an unfinished fifth of vodka swaddled in a pair of his workpants in the corner. Typical after-binge mess, really—nothing unfamiliar about any of it, except maybe the walls. Someone had decorated his wallpaper with crude crayon drawings of a figure on horseback.

"A bottle is just a symbol," Moody said, quoting from their A.A. guidebook. "All my problems are of my own making."

"Save it," Tom said. "I'm not here to give a temperance lecture."

"Glad to hear it," Moody said. "Maybe you can tell me something useful for a change."

Tom nodded toward Moody's brown fedora on the floor by the couch. "You threw up in your hat," he said.

Moody peered over the armrest. "That's good to know."

He struggled to his feet and opened the door for Tom, who entered cautiously, easing empty bottles aside with his polished brown dress shoes. Moody couldn't blame him for taking care. Tom was a meticulously clean man, and the white linen suit he wore every Sunday didn't have a spot on it. Moody's place was a booby trap for clothes like that. As Tom neared the couch, something on the side of the tomato crate caught his eye. He bent down to examine it more closely, then plucked out a box of crayons someone had wedged between two slats. He set it on top of the crate beside the empty whiskey bottles.

"Stinks in here," Tom said.

"That's me," Moody admitted. He scratched at the anchor tattooed on his forearm.

"Stick your head under the faucet. Slap on some Old Spice."

Moody shuffled into the back room and turned on the water tap in his utility sink. He let it run for a moment to clear out the rust and then leaned his head into the icy stream. The cold shocked him fully awake. He blotted his face and bare scalp with a stiff washrag as he walked back into the front room.

"How'd you get the liquor?" Tom asked.

Moody didn't want to say. Sammy Statten was shy about his bootlegging and kept a small, discreet clientele. Sammy was the sexton over at First Presbyterian, and he and Moody had struck a bargain—Moody would help dig Presbyterian graves in exchange for home deliveries. Moody didn't want any of his A.A. buddies to know about that.

"I'm more curious how I got the crayons," Moody said. He squinted at the artwork on his walls.

Tom took off his tortoise-shell spectacles and wiped them with his handkerchief, then balanced them back on his nose and studied the sketches. "Looks like you flunked kindergarten," he said. "Maybe you ought to just hang a picture."

He tipped the ladder-back forward, dumping the gin bottles to the floor. Moody winced at the racket. Tom dusted the seat with his handkerchief and settled himself onto the chair. He crossed his arms and narrowed his eyes at Moody.

"So how come I wasn't invited?" Tom asked. That was the standard A.A. drill. If Moody ever felt tempted to take a drink, he was supposed to call Tom to talk him through it.

"Beats me," Moody told him. He sat heavily on the couch and cupped his face in his hands. "I'm hazy on the details."

Moody couldn't bring himself to say more, because the parts he remembered were too disturbing. Somewhere between his second and third pint, his dreams had merged with the real world, and a dead man had appeared in his yard. A dead man on a swaybacked horse. He'd had hallucinations before, but this one was more vivid than usual, and he feared what might be happening to his brain.

Pugilistic dementia. Doc McKinney had told him all about it at the Baptist social one Sunday afternoon while they both loaded up their plates with potato salad. He couldn't remember how they got onto the topic in the first place. Maybe Moody had said something about the fights he'd been in over the years, although that wasn't likely. He tended not to talk about that part of his past, though it seemed to be the main thing people were curious about. But however it had come up, the Doc explained that if the brain got battered one too many times it would begin to shut down, slowly, like lights blinking out in a neighborhood late at night. Moody had heard of fighters becoming punch-drunk, slurring their words and forgetting their own names. He had pushed his luck in that regard for much of his life, brawling with strangers and even his own shipmates in some of the most inhospitable ports in the world. No telling what kind of damage he'd suffered. And now that he knew there was an actual medical term for it, it seemed even more ominous.

Alcohol, the Doc had warned him, would speed the process.

Still, he had pretty much managed to put it out of his mind until the previous night, when Herb Gatlin paid him a visit. He and Herb had been pals ever since Moody had first moved into Stockyard Row, eight years earlier. News of Herb's death was part of what had pushed Moody toward taking that first burning swig.

But he couldn't put it all on Herb. Losing his job had been a big part of it. They hadn't fired him yet—not officially. But what choice would they have, with the church in ruins? His last chore for First Baptist would probably be to dig Herb Gatlin's grave.

As soon as he realized that, he had written out his order on a scrap of a grocery sack, stuck it in an envelope, and paid a neighbor boy a nickel to hike up to First Presbyterian and deliver it. Then later that evening, when he was almost too drunk to stand, he'd heard the clop-clop of hooves coming up the street. He went outside to look, and there came Herb, ambling up the hill on his old gray swayback. Moody stared at him, dumbfounded.

That was a big wind came through here, Herb said. *Glad to see you're okay.*

What could he have meant by that? Then Herb had just plodded away on his ghost horse and Moody had stumbled back inside.

That must have been when he drew the pictures on his walls. But why would he do a thing like that? Maybe to make himself remember once he sobered up. Sure, that had to be it. But where had the crayons come from? He didn't remember buying any. He wouldn't buy any, in fact, ever. Crayons reminded him of the funny papers and comic books and cartoons, all of which he despised. So they must have come from somewhere else. But there wasn't anywhere else. Which meant they came from nowhere.

Which made no sense.

So it appeared that a haint had come into his yard. That was something he could almost make himself believe. He didn't have to be a practicing Baptist to know there was a spiritual side to the world. People everywhere, in all sorts of religions, believed in some kind of ghost. But no religion he'd ever heard of would claim a box of crayons could materialize on a tomato crate. There was no spiritual basis for a thing like that. Water into wine, sure, but that was a transformation, which was a different thing entirely. Not even Jesus could spin crayons out of thin air.

Of course, every accomplished alcoholic had blackouts, or he wasn't doing it right. He must have gone out for crayons in some kind of trance. And that ghost in his yard—well, that was just brain cells dying off by the thousands. Pugilistic dementia had caught up with him at last.

"I guess we'll both have stories to tell at the next meeting," Tom said.

"You too?" Moody asked.

"Night before last. I slid all the way back to Step One."

Moody understood the problem. All twelve steps were tough, and he'd stumbled over them all on a daily basis. But right now Step Two was the one he wished he could get a grip on: Come to believe that a Power greater than ourselves can restore us to sanity. The truth was, Moody did believe in that Power. But sanity still seemed a long way off.

"Last night was rough," he said. "I saw things."

"Like what?"

Moody didn't like talking about it, but part of Step Five was to admit things to another human being. If he wanted to get better, he had to open up more. He had to confess the exact nature of his wrongs.

"Like the stuff I drew on the walls."

Tom looked at the drawings again.

"So you saw a guy on a horse. What's the big deal?"

"I was delirious," Moody told him. "The guy and the horse weren't real."

Tom frowned and stepped over to the open doorway. "If the horse wasn't real, how'd he manage to take a dump in your yard?"

"What?"

Tom pointed toward the muddy stretch out near the street. "Between the hoofprints, genius."

Moody crossed to the door and stared out at the mound of horse droppings. "I'm confused," he said.

Tom laughed. "That's why drunks aren't considered reliable witnesses."

Moody didn't know what to think. His alcoholic fantasies had left hoofprints halfway to his door. None of the program's twelve steps had an answer for anything like that.

"What say we go to church," Moody said, and he retreated to the bedroom to rummage for his suit.

He felt better once they were out in the open air. The day was spring-like, breezy and cool, with a blue sky and the first buds bursting on the trees. He was amazed at how much storm debris still cluttered the streets. There were mountains of it heaped up along the curb—boards, mattresses, sections of roof, crumpled metal lawn chairs, tree limbs and brush, shop signs, broken toys, tires, ruined clothing, a dog house, and countless cardboard boxes. It was like some great ship had capsized on tall seas, and the tide had spread its wreckage along the shore. He couldn't help wondering if there were bodies. A downed ship always left bodies in its wake.

They paused on the corner of Elk and Green to survey the condition of the square. Moody reached into his coat pocket for his corncob pipe, and Tom pulled out his Camels. Tom struck a light on his shoe and passed the matchbook to Moody.

"Your eye is in crooked," he said as Moody tamped the tobacco in the bowl. Moody lit the pipe and handed the matches back to Tom.

"Thanks," he said, and carefully took out his glass eye. He examined it for dirt, then polished it on his lapel and slipped it back into place. He blinked a few times and turned to face Tom.

"How about now?" he asked.

"That got it," Tom said.

"I need a new one," Moody told him. "There's a hairline crack running right through the center."

"How'd that happen?"

Moody shrugged. "Dropped it in a cook-pot, then ran cold water on it."

"That was stupid." Tom blew out a long stream of smoke and tapped his ash onto the sidewalk. "You ought to get Doc McKinney to order you one."

"I'm a little strapped for cash." As soon as the words left his mouth he regretted saying them.

"You know how we can fix that," Tom said.

When Moody didn't answer, Tom stepped off the curb and headed across the street. Moody sighed and followed along after him.

"All this crap piled in the streets reminds me of Chicago," Tom said as he stepped up over the curb.

He knew what Tom meant. They'd shared a binge there the winter of '29 when Moody was on shore leave from a freighter out of Lake Michigan. Tom had driven up to meet him at the Navy Pier, and they'd proceeded to hit every speakeasy along Michigan Avenue. But what Tom had marveled over most was the three-day blizzard that brought the city to a standstill. Moody had taken it in stride, having already sailed the Arctic, but Tom had never seen weather like that before. The winter plows had worked round the clock, day after day, to keep the roads open, piling the gray snow so high a man couldn't see over it.

But Moody didn't want to talk about Chicago. He knew what Tom was up to.

"I'll remember that trip to my dying day. Cesar Romero and Elzie Segar." He shook his head and smiled. "I'll tell you what, we were stepping in tall cotton."

He paused, but Moody wouldn't take the bait.

"That Elzie Segar was quite a character." Another pause. "The man gave you a gift, Moody. I sure wish you'd take advantage of it."

Some gift.

Moody and Cesar Romero had been shipmates, but Romero had announced he was quitting. He hated working in the galley, as any sane man would, and that's where he and Moody had been stuck the past two years. Moody hated it too, but ship's cook was about the best job a one-eyed sailor could get. Romero drew galley detail because nobody liked him. He was a handsome kid, and bright, a real talker, with no noticeable scars or deformities, so he didn't fit in with the rest of the crew. Now he said he wanted to go to Hollywood and break into the movies. Moody tried to tell him what a bad idea that was. No matter how bad galley work might be, at least it brought a paycheck. But Romero wouldn't listen—he was determined to make himself into some kind of matinee idol. And the crazy thing was, the son of a bitch actually did it. It took him a few years, but in 1933 he landed a role in a picture with William Powell and Myrna Loy. *The Thin Man*. Lots more after that.

But this was their last leave together, Romero was still just a nobody like Moody, and they were set for a high time on the town—especially with Tom driving up from Tennessee with a load of moonshine in his trunk.

They stood there on the pier, Moody and Romero, with the wind knifing in off the lake, smoking their pipes and gabbing while they waited for Tom to show up. His glass eye bothered him in the cold, and that made Moody irritable, so when a skinny landlubber in a green trench coat came up and interrupted the conversation, Moody had given him the brush-off.

"Are you a sailor?" the guy had asked, which at that moment seemed like the most ridiculous question Moody had ever heard in his life. He had on a sailor's peacoat, a sailor's cap, and bell-bottom trousers. Plus he was standing on a pier in front of a ship. What the hell were the options?

You think I'm a cowboy? Moody had answered.

He fixed his good eye on the man, daring him to make some kind of crack. He didn't know why, but he felt ready to take the chump apart. Sometimes the mood just came over him, even when he was sober. Romero saw what was coming—he'd pulled Moody out of brawls on six continents—so he stepped in and put a hand on Moody's shoulder.

But then the man did something unexpected. He laughed. Not the kind of laugh that invites a smack in the mouth, but a genial, good-natured laugh, with no slick attitude behind it.

"You're right," he said. "That was a stupid question." He tilted his head to the side. "You're quick to take offense," he observed. Again, the man's tone was somehow innocent enough that Moody didn't feel obliged to knock him on his ass.

He shrugged. "I am what I am," he said.

The man smiled broadly and clapped Moody on the shoulder as if they'd been friends all their lives. "That's okay with me," he said.

Moody dropped his guard, he couldn't help it; pounding this guy would have been like beating a puppy, and before he knew it, the three of them were standing there as chums, stamping their boots in the bitter cold and telling jokes and trading stories. The guy said he was from downstate, in town on a business trip. At some point he thought to introduce himself.

Romero's eyes got big.

"You're Elzie Segar? The cartoonist?"

Elzie nodded his head. He seemed a little embarrassed that Romero knew who he was, which made Moody think the guy must be all right.

"This man's famous," Romero said to Moody. "He does that strip in the funny papers about the Oyl family."

"*Thimble Theatre*," Elzie Segar said.

"Never read it," Moody said.

Romero laughed. "He draws the funniest looking people you ever saw."

And that had been how their last shore leave had started. Soon Tom showed up with the booze, and Romero invited Elzie to come along for the celebration. That damned Romero. Always the talker. He spent the whole night telling tales about Moody and his missteps—the fights in Hong Kong and Bremen and Capetown and Cairo. Romero was a natural storyteller and he made the violence sound funny and exciting, which wasn't how Moody remembered it at all. But it was Romero's night, so while the snow piled up outside the bar, and Elzie Segar's head filled with ideas, Moody just kept his trap shut and smoked his pipe and continued drinking.

Now, twenty-three years later, he knew he should have followed his first impulse. He should have decked Elzie Segar the second he opened his mouth.

The ruins of Rexall Drug loomed ahead of them on the right, and Moody felt sad to see the fire-gutted building. The Rexall had been his favorite store when he was a kid because they had a section for toys and sporting goods. It was also a great place for cherry Cokes. He'd even worked there as a stock boy when he was thirteen, saving his money for a fielder's mitt. He had dreams of being a star on the school team, of hearing crowds in the bleachers call his name, and he remembered the joy he felt when he finally paid for the glove. It hadn't occurred to him that a boy with only one eye wouldn't have enough depth perception to play real baseball. Wasted money, wasted effort. In the end, he'd burned the glove in the furnace in the Rexall's cellar.

"You're not too old to fight," Tom said. "And I can guarantee you five hundred dollars, win or lose."

Moody snorted. "Yeah, win or lose, like it could go either way."

Tom squinted away across the square. "Anything's possible. David beat Goliath."

"Only because he kept his distance. For God's sake, Tom, it's Jersey Joe Walcott, the world heavyweight champ. I've seen him in newsreels. He could take me apart before I even said howdy."

"It's an exhibition, Moody, not a real fight. You'd only be like a sparring partner."

"I'd be like a punching bag."

Tom grabbed Moody's arm. "Do you know the kind of crowd this could draw?"

"He's the heavyweight champ. I'm pretty sure he can draw a crowd all by himself."

"By himself he's just a celebrity making a public appearance. Add your name to the card, and we've got a public event. A full-scale spectacle. Two legendary brawlers squaring off in the ring. People will tell their grandkids."

"But it's not my name you want on the card," said Moody. "You want the name that damn cartoonist hung on me."

Tom threw up his hands. "Why is that such an issue with you?"

"Because the son of a bitch had no right. He turned me into a comic strip character, Tom. A goddamn cartoon."

He knew Tom wouldn't understand. How could he? How could anyone? He felt like a specimen in a jar, even here in his own hometown. People watched him in stores, stared at him on the street, engaged him in annoying conversations in line at the movie theater. Children whispered and pointed and giggled when they saw him, even in church, and sometimes the braver ones challenged him to show off his strength, daring him to pull a parking meter out of the sidewalk or uproot a tree or lift somebody's pickup truck. He couldn't go near a bar anymore, because there was always some drunk wanting to prove himself. And they all thought they knew him because they'd read some outrageous distortion of his life in the funny papers, almost none of which was true. The skinny girlfriend, the spinach, the fat unshaven brute he always tussled with—all that was bullshit.

But what angered him most was his own weakness, his own inadequacy in pitting himself against this cartoon image. Step Four of the program required him to conduct a searching and fearless moral inventory of himself, and every time he tried it, the answer always came back the same: The comic strip version was by far the better man.

"You don't have to decide right now," Tom said. "You can let me know Tuesday night. I just need enough lead time to get it in the newspaper."

As they rounded the corner onto Mulberry, Moody's chest went hollow. He knew First Baptist had been slammed hard, but he hadn't anticipated the extent of the devastation. Except for the arch at the entryway, not a portion of the church stood more than five feet high. Repair wasn't even a question; the remains of the sanctuary would have to be bulldozed away, scraped clean right down to the earth. A completely new structure would have to be erected in its place.

Maybe he could sign on with one of the construction crews, help in the rebuilding. He thought he might like that. True, he was a lousy carpenter because of his bad eye, but he could still hoist a bag of cement better than most. He had the forearms for it.

The congregation had shown up in full force this morning, which didn't surprise Moody. People claimed to prefer beauty over ugliness, a field of flowers to a landscape of catastrophe, but Moody had been in enough salvage operations to know which drew the longest stares. Most of the congregants had gathered in the lot on the leeward side of the former sanctuary, but a number of the elders milled around in the rubble, picking through the bricks and broken plaster for whatever might be saved.

At the top of the concrete steps, Reverend Tyree stood smiling in the demolished entryway. He wasn't wearing his robes—Moody guessed they may have been lost to the tornado. But his suit coat was filthy, stained on both shoulders and in streaks down the front. His hair was uncombed and stuck out wildly on the sides.

"Heck of a day, Reverend," Tom said as the two of them climbed the steps toward him.

"Hell of a day, Mr. Parsons," the reverend answered, still smiling. There was a fire in the reverend's eyes that Moody hadn't noticed before. "Our Redeemer has left us without a pot to piss in."

Tom laughed, but Moody felt vaguely uncomfortable.

"It'll be all right, though," the reverend said, leaning toward them. "I've taken steps."

"That's . . . real good," said Tom. He glanced toward the congregants assembled in the side yard, then turned to Moody. "Guess I'll head on over to First Presbyterian," he said. "I'll meet you back here after services." He reached out to shake Reverend Tyree's hand, but the reverend was too lost in thought to notice. "Sorting out your sermon, Reverend?" Tom asked.

The reverend focused his gaze on the pile of rubble and smiled. "The Book of Revelation," Reverend Tyree said.

"Ah, the Apocalypse," said Tom, nodding. "Always a relevant topic."

"God granted me a vision," the reverend said. "I've seen the Fourth Horseman."

Tom gave Moody a look, but neither of them spoke.

The reverend spread his arms as if he were addressing multitudes. *"And I looked, and behold a pale horse,"* the reverend intoned, *"and his name that sat on him was Death, and Hell followed with him."*

Then it came into Moody's mind that Herb Gatlin's gray swayback had looked awfully pale in the moonlight.

Maybe the end really was coming.

"I saw him, too," Moody said.

Tom laughed again, but the reverend stepped in close and looked hard into Moody's glass eye. He suddenly seemed angry.

"Then cast out your devils," he demanded.

Moody didn't know what to say. He glanced over at Tom for help, but as he did so, the reverend lunged forward and wrapped Moody in a fierce embrace, pinning his arms to his sides. As the reverend lifted him from the cement, Moody closed his fingers into fists, but he didn't struggle. The reverend was a small man and would have to set him down soon enough.

Maybe the reverend was trying to flush out whatever devils Moody had been storing up. When he was young, he'd seen the evangelicals act this way on the Chautauqua circuit, trying to cleanse the afflicted. Maybe that's what the reverend was up to now.

Or maybe he was just plain crazy, done in by the shock of losing his church. But Moody chose not to think so. He took it on faith that this man now squeezing the breath out of him was some kind of new spiritual guide, the very one he had prayed for, in fact, an embodiment of Step Eleven in the program, a blessing placed in his path to improve his conscious contact with God.

He would give himself over to this baptism. He would not strike out in anger. He would allow himself to stand powerless in the face of a hostile world.

"Easy there, Reverend," he heard Tom Parsons say. But there would be nothing easy about it.

Andy Yearwood

As Andy Yearwood fastened the crane's hook to the trunk of the hackberry tree on the roof of *The Observer* office, he tried hard to forget his fear of heights. The roof had a steep pitch to it, and he was near enough to the edge to imagine a better-than-average chance of falling. Even if he kept his footing, there was still the danger of being swept from the roof by branches if the hackberry became prematurely dislodged. He might survive the basic fall only to be crushed beneath a ton of raw timber—just like Herb Gatlin.

He'd interviewed Mary Jean about her ordeal in the storm, and the last thing she remembered before being dropped into the well was the tree coming down over the top of them. She had cried when she told him that, which had made Andy uncomfortable. The worst part of his job— besides what he was doing right now—was having to talk to people about the terrible things that had happened to them— especially when it meant talking to someone like Mary Jean, whom he had known most of his life. They'd even worked on the high school newspaper together. They hadn't been particularly close, but Mary Jean had been best friends with Patty Hart, the editor-in-chief, so he had spoken to her often, fishing for information.

Patty Hart had been the sole reason for Andy's interest in high school journalism. He had signed up to work on *The Old Maroon and White* his sophomore year because Patty Hart was already a staff member, which meant they would attend the same after-school meetings. He'd chosen to be a sports reporter because Patty was also a cheerleader, so covering the football and basketball teams guaranteed him an excuse to talk to her at the games. Andy had spent three years trying to work up the nerve to ask her out, but he never managed it. He was shy by nature. Not a good trait for a reporter, he realized.

What he really wanted to be now was an editor. Then he wouldn't have to talk to so many people and he could still have opinions. But he understood that being a reporter was the necessary first rung of the professional ladder. Of course, the ladder at *The Observer* had only two rungs, and Tom Parsons would always occupy the one above him.

Andy began to feel clammy. He was a little more than two stories off the ground, maybe twenty-five feet, which hadn't looked so bad just ten minutes earlier, when he was standing on the sidewalk with Mr. Tom. He'd seen movie cowboys leap from higher places plenty of times, and they always landed softly. They would hit and roll, then come up with guns blazing. But maybe there was a trick to it. Or maybe leaping off a rooftop was one of those things that always looked easier when someone else was doing the jumping.

Mr. Tom hadn't forced him to climb up on the roof. Dickey Bagley had given them the use of his crane, and he'd even sent along his younger brother Lloyd to operate it, but supplying a crew to handle the peripheral details—like securing the tree to the crane—had been left up to Mr. Tom. He, in turn, had passed that responsibility along to Andy, who, in an ill-considered burst of bravado, had announced he would handle it himself.

If Andy had known ahead of time that Lloyd Bagley was part of the deal, he might not have been so quick to volunteer. Lloyd had terrorized him in high school. The two of them had started freshman year together, though Lloyd had been two years older because of the grades he had failed. They'd sat next to each other in freshman geometry, and the first week Andy refused to let Lloyd copy his homework on vectors. For the rest of the year Lloyd had routinely knocked Andy's books from his arms in the hallways. Sometimes he had even tripped Andy on the stairs. The problem resolved itself sophomore year when Lloyd dropped out to work for his brother, and Andy had made a habit of avoiding him on the street ever since, ducking into stores or turning corners whenever he saw Lloyd hanging around the square.

But Lloyd Bagley notwithstanding, Andy was glad of this opportunity to prove himself to Mr. Tom, who had taken a great chance in hiring him. Being 4-F was a social handicap in Lincoln, and after the draft board had declared him exempt from military service, people he'd known all his life had begun to regard him with suspicion—as if anyone his age who wasn't fighting in Korea might be a communist sympathizer. When news got around about Friday's fire-truck fiasco, they would mistrust him even more. But Mr. Tom still seemed to have faith in him.

So here he was, risking his life to impress his boss. But as each chilling glance over the edge made him more and more lightheaded, he wondered what the hell he had been thinking. If this were high school and his boss were still Patty Hart, the risk might have been worth it. But Patty had abandoned her interest in journalism when she married Bryce Hatton.

Now, crawling around on this rickety roof, it bothered Andy that his career path was the result of a failed high school crush. He doubted whether many journalists had started out that way. Fewer still would have been stupid enough to volunteer for roof-clearing duty on a windy day.

He should be inside, safe, setting type for the story of the body-snatcher who broke into the dime store and made off with the mystery corpse. That one had everybody guessing.

But typesetting would have to wait—he was already on the roof, growing dizzier with each heartbeat, and if he didn't get the chains secured quickly, there was a good chance Lloyd Bagley might shift the crane, just to rattle him. Of course, whatever happened, Tom Parsons wouldn't see it. Mr. Tom had been called away to the jailhouse to talk to the sheriff about some problem with the upcoming boxing exhibition, which *The Observer* was now promoting as a fundraiser for the town. So much for impressing the boss. Lloyd Bagley was his only witness.

He finished hooking the chain and then carefully crept up the slope to the peak of the roof. "I think it's ready," he called down to Lloyd, who sat eating a sandwich in the cab of the crane. Lloyd carefully rewrapped the remainder of his sandwich before shifting the crane's hoisting mechanism into gear.

A chill went through him as he realized another way that Lloyd was a danger to him now. This was the guy who had failed geometry because he couldn't grasp how angles worked, and here he was operating the crane Andy's life might be attached to. What if Lloyd were too incompetent for the job? What if he didn't maintain his equipment properly? He'd certainly never seemed like a stickler for details, and when it came to heavy equipment, overlooked details could get somebody killed.

Andy tried to envision everything that might possibly go wrong with the next part of the procedure. He imagined the chain snapping, or the hook slipping loose, or the trunk tipping vertically to make hoisting it too awkward. He imagined the roof collapsing beneath a poorly timed shifting of the arm of the crane. He imagined the crane itself buckling. He imagined Lloyd pulling the wrong lever and swinging the tree into the side of the building on the way down. He even imagined an oversized limb piercing the shingled roof and snagging an attic truss, causing the entire building to topple. He tried to anticipate every scenario of disaster so he'd be ready with the proper response. The only one he didn't foresee was the one he now saw unfolding before him.

As Lloyd engaged the mechanism to lift the tree, Andy scooted to the secure center of the roof, straddling the peak.

The tree rose before him, perfectly balanced between the twin chains Andy had looped around opposite ends of the trunk. Then, as the tree pulled away from the roof, suspended securely from the arm of the crane, a gust of wind came whistling in from the west, catching the broad, leafy canopy full force. The tree began to rotate, turning hard to the north like the needle of a giant compass.

Andy understood his predicament at once. He was blocked from Lloyd's view by the roofline, and, if he called out, Lloyd wouldn't hear him over the roar and whine of the crane. He was on his own, and as the mass of branches swung slowly toward him, Andy had plenty of time to consider his options. The problem was that all of his options appeared to be fatal.

If he scrambled down the steep roof to duck beneath the sweep of the limbs, he couldn't keep himself from sliding over the edge. That was Newton's First Law, one of the few things he remembered from Mr. Gregor's physics class: A body in motion tended to remain in motion, all the way to the ground. On the other hand, if he stayed where he was, the canopy would rake across him, scraping him from the peak like gum from a desktop.

The third option he arrived at by default. As the limbs engulfed him, sweeping him toward the inevitable drop, he clawed blindly through the leaves for a sturdy interior branch. He found one and held tight as the tree scooped him from the rooftop and carried him out over the back alley. If he lost his grip or the branch broke, he would plummet a full three stories to the gravel-packed parking lot.

Oddly enough, he didn't feel afraid. Before, when he'd been perched in relative safety, he had terrified himself with expectations—this might go wrong, that might go wrong. But now all the hypotheticals were behind him. Something had indeed gone wrong, the danger was real, and yet, for the first time since he'd set foot on the roof, he felt calm. He was doing what needed to be done under the circumstances, simple as that. He felt as comfortable as if he were riding the Ferris wheel at the county fair.

That confidence stayed with him as the crane carried him smoothly over the roof to the front of the building and slowly down to the center of the blocked-off street. As Lloyd settled the hackberry tree gently onto the pavement and shut down the crane, Andy crawled out from the green web of branches, smiling. He was relieved to be back on the ground, certainly, but he also felt something more. He felt inexplicably happy. Not just happy he'd landed safely, but deep-down happy. His skin tingled, though he realized most of that was probably from the adrenaline rush. But this was more than just an eruption of chemicals in his brain. For once in his life, Andy had ridden out a crisis without giving way to panic. He had coped with the unexpected. Maybe this was the fork in the road he'd been waiting for.

Lloyd leaned out of the cab and scowled down at him. "What the heck do you think you're doing?" he demanded.

"Hitching a ride, I guess," Andy said. The sky was blue as a party balloon, and the breeze tickled playfully against his face.

"If you were on my regular crew, I'd fire you for that."

Andy felt giddy. "If I were on your regular crew, I might give a shit."

What had gotten into him? Lloyd Bagley wasn't the sort to take that kind of lip, especially not from him. But somehow he didn't care.

Lloyd seemed equally surprised.

"That's a mighty rude thing to say," he said, climbing down from the crane. "I'm just telling you, we don't allow any horseplay on this machinery." He unbuttoned his cuffs and began to roll up his shirtsleeves.

Andy straightened, ready for the first blow. "I'm not afraid of you, Lloyd."

Lloyd tilted his head to the side. "I didn't know you were supposed to be."

Andy stood his ground. "You should. You did a pretty good job making sure of it."

"When?"

"All through ninth grade."

A glimmer of recollection rose into Lloyd's eyes. "Oh. Yeah. Sorry." Lloyd walked past him and ducked carefully into the thicket of branches and began unhooking the chains.

"Sorry?" The word stunned him. He hadn't imagined Lloyd Bagley could ever be sorry about anything.

"I had a lot of frustrations when I was a teenager," Lloyd said from behind the wall of leaves. "But I converted to Anabaptist two years ago."

"Anabaptist?"

"Well, Mennonite, if you want to know the particulars." He tossed one of the chains out to the pavement at Andy's feet and then worked his way along the trunk to the second set.

"You're a pacifist?"

"Clear through. And a whole lot happier for it." He pulled back a branch and looked out at Andy through the opening. "Just wish I'd come to it before losing so many teeth in bar fights."

"I can't believe this," Andy said. He couldn't tell whether he felt glad or disappointed.

"If I'd known you was walking around scared of me, I'd have said something sooner," Lloyd told him. "But seems like we never ran into each other."

"But you were awful in high school," Andy said. "How could you just change?"

"It was a big jump, all right." He tossed out the second set of chains and stepped back through the branches to the open street. He brushed off his shirt front, though there was no debris on it. "I guess Dirk Willems made the difference."

"Who's Dirk Willems?"

"Early Mennonite martyr. Great story. There was a price on Dirk's head—you know, just for being a Mennonite—and this bounty hunter was chasing him across a frozen river. Well, the bounty hunter fell through the ice. So what does Dirk Willems do?"

"Goes back and saves him."

"You got it. And they still burned him at the stake." Lloyd shook his head. "It's a shame when people don't recognize the human spirit."

"So that story made you a convert?"

"It showed me the kind of person I want to be. I don't know why it took me so long to get it. I mean, what he did was exactly the kind of thing Roy Rogers or the Lone Ranger would have done, but the concept never clicked for me until I heard about Dirk Willems. The guy knew he'd be burned alive if he went back to save his enemy, but he did it anyway. He stayed true to his better nature."

So the bully Andy had been dodging for years was nothing but a phantom he'd conjured up on his own. Lloyd Bagley had gone from front-page thug to back-page human interest story, and though part of Andy was happy for the transformation, part of him also felt cheated. He'd invested a lot of effort into hating a man who didn't exist. He'd already written out Lloyd's obituary a dozen times, figuring he needed to be ready for the inevitable day when a drunken Lloyd Bagley would drive his truck into a bridge abutment. He had relished the idea of having the last word on his tormentor's sorry life. In different versions he had been sometimes charitable, and sometimes not, depending on how magnanimous he felt. Maybe the final version would describe Lloyd's death as a tragic waste, or maybe it would brand him as a redneck jerk who wound up just the way everybody hoped he would. But he knew that whatever judgment he passed would be taken as the truth.

Now all that power was gone. Lloyd Bagley was one of the good guys. Lloyd Bagley would come back for him if he ever fell through the ice.

"Maybe the newspaper could do a story on you," Andy suggested.

Lloyd looked down at the pavement and shrugged. "Don't see much reason. I'm a crane operator. I pick things up and put things down."

"I think we can make it interesting enough," Andy assured him. "We'll put in Dirk Willems."

Lloyd smiled. "Well, yeah, that would be all right." He glanced back at his crane. "I need to get the equipment back to the yard," he said. He nodded to the fallen hackberry. "What y'all need to do now is cut up the trunk so you can haul it out in pieces."

"All taken care of," he lied. He was sure he could put a crew together to make that happen. It was a new world, and he could do anything that needed to be done.

"All right then," Lloyd said. He picked up the chains and dumped them into a storage box mounted on the back of the crane, then climbed back into the cab. He started the motor and engaged the winch. Andy watched the thick cable of chain ascend slowly up from the hackberry, like a giant fishing line with an empty hook. When the chain had fully rewound, Lloyd engaged another mechanism that made the derrick retract and tilt, giving the crane enough clearance to pass below the utility lines at intersections.

Andy knew that some of the big cities had fire trucks with that sort of complex engineering—trucks with extension ladders that could reach the upper stories of buildings. Lincoln's fire truck was a relic from the '30s. At some point as fire chief he should start a campaign to raise money for a more modern vehicle, though not right now. Now it would be too easy for people to laugh at any suggestion he made about the need for an upgrade. They would say it didn't matter how old a truck was if it only sat in the firehouse.

Maybe he should get some spare keys made.

Lloyd carefully pivoted the huge machine toward Church Street. Andy waved as the giant machine lumbered away, though Lloyd didn't look back to see it. That was okay, though. It wasn't really Lloyd he was waving good-bye to.

His next item of business was to arrange for the tree's removal so the street in front of *The Observer* could open to traffic again. Not that there was any pressing need. Even on an ordinary Sunday, nothing would be open downtown, and these days were far from ordinary. The tree could probably remain in the road for a week without causing an inconvenience.

Maybe he'd write some preliminary notes for a story about Lloyd Bagley's conversion experience, outline the article while the details were fresh in his mind. He felt sure Tom would go for the idea. Anything that put a good light on the community was worth a few column inches. Too bad they couldn't run Lloyd's picture. The big papers had that kind of capability, but *The Observer* was strictly a galley and plate-block printing operation, so they couldn't run photographs. Someday, maybe.

As Andy hopped up the three dark wooden steps to the front office, he felt he understood something about Lloyd's epiphany. Things could happen in an instant that would forever alter the way a person saw the world. He found that a comforting notion.

Most of his comfort evaporated when he stepped through the office doorway. A one-legged man in soiled work clothes sat quietly at the typesetter's table in the back of the room, a crutch-sized tree branch propped against the wall beside him.

Andy froze. He knew who the man was. He'd already type-set his obituary. It lay in galley form on the very table where the man now sat.

Herb Gatlin looked up at him and offered a pleasant smile. "I saw you were busy, so I just came on in here to wait." He patted the thigh above his missing leg. "Sometimes I need to take a load off."

"Sure," Andy said, though he wasn't sure of anything.

Herb Gatlin reached out and tapped a thick finger on the galley beside him. "This obituary's real nice," he said. "Kind of spotty on my next of kin, but otherwise I'd call it a generous account."

"If there's any mistakes in it, you can make all the corrections you want," Andy said.

Herb Gatlin chewed his lower lip for a moment and then nodded. "I guess the main mistake is I'm not dead."

Andy felt like an idiot. "Oh," he said. "Right."

"So I was kind of hoping you'd hold off a while on running it," Herb Gatlin went on. "That's sort of why I came by."

"Of course," Andy said. "We'll hold off as long as you want."

"How about we just wait until I'm dead," Herb Gatlin suggested. "That ought to be long enough."

"Absolutely," Andy said. "We'll just file it away for the future. And you can still make changes."

"No, I think it can run pretty much as-is. You did a fine job with it. I thank you for that."

Andy stepped past the hat rack to the pair of cane chairs that served as the paper's interview area and took a seat. "Mr. Tom told me once to write every article like I expected the people in it to show up at the office someday," he said. "I guess that applies to obituaries, too."

"Them most of all," Herb Gatlin said. "But like I say, I've got no complaints about mine. Except for what I guess you'd call the basic premise."

Andy felt the blood rise to his cheeks.

"Mr. Tom helped me with it," Andy told him. "He said you and he went way back."

"That's true," Herb Gatlin said. "I used to date his younger sister. We even worked together for a while, Mr. Tom and me, right here in this office. The Parsons family was always mighty good people."

"You used to work for *The Observer?*"

"Yep, twenty-odd years ago. Back when Mr. Odell Parsons was running things. That was Tom and Ellen's daddy. I was a typesetter."

"That's my job now."

Herb smiled again. "Well, that's okay. I figured they'd replace me."

"Why'd you quit?"

Herb Gatlin squirmed sideways in his seat and let out a sigh. "Couldn't stand being cooped up all day. I was more the outdoorsy type." He gazed around at the unpainted lathe-wood walls, and Andy could see from his face that Mr. Gatlin still thought he'd made the right choice.

"How about Mr. Tom's niece?" he asked suddenly. "Is she all right?"

"You mean Mary Jean?"

Herb Gatlin nodded. "She was in a pretty tight spot, last I remember. I hope she and that baby came through okay."

"She's fine. They're both fine. She had the baby that very night. A little girl."

Herb let out a long breath. "That's mighty good to hear," he said.

"Mary Jean thinks you're dead," Andy told him. "Everybody does."

Herb Gatlin laughed softly. "Yeah, the obituary kind of tipped me off to that." He leaned forward and rested both forearms across his good knee. "Maybe you could run an announcement letting people know I'm still around," he said. "I've been getting some mighty odd looks."

"That's no problem," Andy told him. "Mr. Gatlin, you're front page news—and these days, that's saying something."

Herb Gatlin took hold of the makeshift crutch beside him and pulled himself to his feet. "I appreciate your help, Mr. Yearwood."

"Maybe you could give me an interview about what happened," Andy said, pushing himself up from his chair. He quickly crossed to the old roll-top desk on the opposite wall and rummaged through its drawers for pencil and paper. He found dozens of brass shell casings for Mr. Tom's .22 pistol, and a handful of loose cigarettes, but, typical of *The Observer*'s modus operandi, nothing useful.

"How about we do that tomorrow?" Herb Gatlin asked. "I'm still a little stove up from wrestling with that twister."

Andy thought of the children's story of Pecos Bill, how he rode a twister like it was a wild horse until he tamed it to a gentle breeze. Maybe he could work that into the article. Herb Gatlin was Lincoln's real-life Pecos Bill.

"That's fine," he said, sliding the last drawer shut. Herb Gatlin began to hobble toward the door. "If you need anything else," Andy told him, "you just let us know."

Herb Gatlin paused at the entryway, then swiveled back around to face him.

"Well, I might could use some help finding my leg," he said. "Maybe you could ask folks to keep an eye out."

Andy slumped back against the edge of the desk. "My gosh," he said. "I can't believe I didn't think to say something sooner. Your leg's already turned up. Di. McKinney identified it. That's how come people thought you were dead."

"Where is it?" Herb Gatlin asked.

Andy looked at his watch and winced. "That's another thing I probably should have mentioned," he said. "It's at your funeral."

Herb leaned his weight into the fork of his branch and took an awkward step toward him. "They're burying my leg?"

"Yes sir, they are."

"Whose fool idea was that?"

"I don't know who came up with it. Charlie Monahan, most likely, trying to drum up a little business. But I know Mrs. Mc-Kinney donated one of the Parsons family plots in Rose Hill on account of your saving her daughter."

Herb Gatlin let out a sigh.

Andy didn't know what to say. Here he was, right back at his least favorite part of the job—talking to people in their worst personal moments. Herb Gatlin, as far as he could tell, was a decent fellow who never caught the right break. Now he couldn't even get his leg back without a court order to exhume a body.

"Maybe it's not too late," Andy suggested. "There was supposed to be a graveside service about a half hour ago. Maybe you could stop them before they fill in the hole."

"Not much chance of that," Herb Gatlin said. "I'm about as fast as a pogo stick."

"No problem there," Andy said. He reached into his pocket and drew out a set of keys. "I've got access to a fire truck."

As he roared out High Street toward Rose Hill with Herb Gatlin strapped into the passenger seat beside him, Andy felt being fire chief was finally paying off. Since he'd first been appointed—at Tom Parsons' insistence—there had been only one fire in the county, and he'd botched that one completely. But firemen were community volunteers with a broad range of obligations, and delivering Herb Gatlin to his own funeral was at least as important as getting cats down from trees. As long as he didn't wreck the truck, he knew the mayor would approve of what he was doing. Besides, he'd meant it when he said Herb Gatlin was front-page news, and it was his job to stay with the story. He tried to imagine they were like two Western heroes riding to the rescue, but none of the pieces really fit. This kind of situation didn't usually come up in Westerns.

The truck was too large to pass through the stone arch at the cemetery gate, but Andy was able to park broadside in the semicircular pull-off, blocking the entrance from any further traffic. He didn't want the mortuary crew to leave the grounds prematurely.

While Herb used his makeshift crutch to climb down from the cab, Andy scanned the hillside for signs of a funeral. There were no concentrated crowds, just a scattering of Sunday afternoon mourners loitering beside family headstones. A caretaker pruned rosebushes along the far perimeter, and another mowed the grass beside the gravel pathway that meandered up through the heart of the cemetery. Early daffodils bloomed along the low rock walls that crisscrossed the lumpy slope.

"It's over there," Herb Gatlin said, and pointed toward the original section of Rose Hill, the eastern side, where some of the old-growth trees from the early days of the county still spread broad limbs over the various family plots.

Andy's view was partially obscured by an elm tree, but he saw that Herb Gatlin was right. He couldn't see the grave itself, because it was up the hill from them, but he could see the dirt pile. A lone woman stood on one side of the pile, looking down. Two workmen stood on the other side of the pile smoking pipes, apparently waiting for her to finish her good-byes.

"I think we're in time," Andy said, hopping down from the truck. "I'll run on ahead and make sure they don't start filling in the hole."

"Thanks," Herb Gatlin said, fitting his crutch firmly beneath his arm. "I'll be along directly."

Andy passed beneath the stone arch and veered onto the footpath that cut straight uphill through the eastern side of the cemetery. The gravesite was a couple of hundred yards away, and as he jogged up the uneven slope, he rehearsed in his mind what he would say once he got there. This was a stop-the-presses kind of intrusion, but he didn't want to shock the woman at the grave, who, as he made progress up the path, he recognized as Mrs. McKinney. The trouble was, he couldn't think of a non-dramatic way to break the news. Every way he practiced it sounded like something from an old horror movie.

The two workmen, he realized, were Moody Smith and Sammy Statten, both of them hearty sorts who could take anything in stride. Maybe he should address his revelations to them.

As he neared the grave, Mrs. McKinney turned away and, to his relief, began walking back up the hill, toward the parking area at the upper gate. Moody Smith and Sammy Statten tossed their pipes aside and picked up their long-handled shovels.

"Hang on there a minute," Andy said, hopping over the small rock wall at the edge of the Parsons family plot. His heart pounded wildly. The climb had winded him, and he bent forward, his hands on his knees, to catch his breath. The small polished casket lay snugly at the bottom of the pit. "You've got to stop what you're doing," he said.

"Bad time for a fire drill, Chief," said Moody Smith, slicing his shovel blade into the mound of red earth.

Sammy Statten gave Andy a polite nod, but he, too rammed his shovel into the side of the pile.

"Herb Gatlin's coming for his leg," Andy told them. "You've got to bring up the casket."

Both men stopped in mid-shovel.

"Don't like the sound of that," Sammy Statten said.

"Boy thinks he's funny," Moody Smith muttered, and slung the first spray of dirt down onto the tiny coffin.

"I'm serious," Andy said. He looked back over his shoulder to make sure Herb Gatlin was making progress up the hill. "He's right behind me. See for yourself."

Moody Smith leveled a hard look at Andy, then stabbed his shovel upright into the fresh dirt and stepped around to the foot of the grave. He put his hand to his eye to shield it from the afternoon sun and stood there for a long moment, staring into the glare.

"Son of a gun," he said at last.

"What is it?" Sammy Statten asked.

"You can forget what I was saying about the Apocalypse," Moody Smith told him. "Guess it ain't the end of the world after all."

"That's okay by me," Sammy Statten said. He dropped his shovel beside the pile and stepped over beside Moody Smith to see for himself.

"Looks like Mr. Herb, all right," Sammy Statten said.

"I expect this'll be a blow to Reverend Tyree," said Moody Smith. "He really had his hopes up."

The three of them watched silently as Herb Gatlin left the winding cemetery path and picked his way among the tombstones directly up the slope toward them. At last he struggled up over the final rock wall and stood beside them, breathing hard.

"Moody, what the heck are you doing?" he asked.

"Giving your leg a decent burial," Moody Smith answered.

Herb Gatlin took a couple of breaths. Andy could see by his tight frown that he was thinking something over.

"But you knew I was still alive," he said. "I came by your place last night."

Moody Smith looked down and scuffed his boot in the dirt. "I thought you was a pink elephant," he said.

Herb Gatlin narrowed his eyes at Mr. Statten. "Sammy, you need to cut Mr. Moody off. Or scale him back, anyway."

Sammy Statten shot Andy an uneasy glance, then nodded. "Yessir, you right about that," he said. "Once he start drinking,

he don't know what's what. He bought up everything I had
with me. Even took the box of crayons I was bringing home
to Jerry Lee."

"Them crayons was yours?" Moody asked.

"You know they was."

Moody shook his head. "Damn. You boys are taking all the
magic right out of my life."

A flock of starlings passed noisily overhead, banking er-
ratically through the windy sky above the cemetery. They all
watched as the birds settled into the branches of a massive oak
at the bottom of the hill. The sharp chirping died away.

"I'd like my leg back now," Herb Gatlin said.

Moody Smith and Sammy Statten looked at each other,
then down into the hole.

"Oh, man," said Sammy Statten.

"What's the problem?" Andy asked.

"Coffins don't come out as easy as they go in," Moody Smith
told him. "That one's tucked in there pretty snug. Be hard to
get it back out without doing some damage."

"We need different equipment," Sammy Statten said.
"Something to hook under the handles and lift it straight up."

"I've got a couple of fire axes on the truck," Andy told them.
"They've got hooked blades on one side."

Moody Smith raised his eyebrows. "That might could work."

"I'll go get 'em," Sammy Statten said. He jumped the wall
and trotted away down the hill.

A muffled cry came from somewhere behind them, and they
turned toward the parking area in time to see Mrs. McKinney,
the horror still evident on her face, stumble sideways into an oversized concrete angel playing a lyre. She grabbed its elbow to keep
from falling, then straightened up and stood like a statue herself
in the middle of the Crabtree family plot, staring down at them.

"Ellen McKinney seems a bit taken aback," Moody Smith
said. "But I guess that's a natural reaction, seeing you fresh
from the dead."

"She's seen me worse," Herb Gatlin said softly.

Having collected herself enough, apparently, to investigate the situation, Mrs. McKinney began to stalk down the slope toward them. They waited for her without moving, and, though he didn't know why, Andy felt like he was back on the grammar school playground, about to be scolded by the teacher for throwing a rock through a window.

She slowed as she drew near and stopped just outside the low rock wall that marked the upper border of the Parsons family plot. She stood for a moment composing herself.

"Afternoon, Miz McKinney," Andy said. She didn't seem to hear him, but kept her gaze steady on Herb Gatlin, which Andy considered understandable, given the circumstances.

"You're still alive," she said. Her voice was flat, pressed into such a neutral tone that Andy couldn't tell if she were pleased or annoyed.

"Yes, ma'am," Herb Gatlin answered. "Just a bit banged up, is all." He cleared his throat as if he had more to say, but then he just stood there, quietly, staring back at her across the open grave.

"We had a funeral," she said.

Herb Gatlin nodded. "I appreciate that."

"It was a fine one, too," Moody Smith added. "Reverend Tyree was a no-show, so we opened up the eulogy to volunteers, like the Quakers do. I even said a few words myself."

Herb Gatlin kept his eyes on Ellen McKinney.

"Nice of you to put me here with your family," he said.

"It was the least we could do," she said, her voice so low and humble she might have been apologizing. "We owed you . . ." As her voice trailed off, Andy thought she seemed sad, though he knew he must be wrong.

"I'm honored beyond words, Ellen," Herb Gatlin said.

"We're not a big family," she said. "There's plenty of room here, whenever you need it."

"There's other generations to come," he said. "They won't have a clue who I am, or what I'm doing here. Might seem kinda strange."

"I never knew you to care much what people thought," she said.

He shrugged. "I don't like to intrude."

"It's not an intrusion," she told him.

Herb Gatlin let out a small sigh.

"This ain't where I belong," he said.

A sharp breeze gave Andy a sudden chill, and, though he didn't know why, he felt a great shift in the afternoon's possibilities, almost like the opening or closing of a door.

Sammy Statten came huffing up beside them, an axe in each hand. "These ought to do the trick," he said.

"I just hope we aren't too late," Moody Smith said, taking one of the axes. "That leg could be halfway to Hades by now."

Sammy Statten knelt at one end of the grave and reached the axe as far into the hole as he could, then straightened up, smiling.

"It's just long enough," he said. "If we crumble the sides a little, we can get the hook up under the handles."

Moody Smith peered into the grave. "Wonder what kind of resale value this'll have."

"Pretty good, I reckon," said Sammy Statten. "Hard to find 'em used."

The two men lay on their bellies and began to fish the hole with Andy's fire axes.

Mrs. McKinney turned without another word and began to trudge slowly back up the hill. Herb Gatlin stared after her.

As Andy watched Mrs. McKinney pick her way among the tombstones, he noticed another woman halfway up the slope, sitting on the grass beside a recently mounded grave.

It was Patty Hatton. Patty Hart.

The world was built on uneven ground. A man could be buried before his time. He could wind up in the wrong family plot. Nothing about this day had been expected, and for the first time in his life, Andy realized how quickly opportunities could slip away, or return unannounced, or slip away again. A sudden gust, and a tree could take him soaring over rooftops.

Enemies could turn back to save him. Carpe diem, a phrase he'd learned in Latin class. But he had never seized the day, not once, not in all the days time had offered him so far.

He would ask out Patty Hart. Today, while the sun still warmed his blood. He would wait until she got to her feet, because he didn't want to intrude—Herb Gatlin was right about that. But when she turned away from whoever she was mourning, he would follow after her, strike up a conversation, remind her who he was. Maybe she wouldn't remember him, or maybe she would still overlook him, as she had in high school. But maybe not. People learned a lot once they got out of high school. He had, anyway. Maybe she had, too, and now there would be more to talk about than how the football team was doing.

He would invite her to the boxing exhibition, if she had an interest, or to the drive-in if she didn't. This weekend there was a double feature of Cesar Romero movies—*Jungle* and *The Lost Continent*. They could lose themselves in exotic adventure. Or, if she felt inclined, they could ignore whatever story played out before them on the screen, and start one of their own. They could turn off the speaker. Explore one another in the darkness. Anything was possible. All he had to do was ask.

Sheriff Tune

As Sheriff Buddy Tune crossed the state line into Alabama, it occurred to him that he had a certain fondness for criminals. Why else would he be driving halfway to Huntsville to have lunch with Marty Raby? Only the day before, Marty had betrayed the sheriff's trust, fled the lockup, stolen an automobile—again—and left the state as a fugitive with a bleak and uncertain future.

It was a shame, really. Marty Raby was as nice a fellow as the sheriff had ever run across, polite almost to a fault and possessed of a cheery disposition that would have made him an ideal scoutmaster. He wasn't violent or crude or mean. He just didn't seem able to abide by the law.

The sheriff had known a few guys like Marty during the war. Every last one of them got killed, usually for stupid reasons. Picking flowers in a minefield, that kind of thing. He remembered Hank Blevins, a private from Kansas, who lost the top of his head to a sniper in Italy when he stood up in his foxhole to work out a charley horse. But some people were like that—just too innocent to understand that the world was full of consequences, none of them pretty.

Sheriff Tune's wife had been just the opposite. Judy saw consequences in everything. More than two decades ago she had begged him not to run for sheriff, saying she couldn't handle that much worry. Maybe he should have listened. After three years of waiting up nights, she left him for a shoe salesman and moved to Memphis.

He pulled off the highway into the parking lot at the Dreamland Barbecue and parked alongside the low, cinderblock building. The lot was fairly large, covered with pencil-sized black rubber strips of shredded tires. He didn't know why Dreamland used shredded tires in their parking lot. Maybe it was just cheaper than gravel. In any case, it gave the place a different feel, as if Dreamland were somehow set apart from the rest of the world. Smoke from the barbecue pit out back drifted lazily around the sides of the building, thickening the air with the aroma of slow-cooked pork.

Sheriff Tune pulled the screen door open and stepped inside. The dining area was dark, the only light coming from whatever afternoon sun spilled through the doorway, and he blinked a few times while his eyes adjusted to the shadows. The afternoon lunch crowd was just beginning to thin, and he took a seat at an unbused table in the corner by the kitchen. He scanned the room for Marty, but didn't see him. Maybe he wouldn't show. That would be typical.

The busboy emerged from the kitchen and propped his collecting tub on the edge of the table, then began to clear away the glasses and plates from the previous diners.

"You want the sandwich or the plate dinner?" he asked. "I recommend the dinner. Comes with hushpuppies and slaw."

Sheriff Tune squinted up at the grinning busboy. It was Marty.

"I'll have the dinner, then," Sheriff Tune said. "And some sweet tea."

"Coming right up," he said, still grinning, and hustled away through the swinging kitchen door.

This was bad. Marty Raby's sense of the future stretched about five minutes longer than a newborn pup's. If he already had a paying job, he'd never see the long-term wisdom of coming back to Lincoln and turning himself in.

Of course, he could always talk to the owner of Dreamland, tell him Marty was a fugitive. That might cost Marty his job and send him back across the state line. But even as the idea came to him, Sheriff Tune dismissed it. He couldn't do a thing like that to Marty any more than he could drown a sack of cats.

Marty came back through the doorway with two plates of barbecued pork and set them on the table. "I'll be right back with our drinks," he said, and disappeared again into the kitchen.

Maybe Marty's job situation would change of its own accord. Sheriff Tune knew enough about the restaurant business to know that busboys weren't supposed to eat with customers, especially not before the lunch crowd had cleared out. Maybe Marty would get himself fired just for being Marty.

He re-emerged from the kitchen with two tall glasses of tea and two bundles of silverware, all of which he placed carefully on the table before swinging his leg over the back of the chair and sitting down.

"Well?" he asked. "What do you think?"

"Don't know," Sheriff Tune said. "Haven't tasted it yet."

"Not the barbecue," Marty said. "Me. What do you think of me getting a job this quick?" He shoveled a forkful of pork into his mouth.

"I think that might interfere with your jail time."

"That's the idea," Marty said, wiping his chin with his napkin. "I can pay my own way now. Dreamland is my cousin Albert's place, and he said I could bus tables here as long as I liked. So I don't have to be a burden on the county anymore." He picked up a hushpuppy and bit it in half.

"We didn't lock you up to be charitable, Marty. It was a punishment."

"Didn't feel like punishment," Marty said, a slight pout creeping into his voice. "I liked it there." He popped the other half of the hushpuppy into his mouth and scooped up a forkful of slaw.

"Then come on back," Sheriff Tune said. "I can drive you up there after lunch."

Marty frowned. "I thought you'd be happy to see I landed on my feet."

Sheriff Tune picked up his fork and poked at his shredded pork. It looked like the barbecue Judy used to make for the Fourth of July. "You're a fugitive, Marty. You need to square things with the law or you won't ever be able to come back home."

"It's not like I moved to Mongolia," he said. "My folks don't live but six miles up the road. Besides, I'm not a criminal down here; I'm just an ordinary taxpayer. Like Frank James, only in reverse."

Sheriff Tune knew the story. Frank James had lived for a while in Lincoln after his brother Jesse got killed. He was a model citizen as long as he was in Tennessee, but from time to time he'd cross the border into Alabama to rob banks in the Huntsville area. Then he would come home to Lincoln and blend back into the community. He'd tell jokes at the barber shop and tip his hat to people on the street. Of course, he did eventually shoot a man on the courthouse lawn, a trouble-maker from out of town, but for some reason nobody had held that against him. The sheriff back then must have judged it self-defense.

"You ain't Frank James," said Sheriff Tune.

"I sure didn't think you'd begrudge me a fresh start," Marty said, crumpling his napkin.

Judy had said the same thing to him once, on the day she left town. He had asked her not to go. *I sure didn't think you'd begrudge me a fresh start.* That was the last thing he ever heard her say.

But he and Marty still had plenty to discuss.

"How can you start fresh with arrest warrants hanging over your head?" he asked.

Marty waved the notion away with his fork. "We've all got something hanging over our heads—diseases, bankruptcy, un-happy marriages." He took a long swallow of tea.

"But people don't choose those problems, Marty, they just happen."

"Well, you chose to be sheriff," he pointed out, "and that's not all amens and thank-yous. People get shot in your line of work. I figure my burden's not so bad in the larger scheme of things."

Sheriff Tune had no answer for that, so he took a bite of barbecue. He wouldn't admit it to Marty—any more than he could have admitted it to Judy—but sometimes he didn't much like his job. The danger didn't bother him—he'd learned how to deal with that in the war. But he hated having to confront people at their worst—the drunks, the bullies, the wife-beaters—and it depressed him to see on a daily basis how low human beings could sink. He also hated to see good souls like Marty make such huge mistakes with their lives.

The politics, too, disgusted him. He had to keep the pillars of the community happy, or he'd never get re-elected. That meant putting up with every complainer in town—even crackpots like Reverend Tyree.

He couldn't prove it, but he was sure Reverend Tyree was responsible for the broken display window at the five-and-dime and for the missing body. No one else had a motive for that kind of vandalism—if the reverend's ravings about the end of the world could be called a motive. But the tornado had pushed the man over an edge of some kind, he could sense it. He would have to keep a close eye on the reverend from here on out. Once a person had stooped to body-snatching, he was liable to do just about anything.

"Speaking of burdens," Marty said, "how's Bryce doing?"

Sheriff Tune took another forkful of barbecue and a sip of tea. "He broke a few things, but he'll live. We might have to postpone his trial. But I figure he's probably looking at seven to ten years."

Marty looked down at his lap and sighed. "I couldn't stop him," he said. "I feel real bad about that."

"Not your fault, Marty," said Sheriff Tune. "You probably saved his life calling that ambulance."

Marty brightened. "You think so?"

"Sure. I was real proud of the way you handled things. I'd have recommended you for a reduced sentence if you hadn't stolen the McKinney's Packard."

"That Ellen McKinney is a nice lady," Marty said. "I remember when she was Ellen Parsons. I took her to a dance once, if you can believe it. Her and me went to the same high school."

"We all went to the same high school, Marty," said Sheriff Tune. "There's only one in the county."

"Maybe she won't press charges," Marty suggested. "I didn't really mean to steal her car. That's just sort of the way things unfolded."

"I don't know," said Sheriff Tune, absently spearing a hushpuppy. "Losing a new automobile is kind of a big deal to most folks."

"Well, that's a real shame, if you ask me," Marty said. "People like that are just victims of their own material possessions." He shook his fork at Sheriff Tune for emphasis. "They're the real prisoners."

"That's one point of view," said the sheriff. "But it's not the one that makes car theft illegal."

"If somebody took my car, I wouldn't want them arrested for it," Marty insisted. "I'd just figure they really needed it."

"Not everybody's as liberal-minded as you," said Sheriff Tune.

"How about the Indians?" asked Marty. "They thought the land belonged equally to everybody. They believed in community property."

"Maybe so," the sheriff said. "But I bet they still scalped horse thieves."

Marty frowned. "That's a good point." He dug into his pants pocket and pulled out a set of keys. "The Packard's out back, by the barbecue pit. Tell Mrs. McKinney I'm sorry I borrowed it without permission." He dropped the keys on the table in front of Sheriff Tune.

"You didn't damage it, did you?" the sheriff asked.

"I left the windows down," he admitted, "so it'll probably smell like pork for a while. But that's not such a bad thing."

"This is a mighty good first step, Marty," he said. "Maybe you're right, maybe the McKinneys won't press charges. I'll talk to them."

"That's kind of you, Sheriff. I appreciate it."

"Tell you what. If I can get them to overlook the car theft, would you come back and finish out your sentence?"

Marty rubbed his chin. "I don't know. There's still the jail-break to consider. That'll probably get me another year."

"Trustees earn privileges sometimes," the sheriff said. "Suppose we just say I gave you a furlough to visit your family."

Marty's face loosened. "You'd be willing to do that for me?"

"If this works out, you'll be a free man by August."

Marty sat quietly for a long moment with his head bowed. When he looked up, his eyes were wet. Sheriff Tune shifted his attention to his plate of barbecue. He scooped up a ragged forkful of pork and stuffed it into his mouth.

"The food here's pretty good," he said, finally.

"Lunch is on me," Marty told him.

Sheriff Tune watched his rearview mirror all the way back to Lincoln, making sure Marty was still behind him in the McKinney's Packard. Marty's surrender was the first good thing that had happened since the tornado. Of course, it wasn't a done deal yet. If Doc McKinney wanted to be a hard-ass about the car theft, the sheriff would have to give Marty a ride back to Dreamland, which was part of their deal. Maybe that wasn't exactly enforcing the letter of the law, but sometimes the law wasn't human enough. When a man acted in good faith, he deserved consideration, even if he was an escaped convict.

Of course, that was exactly the kind of gesture that could cost him an election. But he believed part of his job was to make judgment calls—to apply the full weight of the law to those who deserved it, and to go easy on the rest. Mrs. Crabtree wanted him to arrest someone for killing her dog, which was ridiculous. Some dogs needed killing, and that Boston terrier of hers was high on the list. Luckily, Mrs. Crabtree wasn't the sort to take an interest in her neighbors, so even though she'd been able to provide a description of Chester's attacker, she didn't realize it was probably Jerry Lee Statten who had climbed the wall into her yard. Jerry Lee was a good kid who shouldn't get in trouble for defending himself against a mean little shit of a dog. As far as Sheriff Tune was concerned, the killing of Chester Crabtree would remain forever unsolved. But that, too, was the kind of judgment call that could cost him votes.

Jerry Lee's father, Sammy Statten, could also hurt him come election time. There were those who didn't appreciate the sheriff's turning a blind eye to Sammy's bootlegging business. On the other hand, there were probably just as many who were happy to see him let Sammy slide, so maybe that one balanced out.

But there was still the Bryce Hatton affair. Gambling was illegal in Lincoln, so it didn't look good that the sheriff himself had been at the poker game where Walter Hatton got shot. Everybody knew they weren't playing for matchsticks. Reverend Tyree in particular had made a big stink over that one.

The more he thought about it, the more he became convinced he'd never get re-elected. But maybe that wouldn't be such a bad thing. He could do something else with his life.

But what? The only other thing he really enjoyed was singing in his barbershop quartet with Jimmy Vann, Flaps Pittenturf, and Morgan Motlow, and that was sure no way to make a living. He was too old to run off to Nashville to break into the music business—the world didn't need any more middle-aged crooners. Still, with the exception of selling shoes in Memphis, he could be open to just about any opportunity that might present itself.

He pulled his car into his reserved space in front of the jail while Marty circled around to the visitor parking area along the east side of the building. He felt a rush of well-being when he climbed out of the Plymouth—the day was bright and cool, a perfect preview of spring. He walked around the corner of the jailhouse to join Marty so they could enter the building together—he didn't want some startled deputy to overreact at the sight of a recent escapee.

What he saw when he rounded the corner stopped him in his tracks.

Marty stood on the sidewalk, his hands on his hips, staring at two cars parked side by side in the visitor spaces. One was the brand new Packard sedan he had driven up from Dreamland, its yellow body gleaming in the sun beneath its shiny black hardtop. But beside it was a second yellow and black Packard, and except for its Ohio license plates, the second automobile was identical to the first.

"Quite a coincidence," Marty said, marveling at the twin upscale automobiles.

Sheriff Tune knew better. The more likely explanation was that some wayward tourist had taken the scenic route on his way to a week of sunshine in the Gulf, and an overeager deputy had spotted the distinctive Packard and made a bad arrest. A mistake like that would mean bad publicity for the department. Maybe even a lawsuit against the county.

"When we get inside, I'd like you to go on up to your cell," he said, taking the Packard's keys from Marty's hand. "I may have some procedural matters to take care of."

Marty kicked at a pebble on the sidewalk. "I'm costing you a lot of paperwork, aren't I?"

"Don't you worry about it," the sheriff said. "Your paperwork might turn out to be the bright spot of my day."

He wasn't kidding. At the sight of the second Packard, a heaviness had risen in his chest that couldn't be blamed on Dreamland barbecue. Angry people would be waiting in his office, and he would have to find a way to make things right.

They entered the front hall and Marty immediately headed for the second floor, taking the stairs two at a time like a kid home from vacation. Sheriff Tune paused by his outer office door, listening to the voices competing inside. Tom Parsons, it sounded like, and his brother-in-law, Doc McKinney, along with young Merle Phagan, his newest deputy. No one sounded happy.

"Hello, gentlemen," he said, stepping into the room. He knew he wouldn't have to ask any questions. Everyone would be eager to tell his side of the story.

Doc McKinney rose from his bench by the holding cell. "Sheriff, your deputy won't release my automobile," he said.

"I told you, that's not your car," Tom Parsons said, leaning forward in his chair and putting his face in his hands. "Lord, this is a disaster."

"We don't know whose vehicle it is," Merle said. He slumped in his chair like a sullen eighth grader.

"It's mine, obviously," said Doc McKinney. "I think I ought to know my own Packard."

"I noticed Ohio plates," said Sheriff Tune.

"That's what they do sometimes," said Merle, pretending to busy himself with a stack of arrest reports. "They change the tags so we won't know the car's been stolen."

"Merle, if you arrested somebody, I hope you had more to go on than that," the sheriff said.

Merle looked up at him. "Yes sir, I did. The driver had no registration. If the registration's not with the car, you've got to figure something's wrong."

"Did he have an explanation for that?" the sheriff asked.

"Not a good one," Merle said, picking nervously at the veneer on his desktop. "Said he just bought the car last week and they hadn't mailed it to him yet." His eyes widened, and his words tumbled out in a rush. "But he didn't have a bill of sale, either, so I didn't have much choice but to arrest him. I mean, come on, Sheriff, a Negro driving a fancy car like that, you know something's gotta be up. And I don't care who he claims to be."

Sheriff Tune didn't like the sound of that.

"Just who did he claim to be?" he asked.

Merle shifted uncomfortably. "Why should that matter? People can claim to be anybody." He picked up a clipboard from his desk and scanned the arrest form. "According to his driver's license he's Arnold Raymond Cream." He glared over at Tom Parsons and jabbed his finger at the form. "That's a documented fact."

Tom let out a quiet groan. "Arnold Cream is his real name, Merle, not the name he fights under." He looked up at Sheriff Tune. "Your boy here just arrested Jersey Joe Walcott, the world heavyweight champ."

"That hasn't been established," Merle said.

"It's been established plenty," Tom told him. "He took the title from Ezzard Charles last July. Watch a newsreel, for God's sake."

"Why was Jersey Joe Walcott driving my car?" asked Doc McKinney.

"He wasn't, Doc," the sheriff told him. "Your Packard's outside. You can take it home whenever you like." He tossed him the keys. "It's the one that smells like barbecue."

Marty Raby suddenly appeared in the office doorway. "Excuse me, Sheriff," he said, "I'm not exactly sure what to do. There's a new guy living in my cell."

"He's not living there, Marty," said Sheriff Tune. "He's just passing through."

Merle scrambled to his feet. "You aren't supposed to be here," he said, pointing at Marty.

Marty shrugged. "I had a change of heart."

Merle fumbled with the strap on his holster.

Sheriff Tune stepped between the two men. "Merle, if that gun leaves your hip," he said, "you'll be back stocking shelves at the Piggly Wiggly." He turned to Marty. "Tell Mr. Cream I'll be up in a minute to release him."

"You can't do that," Merle objected. "I've already processed him. He's officially under arrest."

"Throw out the file," Sheriff Tune told him. "And then shut the hell up."

Jesus, he couldn't leave this town on its own for five minutes. A simple trip to Dreamland, and now the last remnants of his career were shot all to hell. It didn't matter that the screw-up hadn't been his doing—a sheriff was responsible for his deputies. His hopes for re-election receded into the horizon like a bevy of flushed quail.

"The man was invited here as an honored guest," Tom said, spreading his palms. "What the hell do I tell him now?"

Sheriff Tune thought of what Judy had said to him once, when he asked her how he was supposed to get along without her. *I guess you've got to roll with the punches,* she had told him. That was good advice for anybody, it seemed to him now—for him, for Merle, for Tom, even for the heavyweight champion of the world. They all had to roll with the punches. Because the punches never stopped coming.

Nolla Rae Statten

When she'd finished setting up the fortune-telling tent by the concession stand, Nolla Rae Statten settled herself onto the folding chair at her card table and shuffled the Tarot deck seven times. She hadn't done a reading for herself in more than a year, not since her boy Web had shipped out for Korea. She'd been afraid of what she might see in the cards. But now Web was dead anyway, and she realized there was no wisdom in hiding from things that had already been set in motion. Maybe if she had looked ahead on Web's behalf, she could have faced his death in time to put him on another course. She wouldn't make that mistake with Jerry Lee, and at the moment she was worried that her younger boy might have rabies.

Last Saturday he'd come home with a deep bite on his leg, which he said was from a mean dog in the neighborhood. But he also said he'd killed the dog—which seemed an unlikely accomplishment for a seven-year-old—and that the attack had come when he was doing a favor for a friendly haint. So Nolla Rae wasn't sure what to believe. She knew there had been plenty of rabid skunks and raccoons in the woods this year, and she feared Jerry Lee might have tangled with some kind of diseased animal. Maybe a varmint he wouldn't even recognize. The boy was still young enough to mistake a possum for an odd breed of dog.

Money was tight, like always, so she wouldn't take him to
Dr. McKinney unless the cards told her sickness was on the
way. Of course, no reading could ever be entirely reliable.
Something bad was always out there somewhere, waiting for
a chance to swoop in, and it might be hard to pick out rabies
from all the other darknesses the cards might know about. She
would have to study the hand carefully and try to sort out the
more subtle signs.

She turned over the ten cards for the divination. The sixth
card, indicator of the shaping current, was the Moon. Hidden
enemies. Deception. Danger. The tenth card, revealing that
which would come to be, was the Five of Swords, upside down.
Lord, what a world of troubles that could mean. This card carried degradation and destruction. Reversal leading to infamy
and dishonor. A great loss. In the end, a burial.

But nothing about sickness. Something other than rabies,
it looked like, was taking shape. Something stronger. Something worse.

In another time, these could have been Web's cards. Especially the reversal, infamy, and dishonor. Not Web's, but those
who killed him—the unnamed American artillerymen who read
the wrong numbers on a map and blew up her son by accident.

She had to believe it had been an honest mistake, though
Sammy saw a more sinister hand behind it. "They'll kill any
colored man they can get away with," he had said after he read
the telegram.

He'd been touchy even before Web's death. He'd been
reading the paper—not Mr. Tom's *Observer*, but *The Birming-
ham News*, which he picked up on his trips to Huntsville—and
found out that a lot of Negroes in the big cities were calling for
integration. None of that kind of talk had surfaced in Lincoln
yet, or at least not in public. But according to Sammy, a lot of
the congregations down in Alabama and even some over in
Chattanooga had got fed up with Jim Crow. They were tired
of taking a back seat on the buses and drinking from separate
water fountains. Of course, those weren't issues in Lincoln be-

cause there weren't any bus lines or even any public drinking fountains. But no Negro could get served in a white-owned restaurant. She understood that as a slap in the face, though she preferred to eat at home anyway.

The issue that did make a difference to her was the school system. She wanted Jerry Lee to get a good education so he could make something of himself, but the county's six-room Negro school was a disgrace, a converted tobacco warehouse with gaps in the walls and holes in the roof. Too few books and too few teachers. Not enough coal to keep the boiler going in the wintertime. Sammy told her there was a big court case being decided right now that could change everything, especially for Jerry Lee. Something called *Brown v. the Board of Education of Topeka, Kansas*. Brown was their side, she assumed.

Nolla Rae didn't see how a case in Kansas would make much difference in Tennessee, and she sure knew no court decision could affect how people thought or what they felt in their hearts. If the law suddenly said Jerry Lee could go to a white school to get a better education, she feared for how they might treat him there. That kind of change wouldn't come peacefully, no matter what those Montgomery ministers said. If things kept on the way they were going, everybody had struggles ahead, and not even the Tarot could predict what kind of ugly world Jerry Lee would have to grow up in.

But for now, most whites around town were polite enough, and polite was better than some of the alternatives. She hadn't been called names since she was a little girl, at least not to her face. But she'd learned that no matter what race people were, some folks were just low-down trash, even if they were churchgoers, while others were true Christian souls. In most cases it was easy enough to tell the two apart.

Mr. Tom and Miss Kate, for example, had always been fine people. In all the years she'd worked as their housekeeper, she'd never heard them make a single inappropriate remark, never heard them say anything disrespectful. Once, years back, when Mr. Tom ran his unsuccessful campaign for mayor, she'd overheard a party guest say something about getting the nigger vote, and Mr. Tom had asked him to leave the house. "I don't appreciate that kind of language," he had said.

Mr. Tom had remained a good man, though he didn't take care of himself now that Miss Kate had passed on. Nolla Rae still came in twice a week to tidy up the house and make him dinner, but she suspected that was the only decent food he got. She knew he drank too much, and that bothered her, especially since Sammy was the one selling him the whiskey.

But Sammy had to do whatever he could to make a living, she understood that. She also realized that he had a tougher time of it, being a man and having to work menial jobs around foul-mouthed rednecks. But even he had found a couple of white folks he could tolerate. Mr. Tom's brother-in-law, Moody Smith, was a good man, Sammy had told her, and Herb Gatlin too. Sammy and Moody had dug graves together for the past few years, and now that all this fear of communism was making people so crazy, they'd joined up with Mr. Herb to dig backyard fallout shelters for some of the wealthier families in town. It was a good sideline.

She was glad Mr. Herb hadn't died in the tornado like everybody thought. He was almost a celebrity now that the newspaper had announced his return from the grave. In fact, the only person she knew who hadn't rejoiced in the miracle was Jerry Lee, though she couldn't imagine why. He'd acted sullen ever since hearing the news. But maybe that was just her imagination. Kids could be harder to read than Tarot cards.

The Tarot had brought a little extra income into their lives, and she was thankful for that. She'd bought the deck in New Orleans on a visit to her younger sister, Ella, who worked in a novelty shop in the French Quarter. That was three years ago, and she'd studied up on the cards a lot since then. Some of the more conservative churchgoers in town frowned on her fortune-telling business even more than they did on Sammy's bootlegging, but the Tarot was just another avenue to the Lord's wisdom, as far as she was concerned. That Baptist minister, Reverend Tyree, had tried to make trouble, preaching whole sermons against her, but she just considered that free publicity. Her own minister at Third Baptist, Reverend Jefferson, didn't see anything wrong with what she was doing. She figured Reverend Tyree was just one of those people who had to go on tirades, and he probably couldn't help himself any more than a Chihuahua could keep from yapping at flies. But he couldn't stop folks from wanting to know things outside the Bible, especially young people, who were still open to new ideas. Madame Zubu the Mysterious was a hit with the teenagers, and that was all she needed.

She found that she liked having a second identity. Madame Zubu led a colorful and exotic life, at least compared to what Nolla Rae was used to. Two nights a week Mr. Tom let her use one of the vacant offices in a building he owned on the square, and she had decorated it to look something like the palm reader's room she had visited in New Orleans. She wore a dark blue robe with red dragons on it that she'd bought in the Chinese district of Memphis and a homemade red satin turban with a peacock feather sticking up in the back.

But today she was simply Nolla Rae, dressed in a standard floral housedress she'd sewn from remnants of a discontinued pattern she'd found on sale at a mill outlet. She'd be back tonight as Madame Zubu in her full regalia, but this afternoon all she had to do was set things up. The tent was an odd mix of burlap and canvas—she'd had to go with whatever cheap materials she could scrape together on short notice. Only the day before yesterday Mr. Tom had suggested she might want to set up some kind of fortune-telling booth at the prizefighting exhibition. He said it would add to the atmosphere, but she knew he was just trying to throw some business her way. This would be her most public appearance yet, and she might draw more criticism from Reverend Tyree and his ilk, but since Mr. Tom owned the drive-in where the fight was being staged, she figured she didn't need to worry about anybody else's approval.

It had taken her two full days to make the tent, but that included the moons and planets and stars she had painted on the

sides. She realized her customers might mistake her for an as-
trologer, but the confusion couldn't be helped. The pictures on
the Tarot cards were too complicated for her to draw. Circles
and stars were about all she could manage. She had colored
the planets and moons herself, but she had let Jerry Lee fill in
the stars, because she figured if he painted outside the lines it
would just look like extra starshine. Twinkling stars didn't really
have a specific shape anyway.

Inside the tent was one of Miss Kate's old folding bridge tables,
covered with a tattered piece of white linen that had belonged to
Nolla Rae's mother. In the center of the table was her crystal ball,
which she'd bought second-hand from Delila the Divine, who
had passed through town with the carnival two years back. The
crystal ball really had nothing to do with the Tarot readings, but
people still expected it. They just wouldn't believe Nolla Rae saw
their futures unless there was a crystal ball involved. So she kept
it on the table and laid out the cards around it.

She wished now she could use the crystal ball as more than
just a decoration. A revelation was unfolding in the cards, and
yet she couldn't bring it forward into words. The shadows were
too strong, the pieces too far apart. Something was brewing,
she knew that much—another storm, another whirlwind—but
the substance of it lay just beyond her reach.

Maybe it was better not to know. Maybe she should focus
on the light for a while, and not stare so deeply into the face of
the abyss.

The tent suddenly grew brighter, and Nolla Rae looked up
from her cards to see the silhouette of a woman standing at the
opening, holding the burlap flap to the side. She was slightly
plump, and her brown dress hung on her like a potato sack. Her
hair was pulled back into a tight bun.

"Knock, knock," she said, and if it weren't for the obvious
defeat in her voice, Nolla Rae would have thought the woman
was about to tell her a joke.

"Sorry, ma'am, but we ain't open yet," Nolla Rae said. "Madame Zubu the Mysterious won't be in till later this evening."

The woman glanced over her shoulder and stepped inside the tent, letting the flap fall shut behind her. Nolla Rae leaned back in her chair and studied the woman in the filtered daylight, trying to remember if she'd seen her somewhere before. She was a plain woman, middle-aged, no makeup, with gray hair streaking at her temples. She clutched her black purse against her stomach with both hands.

"I'm looking for my husband," she said. She gazed around the tent as if she expected the man to materialize in a corner. "I'm looking for Reverend Tyree."

Nolla Rae almost laughed.

"He wouldn't be nowhere around here, Miz Tyree," she said. "Madame Zubu and him don't see eye to eye."

"I thought he might have come out to have a look around before the boxing match," she said. "He's talked about it a lot."

That was a likely guess, Nolla Rae realized—the reverend might indeed come to check the place out before the big show. From what Nolla Rae knew of him, he was the kind of preacher who wouldn't hesitate to take the fight to the enemy, and tonight this drive-in would be crawling with the reverend's idea of sinners. He'd probably come sniffing around early to scout a good spot to preach from.

"I saw Mr. Tom Parsons out there a while ago," Nolla Rae said. "Him and some other fellows was rigging up the ropes on the boxing ring. Maybe one of them saw the reverend."

Mrs. Tyree stood still as a church mouse.

"There's nobody there now," she said.

"There better be somebody," Nolla Rae said, rising from her chair. She stepped past Mrs. Tyree through the tent flap into the cool afternoon air. At the far end of the drive-in, Jerry Lee danced wildly around in the ring, swinging his arms at invisible foes. Nolla Rae sighed.

"Oh, well, there's that little colored boy," Mrs. Tyree conceded as she emerged from the tent.

"That's my Jerry Lee," Nolla Rae told her. "Mr. Tom introduced him to the champ. Now he loves playing boxer."

Nolla Rae stood there for a long moment, watching Jerry Lee play, until Mrs. Tyree blew her nose loudly. She turned and looked at the woman, whose eyes were now brimming with tears.

"I don't know what to do," Mrs. Tyree said. "I've looked everywhere I know to look."

Nolla Rae pointed to the low cinder-block building beside them. "Just get you a chair out of the concession stand and settle in," she suggested. "I bet the reverend'll be along directly. He'll need to get used to his new church."

Mrs. Tyree sniffed and dabbed at her eyes with a yellowed handkerchief. "What new church?"

The news had spread so quickly, it didn't seem possible that Reverend Tyree's own wife wouldn't know.

"This here's the new Baptist church," Nolla Rae said.

Mrs. Tyree looked around nervously. "What is?"

"The drive-in," Nolla Rae told her. "Mr. Tom donated the use of the grounds. All the churches that got destroyed will have their Sunday services here until they can rebuild. Baptist at eight thirty, Methodist at ten o'clock, Episcopal at eleven thirty. Folks won't even have to get out of their cars." She pointed to the boxing ring. "Reverend Tyree'll stand right up there on that platform with the choir spread out behind him."

"What if it rains?"

Nolla Rae smiled. "He'll just do his sermon from inside the concession stand. Folks won't be able to see him, I guess, unless they turn their cars around and switch their windshield wipers on. But they'll still hear him through the movie speakers."

Mrs. Tyree frowned. "This all sounds very . . . strange."

Nolla Rae shrugged. "These is strange times," she said. "People have to make do." She stepped closer to Mrs. Tyree. "I'm surprised you hadn't heard. Mr. Tom's drive-in church is the talk of the town."

"Except for work, I don't get out much," said Mrs. Tyree. "I have responsibilities at home."

Nolla Rae had heard rumors about those responsibilities. Word in the backyards was that Mrs. Tyree had to put in a lot of time taking care of Miss Edith, the reverend's invalid mother, who had lived with them for the past ten years. Miss Edith was mostly senile, and bedridden to boot. But she could still throw a tantrum that would wake the neighbors on all four sides.

"I mean I thought the reverend would've said something about it," said Nolla Rae.

"My husband may not know," she said. "He's been gone three days."

A chill went up Nolla Rae's spine. She put a gentle hand on Mrs. Tyree's shoulder.

"Hon, you might need to talk to Sheriff Tune about that."

Mrs. Tyree stiffened. "That man has never shown the slightest respect for my husband," she said. "Sheriff Tune is the last person I'd ever go to for help."

"Help is help," Nolla Rae said, folding her arms. "I 'spect the sheriff couldn't be much further down the list than Madame Zubu."

A red Ford pickup entered the front gate of the drive-in and pulled in behind the concession stand. Sammy rode in the back, his arm draped over the tailgate.

"I have to go," Mrs. Tyree said. "If you happen to see my husband, please don't tell him I was here." She tucked her handkerchief in her purse and hurried away around the side of the concession stand to her own mud-spattered DeSoto.

As Mrs. Tyree pulled back out onto the highway, Sammy hopped down from the bed of the truck and Tom Parsons and Arnold Cream climbed out of the cab. Mr. Tom, dressed in his usual white suit and Panama hat, braced his palms against his spine and bent himself backward to stretch out the kinks. Nolla Rae understood that well enough. She was a few years younger than Mr. Tom, but they both suffered from stiffness in their joints, especially after sitting still too long. That was the hardest part of being Madame Zubu—on busy nights, she had to sit hunched over those cards for hours, and by the time she'd predicted wealth and true love for her last customer, she could barely push herself up from the table.

Sammy was luckier—he stayed as limber as a teenager, even after so many years of hard labor. He still had some of that old teenage sparkle to him, too, it seemed to Nolla Rae, even dressed as he was now, in those same ratty blue overalls he wore to dig graves. Some people got one kind of blessing, some people got another.

Mr. Cream had more than his share of blessings, from the looks of him. He was dressed in a gray three-piece pinstripe and a black fedora, and the way he stood when he got out of the truck, with his feet spread and his hands on his hips, he looked like he might be the king of the world. Of course, he wasn't far from it—world heavyweight champ was no small matter. He drove a fancy automobile, he wore a diamond stickpin in his tie, and he probably lived in a big house back in New Jersey. He could knock a white man down and get away with it. Sammy had told her he was the oldest man ever to win the title—thirty-seven, though that didn't sound old at all to Nolla Rae. When she was thirty-seven she'd had Jerry Lee, and that had certainly been as difficult as any prize fight.

"What's the good word?" Mr. Tom called out to her, tugging his hat brim low against the sun. She couldn't see his eyes, but he was smiling. He'd been as happy as she'd ever seen him the past couple of days, ever since Mr. Cream agreed to overlook his run-in with the sheriff's office and go ahead with the exhibition. For his part, Mr. Tom had offered to donate a third of the proceeds to the Negro school, which had probably raised a few eyebrows around town.

"Caution," Nolla Rae said.

"Caution's a good word, all right," Mr. Tom agreed, picking his way over to her across the tire ruts that surrounded the concession stand. "But is that Nolla Rae talking, or Madame Zubu the Mysterious?"

"Madame Zubu would've charged you a quarter," she said.

"Them's pretty steep rates, Miz Statten," said Arnold Cream, taking off his hat and smiling at her.

"Some words is worth it," she said.

"Don't I know it," he agreed. "The right word makes all the difference—and I'll take win over lose any day."

"We brought you back some barbecue," Sammy said, walking up to join them with a brown paper sack in his hands, grease seeping through the bottom.

"Barbecue's a good word," said Mr. Tom.

"Don't take it in the tent," Nolla Rae told him. "I don't want Madame Zubu's smelling like no rib joint."

Sammy looked around and set the bag on the ledge of the counter at the concession stand.

"Maybe Madame Zubu can tell us how Jersey Joe's next match'll turn out," teased Mr. Tom.

"Oh, I suspect he'll hold his own against our local boys," she said.

Mr. Cream laughed. "You never know," he said. "The next champ has to come from somewhere."

"Maybe that's him yonder," said Sammy, pointing to Jerry Lee, who was still dancing in the ring.

"I meant his next heavyweight fight," said Mr. Tom. "He's taking on Rocky Marciano in September. If I knew a little more about the future, I might make a small wager."

"You can bet Christmas on that one," Mr. Cream said. "I plan on beating him."

"Beating ain't always the same as winning," Sammy said. "You beat Joe Louis back in '47—knocked him down twice— and the judges still let him keep the title."

"That's true enough," said Mr. Cream. "Anything short of a knockout is always a matter of somebody's opinion."

"How come you don't use your real name when you box?" Nolla Rae asked.

Mr. Cream nodded toward the elaborately painted name on the front of Nolla Rae's tent. "Same reason as Madame Zubu the Mysterious, I imagine," he said. "Sometimes we just need a whole new name to measure up to."

"But why Jersey Joe Walcott?" asked Mr. Tom. "Where'd that come from?"

Mr. Cream squinted toward the makeshift ring, where Jerry Lee was now bouncing up and down on the lower rope. "When I was first coming up, folks said I had the same moves as a middleweight name of Joe Walcott. I was from New Jersey, so they just started calling me Jersey Joe Walcott." He smiled sheepishly. "I guess it sounded tougher than Arnold Cream."

Names. They all carried their own baggage, their own magic. *Jersey Joe Walcott* sounded more like a fighter than *Arnold Cream. Madame Zubu* sounded more like a fortune-teller than *Nolla Rae Statten. Popeye* sounded more like a comic strip character than *Moody Smith.* Her own brother Floyd insisted on being called Gas-House, for reasons she never understood. She had even read in a magazine at the beauty shop that the greatest of the Western movie heroes, Roy Rogers, wasn't really Roy Rogers at all, but a man named Leonard Sly from someplace in Ohio. If he'd stayed Leonard Sly, he'd never have been called the King of the Cowboys.

"Mr. Cream, you ready to check out that ring?" asked Mr. Tom.

Mr. Cream took off his hat with one hand and ran his other over the top of his short-cropped hair. "Looks like it's getting checked out pretty good already," he said. Jerry Lee was now hanging by his knees from the top rope, pounding on his chest and hollering like Tarzan. "But yeah, I always like to walk a ring before a bout. Get a feel for the footing."

"It's regulation size," Mr. Tom told him. "But there's no padding underneath that canvas. Might make for some hard landings."

"That's nothing I have to worry about," said Mr. Cream, laughing and slapping Mr. Tom on the back.

Nolla Rae almost gasped. She'd never seen a Negro take that kind of liberty with a grown white man, especially one he barely knew. For his part, Mr. Tom just grinned.

"What about lights?" Mr. Cream asked. "I need to see who I'm whipping up on."

"Sammy rigged up floodlights," Mr. Tom said, pointing to the utility poles flanking the huge movie screen. "I've also got a couple of airplane searchlights to set up, but that's just for show."

"How'd you get hold of searchlights?" Mr. Cream asked.

"I'm the Civil Defense director for the county," he said.

"Mr. Tom's the air-raid warden," added Sammy.

"That must be a big job these days," said Mr. Cream, "with the Russians having the A-bomb and all."

"We're a target zone for sure," said Sammy. "The Redstone Arsenal's just down the road. That's where they build all the rockets."

"There's not much for me to do, really," Mr. Tom said. "I just keep the air-raid shelters stocked with water and canned goods. Once a year I visit the grammar school and tell the kids to duck and cover."

Mr. Cream put his hat back on and pursed his lips. "Duck and cover?"

"If we get attacked, they're supposed to duck under their school desks and cover their ears. That's the official government position on surviving a nuclear blast." He shook his head. "I thought Harry Truman had more on the ball than that. I may have to vote Eisenhower this time around."

Mr. Tom tipped his hat to Nolla Rae and then led the heavyweight champ out across the rutted field, angling across the uniform rows of waist-high speaker poles.

Sammy stepped over to Nolla Rae and put an arm around her shoulder.

"Sheriff Tune stopped me on the street this morning," he said.

"He ain't after you about bootlegging, I hope," she said. "I told you, first sign of trouble and your days running liquor are done." She didn't mean to sound harsh, but she'd never liked his bootlegging to begin with. She couldn't fault him for his effort, especially since they needed the money, but she wished he'd set his career sights higher than just carting illegal whiskey up from Alabama. She knew, though, that if she really wanted Sammy to set loftier goals, she'd have to make that clear as tap water. No man ever strove for more than what he thought the woman in his life expected of him.

"Naw, it's nothing like that." He took in a slow breath. "He just wanted to tell me to keep Jerry Lee clear of the Crabtree place for a while. Looks like the boy might have killed their dog." Nolla Rae could tell he was trying not to laugh.

"What dog?" She knew the Crabtrees had a Boston terrier, but she also knew they never let it outside. It always barked at her from their dining room window whenever she walked past on her way downtown.

"That little black and white yapper," Sammy said. "The one with the pointy ears."

"What was Jerry Lee doing around that dog?" she asked.

"Miz Crabtree sicced it on him. The boy just defended himself." Nolla Rae could hear the pride in Sammy's voice. "Sheriff Tune wanted me to know he's got no problem with what Jerry Lee did. But he said the Crabtrees might make a stink if they spot Jerry Lee around the neighborhood."

Nolla Rae looked across the drive-in field toward Jerry Lee, who was now leaning over the ropes, waving to his approaching hero, Jersey Joe Walcott. The champ waved back.

"I don't give a tinker's damn what the Crabtrees might do," said Nolla Rae, her anger rising at the thought that anyone could sic a dog on her little boy. "I'll put Jerry Lee on their front porch swing if I want to and dare that woman to say a single word about it."

"Nolla Rae, he had no business being on their property," Sammy told her. "We gotta pick our battles, sweetheart, and believe me, this ain't the one to get crazy over."

She knew he was right. The Crabtrees were a respected family in town, and the Stattens weren't anybody at all. They were lucky the sheriff was a just man.

And really, this was good news about the dog. The Crabtrees were the kind of people who would only own a pedigreed animal, one with all the right vaccinations. So even though the horrible creature was vicious, it wouldn't have been rabid. Jerry Lee was in the clear on that score, at least. She wouldn't have to spend his birthday money on shots.

But something untoward was still in the cards, some dark holdover from the recent storm. In just a couple of hours, a dozen local toughs would line up to have their jaws broken by the world heavyweight champion, but that wasn't it—that wasn't the consequence that nagged at the back of her mind. Those boys were merely foolish. The thing she felt approaching was nothing so trivial, nothing so fleeting as a gloved fist connecting with skin and bone. But until the thing arrived and she understood its face, there was nothing she could do. The tornado and its aftermath would be forgotten, for tonight anyway, and a mob of happy survivors would encircle the boxing ring, cheering for every blow they saw. They would crowd the concession stand, buying hot dogs and Coca-Colas and cotton candy to celebrate the night. Some of them, the curious teenagers and their dates, would eventually find their way to her card table and her crystal ball, and Nolla Rae would read their fortunes, one by one, keeping a sharp eye out for whatever gray force was on the rise. Already the sun was dipping behind the movie screen, casting a shadow all the way to the entrance of Madame Zubu's tent. The drive-in would soon spring to life.

The necessary darkness was beginning to gather.

Bobby Malone

Even before he got dropped off at his parents' house, Bobby Malone had begun to worry. The streets near the square were deserted, and all the street lamps were out, leaving the familiar neighborhoods in darkness. The once-familiar neighborhoods. They were different now, he could tell that much from the low, limited sweep of the automobile's headlights. Portions of the town lay in ruins, as if certain blocks had been shelled by artillery. Buildings he'd known all his life had vanished from the landscape, or been reduced to skeletal outlines against the moonlit sky.

He tried to tell himself he was imagining things, that the night was playing tricks on him. After all, there was no rubble in the roadway, which would certainly be the case if the town had truly been hit. He knew what it was to stalk the outskirts of a bombed-out village, where wreckage and debris almost always made the dirt streets impassable. This was something else—it had to be. But he still couldn't shake the feeling that he had somehow brought the war home with him.

Neither Corporal Berman nor his chipmunk of a wife noticed the change, but they'd never seen Lincoln before, even in daylight. Berman had just finished his hitch in Germany where he'd been a file clerk for two years, and now he was on his way

home to Decatur, Alabama, to farm soybeans. He hadn't gone
to Korea like Bobby. Maybe that's why Berman had felt obliged
to offer him a ride from the base.

"Take care of that hand, Private," Berman had said as Bobby climbed from the back seat, dragging his duffel bag out to
the curb. Berman's wife turned her head toward Bobby from
the front seat and stared at him through the window, but she
didn't say anything. She'd said very little all day. He figured she
was mad that Berman had spoiled their reunion by inviting a
stranger along for part of the trip home.

Mary Jean would have come to pick him up, he felt certain,
if he'd had the guts to ask her. But he hadn't even told her he
was on his way home. He hadn't told her about his accident,
either. He'd certainly thought about it, first lying on a cot in
the M.A.S.H. unit at Panmunjom, then in a lumpy hospital
bed in Tokyo. But somehow he'd never mustered the energy to
attempt a letter. He wasn't sure he could write legibly with just
his left hand.

The house was unlocked but dark. He stood in the front hall
and listened, thoroughly, as the army had trained him to do.
His parents weren't home. He gently set his bag beside the stairs
and stepped back out onto the porch, avoiding the boards he
knew would creak. That was his habit now—moving through
darkness as silently as he could. He stood at the porch rail and
scanned the houses across the street. Not a light on anywhere
along the block. He wondered if his watch had stopped, or if
he had somehow lost his sense of time. It should have been no
later than seven o'clock, but the empty streets and darkened
houses gave everything the feel of midnight.

The cool night air drew him down into the yard, and he
walked to the edge of the sidewalk and stood there, forcing
himself to relax. He was a civilian now, safe at home—that's
what he needed to remember. Standing in the open on a moonlit night didn't have to be terrifying anymore. But it was. He
could adjust in time, he knew that. He could relearn how to
stand unprotected without any fear of snipers and how to stroll

through tall grass without testing for trip wires. For now though, the feeling of exposure made his heart pump faster, and the quickened beat of his blood made his wrist throb. He looked down at the white bandage glowing in the darkness. He suppressed the urge to cover it up. Two months ago, a bandage that clean and bright would have been sure to draw fire. Here in Lincoln it would only draw condolences.

Condolences meant conversation. People would ask him what had happened, and he hadn't decided yet what to say. The loss of a hand ought to carry some drama with it, but that hadn't been the case. There had been nothing noble, nothing brave or inspirational in any part of the story. He had simply been on patrol in cold weather when the guy behind him slipped on an icy rock and fell, discharging his rifle. The bullet passed through Bobby's wrist from side to side, pulverizing the bones and leaving his hand attached by only a couple of strips of skin. Nothing to do but hack the rest off and staunch the bleeding. Adios, amigo.

He thought of Herb Gatlin. When Bobby was a boy, Mr. Gatlin had been the only person he knew who didn't have all his parts. Bobby and his friends sometimes debated which option would be worse—losing a leg or losing an arm. Bryce Hatton always argued that it would be worse to gimp around on just one leg, like Mr. Gatlin, but Bobby had believed losing an arm would be far worse. He believed it now more than ever.

In terms of function, there wasn't much difference between losing a hand and losing an arm, he had discovered. Either way, he couldn't throw a baseball or cut his own meat or play his guitar or shake hands like a normal person would. He couldn't be a surgeon or a policeman or even a ditch-digger. He couldn't use certain tools or operate certain types of equipment. He couldn't shift the gears on a truck. He couldn't even tie his own shoes.

All the everyday things wives asked husbands to do would pose insurmountable obstacles for him: hanging a picture, building a doghouse, clipping a hedge. Changing a baby's diaper. Mary Jean would discover a million things he would never be able to do for her. If, in fact, she chose to stay with him.

Something flickered at the corner of his vision, and Bobby turned toward the western sky. Two powerful arc lights swept back and forth, their beams crossing randomly and bouncing off the bottoms of the clouds. He'd seen plenty of lights like that searching the skies above Korea, usually accompanied by sirens. There, the lights meant trouble. Here in the States, they barely meant anything at all. A new department store was holding a grand opening or an automobile lot was having a sale or a carnival had come to town.

He tried to gauge the distance. Probably only a mile or so out the highway. Maybe two. But what was out there? Not much, that he could recall. Just a lot of pasture and farmland. And the Starlight Drive-in. Sure, that had to be it. Something was going on out at the Starlight. Maybe a special double feature or something, with a raffle for door prizes.

Whatever it was, he knew his parents would be part of the crowd. His father always said the only way to run a successful business in a small town was to be involved in the community, and that meant showing up at every Little League game, every high school play, every holiday parade, every fireworks display.

Maybe Mary Jean would be there, too. Maybe his parents had taken her to see a movie to welcome her into the family. Never mind that his mother thought Mary Jean was a slut for getting pregnant in the first place.

He tucked his bandaged stump carefully into the front of his uniform jacket and set off down Garden Street toward the intersection with Route 431. In a matter of minutes, he had turned the corner at Robert E. Lee Elementary and entered the highway just ahead of Dead Man's Curve. The search lights continued to swing wildly about the sky.

He'd barely walked a hundred yards along the main road when he was overtaken by a pair of headlights from behind, from an automobile creeping cautiously around Dead Man's Curve. His first impulse was to take cover—too many nights on guard duty had conditioned him to be wary of any stranger approaching in the dark. He stepped off the shoulder of the road and positioned himself behind a telephone pole, not hiding, exactly, but allowing himself some measure of protection until the vehicle had passed.

It didn't pass. The sedan cruised to a stop alongside him. Bobby stepped out from the pole and peered into the old DeSoto. The passenger-side window was down, and he could see that the driver, a man, was alone. He couldn't make out the man's face.

"Evening, soldier," the man called through the window. "You been doing the Lord's work?"

Bobby didn't know how to answer that. As near as he could tell, the Lord had bypassed Korea altogether.

"I've been in the army," Bobby said. "I just got my discharge."

"You fought communism," the man said.

"Yes sir," Bobby said, though even after losing his hand in the effort, he still didn't know what communism was, exactly.

"That's good. That's serving your country," the man said. "One nation under God."

"Yes sir," said Bobby. Something about the man's voice sounded familiar.

"Get in, boy," the man told him. "I'll take you where you're going."

As Bobby opened the door, the dome light switched on and he got his first clear look at the man in the driver's seat. He appeared disheveled, the way a soldier on patrol looked after sleeping in his clothes for a few days. His sweat-stained shirt was untucked, with the sleeves shoved above his elbows. His thinning hair was matted to his scalp, and Bobby noticed smears of dirt on his face and the backs of his hands. The sudden light seemed to have startled him, and he raised his forearm against the glare, as if shielding himself from a blow. More than anything else, the man looked exhausted, and Bobby might have taken him for some kind of fugitive if he hadn't recognized who the poor fellow was. It was his minister from the Baptist church, Reverend Tyree.

"I'm just going a little ways down the road, Reverend," he said as he climbed inside the car. He awkwardly closed the door with his left hand, extinguishing the overhead light.

"To the drive-in, I'll bet," the reverend said as he pulled back onto the highway.

"Yes sir, that's right," Bobby said. "Looks like big doings there tonight." He wondered if the reverend recognized him at all from the church youth group. Probably not. He'd always had the feeling that the reverend's mind was somewhere else during those weekly meetings.

"It's the place of judgment," the reverend said, his voice wavering slightly. "The Whore of Babylon rises from the bottomless pit."

"Sounds like a good one," Bobby said, though he wasn't too keen on religious films. If he had to get stuck with one, he hoped it would be an action movie like *Quo Vadis* and not one of those sappy tearjerkers like *The Song of Bernadette*. Of course, either way there would be a lot of unfortunate dying. He felt a little skittish about that these days.

He half expected the reverend to ask about his hand. Bobby figured he must look like Napoleon with his arm tucked in his uniform jacket the way it was. But the reverend didn't seem to notice. Maybe his mind was already distracted with other people's problems. He might well have been coming home from helping out at the scene of an accident. Or maybe he'd had an accident himself. It was certainly possible, judging from the look of him.

"I lost my right hand," Bobby told him.

Reverend Tyree turned and looked at him, long enough that the DeSoto drifted off the shoulder of the road. Bobby grabbed the wheel to keep them out of the ditch, but even then the reverend didn't stop staring at him.

"It's waiting for you in paradise," the reverend said, and then calmly steered them back onto the highway.

Bobby released his grip on the wheel and took a breath. These spiritual types could be a little too unfocused, too easily distracted, it seemed to him. One foot planted on earth, the other off tap-dancing in the great beyond. That's why he'd hated it when fundamentalists got assigned to his unit. They were always blathering on about God when they should have been scanning the trees for snipers. Bobby was a believer himself, but he understood that sometimes you just had to deal with the task at hand. He didn't know how some of those guys even made it through boot camp. He wouldn't trust them to sort screws at his father's hardware store. Always daydreaming about the afterlife. Of course, that kind of distraction was excusable for the reverend. His job was to keep his distance from the everyday world.

So his hand was in paradise. Bobby tried to picture that, but it seemed too strange. How could it be waiting for him? Did God keep it in a box or jar somewhere with all the other unclaimed body parts? Would he have to rummage through them all to identify which one was his? Or was it resting on some heavenly tabletop, drumming its fingers, waiting for him to show up? Would Jesus just casually give it to him when he got there, or would there be some kind of ceremony, forms to fill out, bureaucratic red tape? And what if he didn't even make it to heaven? Would his hand be stuck there forever, alone, the only part of him good enough to make it through the gates?

He decided not to say anything else.

They crested the last rise above the drive-in and Bobby could see that the Starlight was packed. The screen was alive with movement, but no movie was playing, and Bobby wasn't sure at first what he was seeing. Then he realized that a boxing match was underway, and a carefully placed spotlight was casting giant shadows of the boxers as they danced around one another in the ring. Parked automobiles lined the fringes of the property, leaving the center of the field open for the mob of spectators. The two arc lights on the flat roof of the concession stand continued to sweep the sky.

Reverend Tyree pulled the DeSoto onto the gravel apron at the entrance of the drive-in and let the engine idle.

"I appreciate the lift," Bobby said as he shouldered the door open. Again the dome light illuminated the reverend's face, but this time he didn't flinch.

"*These shall make war with the Lamb*," the reverend said, "*and the Lamb shall overcome them.*"

"That's a good thought, Reverend," Bobby said as he stepped out into the night. "But those North Koreans don't know much about the Lamb. We might be better off with Eisenhower."

The reverend said nothing, and Bobby wondered if he might have offended the man. But he couldn't help what he knew, and he knew the Communists wouldn't lay down their arms in the name of Jesus. If he were old enough, he would certainly vote for Eisenhower. Sometimes it took a hard-line soldier to straighten things out. He closed the door and patted his farewell on the roof of the DeSoto, then headed up the path toward the ticket booth. The DeSoto continued idling at the entryway. Maybe the reverend was thinking over what Bobby had said.

He was happy to be out of the automobile. Even with the windows rolled down, something in the seats or the floorboards had given off an odor he didn't care for—something that reminded him of his hospital stay, the smell of bad meat doused in alcohol. He didn't know how the reverend stood it.

As he approached the ticket booth, he pulled his wallet from his hip-pocket and looked inside. He was pretty flush right now—the army had covered all his expenses, even after he got shot, so he'd saved most of his regular pay. Now he had a good-sized chunk of start-up cash—though he wasn't sure what he might be starting up. A mortgage, maybe, if marriage was still in the picture. If Mary Jean didn't want him anymore, he'd just give it to the baby for a college fund or something. Surely there was enough to make the kid's road a little easier, however much it was. He'd never actually counted it. Knowing the amount would have made it seem smaller. In any case, he could spare a few bucks for tonight. Harvard wouldn't miss it.

He made out two figures in the ticket booth, a man and a woman, though it was too dark inside to see their faces. The grounds themselves were bright as a ball field with all the drive-in lights, so his own face was clearly illuminated. The woman leaned in close to the screened window to scrutinize him.

"My God, Bobby Malone, is that you?" Her voice was too shrill with excitement for him to recognize, but it wasn't Mary Jean's, he knew that much. The side door of the booth burst open and she came running around the corner toward him, her arms wide. It was Patty Hatton, Bryce's wife, the smile on her face the first sure sign that he'd actually made it home alive. She flung her arms around his neck, and he bent forward to keep the pressure of her hug away from his right arm.

"Hey, Patty," he said. He turned his face toward the other figure in the booth. "Hey, Bryce."

Patty released him abruptly and stepped back. "That's not Bryce," she said quickly.

The figure in the booth slid the screen aside and stuck his head through the opening. It was Andy Yearwood.

"Hey, Bobby," Andy said. "Welcome back."

"Hey, Andy." He looked back at Patty. "Do you guys work here now?"

Patty shook her head. "Andy's just helping out for tonight." She paused to smooth out the pleats in her skirt. "I'm his date."

"You're working the ticket booth on a date?" he asked.

"Mr. Parsons needed help at the last minute," she explained. "The regular girl's mother wouldn't let her come in tonight. They're strict Baptist."

None of this was making any sense. "Where's Bryce?"

Patty looked down at the ground. "A lot's happened lately."

"Bryce sort of killed his cousin Walter," Andy told him. "He's under arrest."

"Me and him are through," Patty added.

"Well, I sure am sorry," Bobby said, which was at least partly true. Walter had been a solid left-fielder and a good teammate, so he hated to hear that he was gone. But Bryce was another matter. Bobby had never particularly cared for him, even though he'd been an usher in Bryce and Patty's wedding. Bryce was a poor sport, plain and simple—a third baseman who tried to cleat the runner on every slide. He guessed Patty would be better off without a guy like that in her life. But what in God's name was she doing in the Starlight ticket booth with Andy Yearwood? Patty was a regular firecracker, and Andy was as bland a guy as he'd ever known, the kind substitute teachers prayed for. Things had gone all to hell around here while he'd been in the army.

Patty's face brightened. "Have you seen Mary Jean yet?"

"No, not yet. I thought maybe I'd find her out here tonight."

"That's a good bet," Andy said. "The whole town's turned out for the show."

"She's here, all right," Patty said, still beaming. "I saw her myself. You go on in and find her. You two have got lots to catch up on."

Now that he knew Mary Jean was here, he didn't feel in such a hurry to find her. What would he say, after all?

I'm back.

I'm crippled.

I've killed people and been glad of it.

"So what's the deal here tonight?" he asked. "Why so much interest in a boxing match?"

"That's the world heavyweight champ out there," Andy told him. "Jersey Joe Walcott. He's taking on all comers."

"For charity," added Patty.

Bobby looked across the crowd to the makeshift ring at the far end of the drive-in, where a large black man was now pummeling a stocky white guy. The white guy looked like he didn't know much more about boxing than how to take a punch.

"That's incredible," Bobby said. "How the heck did they get the heavyweight champ to come to Lincoln?"

"Tom Parsons set it up," Patty told him. "He's donating the proceeds to help folks rebuild after the tornado."

A tornado. So that's what had happened. But leave it to Tom Parsons to try to make things right. When the Masons had run low on funds Bobby's junior year, their baseball team would have gone under if Mr. Tom hadn't stepped in and bought them all uniforms and equipment.

"How bad was the damage?" he asked.

"The square got hit pretty hard," Andy said. "Church Street, too. But your dad's store came through pretty much in one piece. Just lost a front window and a couple of displays."

"I'm sure Mary Jean can fill you in on all the details," Patty said. "But you need to find her first." She turned him around and gave him a playful shove in the direction of the milling crowd.

"I can pay," he said, holding up his wallet.

"Can't take your money," Andy said, grinning. "This here's a drive-in. You're on foot."

"Thanks," Bobby said, slipping his wallet back into his pocket. Patty gave him a final pat on the shoulder, and he set out for the concession stand to start his search.

Funny that neither Patty nor Andy had asked about his arm. Maybe it didn't stand out the way he imagined. Of course, Andy had always been fairly clueless, so that was no real test. And if Patty's choices in men were any indication, she wasn't the sharpest bayonet in the barracks herself. But Mary Jean would notice at once. He just hoped he would see her first, before she had a chance to hide her reaction. Then he would know what she really felt.

He hadn't seen a mob like this since maneuvers at Fort Bragg. The outfits were more colorful, but there was the same excitement, the same bloodlust in the air. He looked again toward the ring just as Jersey Joe Walcott landed an uppercut on the stocky amateur that sent the man staggering backward into the corner post. He fell forward onto his face, and someone rang the bell. A cheer went up from the crowd, mixed with a few sympathetic groans. While a couple of attendants, one black and one white, scrambled into the ring to pull the fallen man to his feet, Mr. Tom—Mary Jean's uncle—stepped up into the ring with a microphone and gestured to him.

"Let's hear it for Wade Miller, folks!" he said. "And if a man's willing to take a drubbing like that, you know he'll do right by you at his automobile dealership!"

The crowd applauded for Wade Miller as he was helped down from the ring. The attendants then sat him on a square wooden table to be examined by Mary Jean's father, Dr. Mc-Kinney, who shined a penlight into his eyes and waved his fingers back and forth in front of Wade Miller's face.

"Next up to face the champ is Lorne Carmichael!" announced Mr. Tom, and the crowd erupted into fresh cheers. "Y'all can visit Lorne anytime at the Pants Barn out on Highway 64!"

A small colored boy climbed into the ring with a cup of water and handed it to Jersey Joe Walcott. Then the boy leaped into the air and swung wildly at some invisible foe while Jersey Joe drained the cup. People in the crowd laughed. The champ handed the cup back to the little boy, who then crossed to the other side of the ring in a series of short hops and crawled out under the bottom rope.

Meanwhile, Lorne Carmichael pulled himself up to ring level, squeezed his three-hundred-pound frame between the ropes, and sat, panting, on the stool in his corner of the ring. Bobby had known Lorne Carmichael all his life, knew his passion for fried chicken and big cigars. What was Lorne thinking? He was huge, but he was no fighter. He'd once passed out in an argument with a supplier over a shipment of bad pants. He couldn't keep on his feet thirty seconds against a stiff breeze, let alone the heavyweight champ. The mere effort of climbing into the ring had clearly winded him. Was free publicity for the Pants Barn worth such public humiliation?

He knew the answer to that, of course. His own father might well be somewhere in line to take one on the chin for his hardware store. Wasn't that what Bobby had been fighting for, after all: free enterprise? The chance to get ahead by doing whatever it took. Competition was a privilege, Coach Lindsay had always said. His drill sergeant, too. Hard work and sacrifice, the good old American way. Those North Koreans had no idea what they were missing.

But Bobby knew what he was missing: a goddamned hand.

He moved up beside the concession stand and eyed the people milling around the service counter. Several faces looked familiar, but he couldn't call up any names. Just as well. One thing he'd liked about the army was not having to talk to anyone, even the guys he knew. Silence had been a virtue there, especially among the enlisted men.

He moved around to the far side of the stand where someone had put up a homemade tent. It was a laughably bad piece of work. Whoever had thrown it together had used the wrong materials from start to finish. Rain would pour through it like a sieve. The staking was all wrong, too—a sudden gust would carry it off like a big box-kite. And the colors were anything but camouflage. "Madame Zubu the Mysterious," in bright red and yellow letters. "She sees all, she knows all." A tent like this would be a death wish anywhere within ten kilometers of Panmunjom.

But Korea was behind him now. That's the part he had to remember. The problem was, he didn't seem to know who he was anymore. A couple of months ago, he'd had a solid grip on things: He was a soldier with a girl waiting for him stateside, and when his hitch was over, he'd be back in his hometown, smiling at customers in his father's store and building a life for his new family. But that clarity had all disappeared with the accidental pulling of a trigger. Who was he now? Maybe he ought to ask Madame Zubu the Mysterious. Maybe she could gaze into his future and tell him what kind of person he would have to learn to be. Of course, the way his luck had been running, she was probably a palm reader.

He turned from the tent and shouldered his way through the crowd, protecting his arm as best he could from inadvertent jostling. The throbbing was getting worse.

Lorne Carmichael crumpled to his knees and rolled slowly onto his side. Mr. Tom bent down to check on him, then patted him on the shoulder and said something to him out of range of the microphone. Bobby could see blood pouring from Lorne's battered nose. Mr. Tom stepped over to the champ and held his arm in the air to signify another victory. The two attendants climbed back into the ring, but they couldn't get Lorne to his feet until Jersey Joe himself lent a hand. The three men eased Lorne out of the ring like he was an enormous egg. Humpty Dumpty, Bobby thought. The crowd offered catcalls and tepid applause.

Bobby thought he recognized the white guy supporting Lorne's left side. Moody Smith, it looked like. Years ago, when Bobby was a kid, he and his friends had thought Moody Smith was Popeye the Sailor, though he couldn't imagine where the idea had come from. Maybe they'd made it up. The guy did kind of look like Popeye, which was certainly no compliment. He also looked like the kind of guy who could take care of himself in a fight. The kind of guy who wouldn't slip on an icy rock with his safety off.

"The next challenger," Tom Parson's announced to the crowd, "is best in his weight class! At three feet seven inches and weighing in at nearly forty pounds, Jerry Lee Statten!"

The colored attendant swung the same little boy up over the top rope into the ring. This time he was wearing a child's set of boxing gloves. Laughter rippled through the crowd. Jersey Joe Walcott met the boy at the center of the ring and crouched down to eye level. The champ bobbed his head a little, blocked a couple of wild swings, then suddenly dropped his guard. The little boy wound up his arm like he'd probably seen in cartoons and gave Jersey Joe a pop on the chin. Jersey Joe flung his arms to the side and fell over backward on the canvas, down for the count. People began to whistle and applaud. Mr. Tom held the little boy's arm in the air. "The new champion!" he announced. The little boy scampered to the edge of the ring, ducked under the rope, and leapt into the colored attendant's arms. The man was probably the kid's father, Bobby realized.

He needed to find Mary Jean.

The best place to begin was ringside, with her father, but the last thing he wanted right now was to deal with Dr. Mc-Kinney, who didn't like him at all. The Doc had opposed their engagement even after he found out Mary Jean was pregnant. He wanted his daughter to marry somebody with a position in the world—some blueblood, maybe, with four middle names and a monocle. Mary Jean's mother had been more willing to reserve judgment, like she figured it was okay for him to start out in the stockroom as long as that wasn't where he ended up. Of course, the verdict was already in on that account—Bobby's career path would have a low trajectory at best. There just weren't many lucrative job options for a one-handed man, except maybe pirate. Maybe he could ask the Doc to get him a good price on a hook.

He decided instead to circle the perimeter, check out the long curve of parked automobiles that lined the outer fringes of the Starlight. After all, a pregnant woman couldn't stand very long in such a raucous crowd—she'd have to have a place to sit. Mary Jean was probably watching the spectacle from the front seat of her parents' new Packard, the one she'd written him about. Her father had ordered it special, with all the options. But what color had she told him it was? Something gaudy. Yellow, maybe.

He worked his way over to the edge of the crowd, keeping his head down to avoid any ill-timed reunions with his old high school classmates or regular customers from the store. His uniform would have made him stand out if anyone had been paying attention, but tonight the focus was on the heavyweight champ and his parade of punching bags, so Bobby was able to amble through to the parking row unnoticed.

A number of people were viewing the show from the relative comfort of their automobiles, especially the elderly and families with small kids. Bobby had barely started down the row when he spotted his father's Studebaker just a few yards ahead of him. Even in the uneven light of the drive-in, the car looked dirtier than he'd ever seen it. Apparently, his father wasn't such a stickler for its appearance without Bobby there to wash and wax it for him every week. His mother sat in the passenger seat nibbling on a popcorn ball, while his father hunched forward over the wheel like he was driving through fog. The last time he'd seen them they'd been in this car, watching him wave good-bye from the bus station in Lewisburg, and for a moment it seemed like he'd never been away. Then, of course, he remembered, and it seemed more like he had never come back.

He passed directly in front of the Studebaker, his eyes focused on the tire-flattened grass at his feet. He listened for the sound of a door opening, or a light beep of the horn, or a sharp rapping on the windshield, any response at all, but there was nothing. A few cars farther along the row he paused and turned around. His parents were still staring straight ahead, watching the ring, the crowd, the heavyweight champ. They had both looked right through him, as if he were a ghost.

Maybe he was. Maybe Bobby Malone was gone for good, nothing left but a husk, roaming the old haunts out of habit. And what better place to come back to than the Starlight Drive-in? This was where he'd impregnated Mary Jean.

He continued along the row, following the curve toward the huge screen of shadows. As he neared the back of the lot, he had his first clear view of the automobiles on the far side of the ring. Among them were what appeared to be two late-model Packards, both with yellow bodies and black tops, parked side by side. He crossed the soggy ground beneath the screen and eased his way carefully toward the two vehicles from behind, the way he had been trained to approach anything that might represent a danger.

One of the Packards was empty.

The other held a disappointment.

Mrs. McKinney was sitting alone on the front seat, her head tilted forward, as if she were napping. For a long minute he stared at the back of her puffy hairdo through the dirty rear window, weighing his options. He briefly considered tapping on the passenger window to ask her about Mary Jean, but reconsidered. Mrs. McKinney always had a draining effect on him, and if he tangled with her now, he'd have no strength left for Mary Jean.

Then a dark thought hit him. What if that wasn't Mrs. McKinney in the car? The back of a head wasn't much to go on, and he'd heard that women always started to look like their mothers at some point. Maybe Mary Jean had changed her hair style. He couldn't walk away without checking.

He moved up quietly alongside the passenger door and peered in at the woman in the front seat. It was Mrs. McKinney, all right, decked out in her usual country-club best, a formal-looking blue dress this time, with polka dots the same bright yellow as her automobile. She wore pearl earrings to match the double strand around her neck, and both her wrists were crowded with gold bracelets. She looked entirely out of place for a boxing match. But she wasn't asleep, as he had first thought. She was staring down at a baby swaddled in a pink blanket in her lap. Bobby stumbled backward against the front fender of the other yellow Packard. Mrs. McKinney glimpsed the movement at her door and jerked her head up, eyes wide and mouth open. Bobby quickly folded his left arm over his chest, the better to hide his amputation. Mrs. McKinney blinked a few times, then slowly rolled her window down.

"Well, Bobby Malone," she said.

"Yes, ma'am," he answered, straightening to something like attention. He thought he smelled barbecue.

"We thought you might be dead," she said, her tone pointedly neutral.

"Not quite," he told her.

She looked him up and down, her face slightly puckered, as if he were a dog tracking mud through her living room. "How long you been home?" There was an accusation in the question.

"I just got in a few minutes ago," he told her. "I came out here to find Mary Jean."

That was the right answer apparently, and Mrs. McKinney's face softened.

"Mary Jean's been through a lot," she said, leaning toward him and lowering her voice.

"Is she all right?" he asked.

She shook her head. "I couldn't even say. You wouldn't believe what all's happened around here lately. Last Saturday somebody stole my car." She gazed at the plush interior around her. "I got it back, though."

Bobby stepped closer so he could see down into the Packard.

"Is that the baby?" He could feel the sweat breaking out across his forehead and on the back of his neck.

She lifted the bundle slightly by the crook of her arm. "This is Mary Jean's little girl, Stella Lucille," she said, more to the infant than to him. Half of the baby's face was obscured by an upturned fold in the blanket, but the part he could see looked pink and fragile. Her head was barely bigger than a softball, and her skin was so translucent he could trace her veins. Her hands were the only other part of her that lay uncovered, and he could see that her fingers, so incredibly small, were curled into the tiniest of fists. He'd never seen a child so brand new.

Mrs. McKinney looked up at him as if deciding something and then smiled. "Would you like to hold her?"

Of course he wanted to hold her, his baby, his Stella Lucille, but he had only one arm, and if he said yes, he'd end up spilling all his secrets. He couldn't let that happen just yet.

"Some other time," he said, shifting uncomfortably.

Mrs. McKinney regarded him for a long moment. "This night air isn't good for her lungs," she said finally. "And I'm sure you have other people to see." She stared impassively through the windshield as she rolled her side window back up.

She was angry now, and Bobby understood that. What kind of a man wouldn't want to hold his own child? She'd given him the benefit of the doubt until that moment, and all he had done was reinforce her darkest suspicions about him. He was, after all, the louse who had stopped writing love letters to her pregnant daughter, probably just when Mary Jean had needed him the most. That was a towering sin of omission. Maybe later Mrs. McKinney would be open to an explanation, but not now. Now he needed to face Mary Jean herself, learn what kind of damage he had done to her with his silence, see if he could square things. See if she even wanted him to square things. All this time he'd worried she would leave him for losing his hand. It hadn't occurred to him that she might leave him for breaking her heart.

He nodded his good-bye to Mrs. McKinney and turned away, toward the boxing ring this time, where Jersey Joe was now launching into a flurry of body blows that sent his latest challenger, Harlow Knowles, of Knowles Wrecker Service, cowering into a corner. The crowd was more raucous now, less tolerant of defeat, and it howled without mercy when Harlow fled the ring. The night itself was charged in ways Bobby had learned to recognize—at Inchon Bay and Seoul and Panmunjom and all the rest. Mary Jean would be perilously near the heart of it, somewhere close to her father.

As Bobby threaded his way toward the ring, the crowd thickened, becoming more boisterous, more intimately massed together, everyone straining forward to hear the crack of bone and see the spurt of blood. The champ was either tiring or becoming bored, because he now engaged his succession of opponents with a cold efficiency, dispatching each one in a minimum of effort, no further pomp or ceremony. The crowd seemed to prefer it this way, clamoring louder as the body count rose. Tom Parsons no longer bothered to climb into the ring to introduce the dwindling line of contestants, but merely announced the names from a folding chair at ringside, with the young colored boy straddling his shoulders. Bobby pushed ahead toward the table at the loser's corner where Dr. McKinney examined, bandaged, and dismissed the parade of beaten boxers.

As he worked his way through the tightening knot of spectators, he looked back toward the concession stand, which was still mobbed with unruly kids and disinterested teens. The line

of fortune-seekers outside Madame Zubu's tent had lengthened and now wound like a serpent through the larger concession-stand crowd. He scanned the distant blur of faces for Mary Jean, knowing he could pick her out as easily as a lighted candle in an empty room. She was nowhere at that end of the Starlight, and he felt an inexplicable sense of relief.

But something else caught his attention, something that sparked the soldier in him back to life. His first impulse was to call out a warning, but he knew there would be no point. The Starlight was too noisy, and it was already too late.

The speeding DeSoto had already roared through the entrance gates and splintered through the corner of the ticket booth, spinning the small structure on its foundation and toppling it into the weeds. In another instant the automobile would slam into the side of the concession stand, the side where Madame Zubu had pitched her tent.

That instant developed like a snapshot in Bobby's mind, one he could examine and evaluate without losing a single tick of the clock, as he had done many times on patrol when his unit had come under fire. Maybe that was a talent all combat soldiers shared—the ability to suspend the normal flow of time, to slow it down to a manageable crawl, parcel it out into as many pieces as necessary, and dwell with each fragment in the space of an ever-expanding moment, absorbing the crucial details of the scene.

Patty Hatton stood in the gravel lane, her hands covering her mouth, staring at the overturned ticket booth. Andy was nowhere in sight.

A score of people along the entry lane, those who had lost interest in the exhibition and had retreated to the outer fringes to pass around brown bags and flasks with their friends, now turned toward this fresh commotion, most of them in time to leap aside as the DeSoto barreled past. Some were too slow, or too unlucky. A bald-headed man in overalls froze in place and got clipped by the front fender, which sent him tumbling headlong into the shadows. Another man turned the wrong way and then tried to change direction, but went down beneath the bumper. The DeSoto rolled over his leg at the knee, crushing it so quickly he didn't even have time to grimace. A young woman smoking a cigarette got jerked aside by a punk in a motorcycle jacket, and both of them fell face first in the gravel. The first few screams started up.

A few people at the concession stand saw what was coming and tried to scatter, but too many others were hemming them in. A few clawed their way savagely past their neighbors, while others flailed like swimmers struggling in a riptide and made no progress at all. Someone tripped over one of the stakes at Madame Zubu's, sending a shiver of motion through the flimsy tent.

Reverend Tyree gave no indication that he saw any of these people at all, neither swerving to avoid them nor swerving to strike them down. Instead, he stared straight ahead, his hands gripping the wheel, his body leaning forward, toward a moment of impact.

At the last instant, he slammed on the brakes and cut the wheels hard to the left. The DeSoto swung sideways and skidded through the last cluster of spectators, slamming into Madame Zubu's tent and crushing it against the cinderblock wall of the concession stand. The wall crumpled inward and a portion of the roof collapsed, sending one of the giant search lights sliding over the edge and down onto the roof of the reverend's automobile. The light sprayed a stream of blue sparks and then went out. The other light tipped onto its side, redirecting its beam to a narrow line of stunned faces in the crowd. A man behind Bobby, from the area of the ring, cried out, while everyone else fell silent.

But the reverend wasn't through. The DeSoto had stalled out after hitting the building, and now he attempted to restart it, cranking the ignition in long, grinding turns. The engine failed to catch on the first two tries, and Bobby wondered why no one had yet dragged the reverend from the car and snatched the keys away from him. Bobby would have done it himself had he been closer. Even with one hand.

He twisted back toward the ring to check on Mary Jean's father. But the Doc had cleared out already, leaving an unconscious fighter on the table at ringside, and Bobby still saw no sign of Mary Jean. The champ stood in the center of the ring, his gloved hands on his hips, staring down the approaching maniac. Moody Smith stood beside him, looking equally determined to hold his ground. But the other attendant, the colored man, leapt over the front ropes into the matted grass beside Mr. Tom, who was just rising from his chair, the child still on his shoulders. Mr. Tom barked something that Bobby didn't catch, but the man ignored him and charged toward the DeSoto as the crowd continued to part. Bobby thought the man would be killed for sure, but at the center of the drive-in, when the machine was nearly on top of him, the man dodged to the side. As the DeSoto rolled past, he threw himself onto the fortune-teller's tent, ripping it free of the bumper.

The reverend kept his focus on the ring and continued to accelerate down the widening lane. By the time the DeSoto had closed to the last twenty yards everyone but Mr. Tom and the little boy had managed to dive clear of its path. But Mr. Tom made no effort to get out of the way. Maybe he didn't understand what was happening, or maybe he was just too old and worn out to dodge cars with a boy on his shoulders. Maybe, like Moody Smith and the champ, he was simply the sort of man who didn't give ground. Bobby had seen that in the army—guys who would stand there, calm as bathwater, in the face of enemy fire. Sometimes they got their heads blown off. But sometimes they were the only ones cool enough to draw a bead on the enemy and keep a position from being overrun. Guys like that were crazy, but good to have around. Mr. Tom had that same unshakable calm about him, even when it was clear what was coming, and as the DeSoto plowed ahead, he turned back toward the ring and shoved the little boy high in the air, up over the ropes, where Moody Smith stepped forward and caught him. An instant later the DeSoto slammed into Mr. Tom from behind, pinning his lower body against the corner post of the ring.

The structure buckled in the middle, which knocked Moody Smith and the kid to the canvas and pitched the champ into the ropes on the back side of the ring, but the corner post held, and the DeSoto went from thirty to zero in less than a heartbeat. The reverend pitched forward into the windshield, cracking it wide open.

Mr. Tom grabbed onto the top rope with one hand and swatted awkwardly behind him with the other, as if the DeSoto were some pesky dog nipping at his heels. His face was half turned, and Bobby was relieved to see no pain there at all. The spinal cord was probably severed. But Mr. Tom did have a look Bobby recognized, that mix of surprise and acknowledgment that comes when the only thought left to think is suddenly, blindingly obvious: So this is how it ends.

Bobby forced his way out through the numbed crowd and started toward Mr. Tom, not to save him, because he knew that chance was gone, but to pry the machine away, if such a thing was possible, and ease him down into the grass, free from all this spectacle. It was the only right thing anyone could still do for him.

Moody Smith, apparently acting on the same thought, scrambled out under the ropes as Bobby approached the ring and put his shoulder to the front fender. "Hang on, Tom," he growled, then strained hard against the full weight of the DeSoto, and before Bobby could position himself to help out, the old man had lifted the wreck and moved it back nearly a foot on his own. That was enough, and Bobby hooked his good arm around Mr. Tom's chest to keep him from falling over as Moody Smith slumped back against the edge of the ring, breathing hard.

But as Bobby dragged the dying man clear of the wreckage and laid him down in the wet grass, the driver's door of the DeSoto creaked open loudly and Reverend Tyree climbed out, blood running down his face, staggered but still strong, clutching a three-foot length of iron in his right hand.

The crowd, still stunned by so much mayhem, began to close around the reverend, but recoiled again as he swung at them wildly with the iron bar.

"Woe to the inhabiters of the earth and of the sea!" he proclaimed, brandishing the bar over his head like a holy relic. *"For the devil is come down unto you, having great wrath!"* Bobby straightened to face him as the reverend lumbered forward. Moody Smith was on the far side of the DeSoto and in no position to help, so Bobby was on his own.

But as he raised his own right arm to absorb the blow, he realized that the reverend wasn't even looking at him. His eyes were fixed solely on Mr. Tom, stretched out and bleeding on the ground between them.

Bobby could have stepped away. Tom Parsons was done for, he knew that. But he also knew that was irrelevant. He grabbed the reverend's arm on the downswing and diverted the blow into the soft earth beside Mr. Tom's head. The reverend wheeled on him at once and swung the rod savagely upward, catching Bobby beneath his chin. He fell backward, a white flash filling his head. He heard watery sounds, and saw hazy, moving lights, and when Bobby's eyes came into focus again, Reverend Tyree was standing over him, ready to strike him dead. But before the rod came down, another man stepped in from the side, the colored ring attendant who had charged the DeSoto, and he smashed the reverend in the temple with what seemed to be a large glass ball. The reverend fell against the DeSoto and slid to the ground, his eyes open and swimming, the iron rod still in his hand.

Bobby's head ached and he couldn't move his jaw. As he propped himself on his good arm and looked around, the crowd began to come alive again, closing in on the injured and the dead. Dr. McKinney slipped into the small clearing from the side of the ring and knelt in the grass beside Tom Parsons. He bent over Mr. Tom and unfastened the lower buttons of his bloody shirt, tugged it free of the waistband, and pulled it gingerly aside. The poor man was split open, and Bobby could tell by the look on Dr. McKinney's face that there was nothing to be done. Blood spread through the white linen of Mr. Tom's pants all the way down to his knees. The Doc put a hand on Mr.

Tom's shoulder and said something to him, too low for Bobby
to make out over the noise of the electrified crowd. Mr. Tom
said something back to him, and then, though it made no sense
at all, he laughed. He actually laughed. Even in Korea, Bobby
had never seen a reaction like that. Then Mr. Tom leaned his
head back in the dirt and became totally still. Bobby knew what
that meant.

Now Mary Jean pushed her way into the clearing, but she
stopped short when she saw her uncle and had to steady herself
against the battered corner post of the boxing ring. The sympathetic anguish on her face was beautiful.

Bobby had his wish: He got to see her first, clearly and completely, before she realized he was there. She looked tired and
frail and frightened, and all he wanted in the world was to have
her look at him now with some portion of that same weight of
love and understanding.

Bobby's right hand began to throb, which was impossible
because it wasn't there. Phantom pains. He was supposed to be
past that. His nerve endings should have learned to adjust by
now, to stop lying to him about the loss. But fire still burned in
every finger, he could feel it, and he held his bandaged stump before his face, trying his best to stare his way through the mystery.

And then she saw him, realized for the first time that he was
here, home from the war. Home from the war, but damaged,
mutilated, crippled. The horror of it filled her face, and his
heart sank, but only for a moment, because there was more to it,
much more. The horror wasn't for herself or for her own cas-
cading disappointments, but for him, for the pain he'd endured,
and the fears he'd suffered through, and she rushed forward
with a terrible cry and threw her arms around his neck and
hugged him there on the ground and sobbed and sobbed and
told him that she loved him.

Herb Gatlin

Herb Gatlin, itching in his threadbare linen suit, sat quietly in the anteroom of Wally McKinney's office, waiting to see about getting a new leg. Not that he hadn't been happy to get the old one back, but it had a lot of mileage on it now, and the independent side trips of the past week had left it with more than a few fresh gouges, particularly along the top. The fit wasn't comfortable anymore.

He shifted on the creaking leather couch, which drew an annoyed look from Mildred Tyree, Wally's receptionist, hunched over paperwork at her desk. She seemed a prickly sort of woman, difficult to talk to even under the best of circumstances, but especially now, after what had happened with her husband. Herb was surprised she'd pulled herself together enough to come in this morning at all.

He wondered if she'd keep her job. Mildred had worked here a good while, going on fifteen years if he remembered right, so maybe she'd made herself indispensable. Still, her husband had killed Wally's brother-in-law. That was bound to put a damper on office chit-chat.

Hard to believe Tom Parsons was gone. Their paths hadn't crossed much the past few years, but Herb had always counted him a friend. Struck down by some crazed imbecile who thought he was the hand of God—hard to imagine divine purpose in a thing like that. But who was to say? Before the tornado, he'd thought nothing in life made much sense. Now he wasn't so sure. Things happened, and you could either see the ugliness or you could overlook it, give God the benefit of the doubt. Maybe ugliness was just a tiny piece of the puzzle, and the big picture wasn't so ugly at all.

The door to Wally's examining room opened and Andy Yearwood stepped out, his arm in a plaster cast from his wrist to just above his elbow. He looked tired, older than he had the day of Herb's funeral. Andy glanced at Mildred, then quickly turned away. That's when he saw Herb sitting on the couch. A look of pure shock flashed across his face, and he caught his breath. Then he exhaled and shook his head, smiling.

"Mr. Gatlin," he said. "I thought you were a ghost."

"I get that a lot lately," Herb said.

"No," Andy said. "That white suit. For a second there I thought you were Mr. Parsons."

Herb looked down at the sleeve of his coat. "He's the one give it to me. Three years ago. Said every man ought to have a suit of clothes on hand, just in case." He smoothed out the creases in his trousers. "I never needed it until today."

"Well, it looks real nice," Andy told him.

"Fits good for a hand-me-down," Herb agreed. He tugged his pant legs up to reveal a pair of shiny brown Wing Tips. "He give me these shoes, too. But the one feels a little tight on me."

"Which one?" Andy asked.

Herb narrowed his eyes at the boy. "The one with a foot in it."

Andy blushed and turned away, pretending to become absorbed in a colorful painting of a duck that hung on the wall beside the couch. The duck was rising from a weedy marshland.

"What happened to your arm?" Herb asked.

Mildred slammed a pencil on her desk and stood up.

"I hate every goddamn sinner in this town," she said, snatching up the Bible she'd been using as a paperweight. Then she strode across the room and shut herself in the bathroom.

"I guess that answers that," Herb said. He felt sorry for Mildred. Die-hard religion could take a lot out of a person, sometimes without putting anything back.

Andy eased over to Herb's side of the room.

"That thing at the drive-in was the worst mess I ever saw," Andy said. "All kinds of people got hurt. More than in the tornado."

"Glad I missed it," Herb said. "That twister was enough for me."

"You going to the visitation?" he asked. "It's right down the block at the dime store."

"I'm not comfortable with that," Herb said, imagining Mr. Tom laid out among the bins of clearance items. "But I'll be at the graveside service later on."

"I have to write his obituary," Andy told him.

"Make it a long one," Herb said. "And use a big font."

Andy sat on the couch beside him. "Miss Ellen owns the paper by herself now." His brow furrowed, as if the weight of this news were hard to carry. "She wants me to stay on and run things. She wants me to be the editor."

"Seems right."

"Not to me, it doesn't. It's too big a job." He raised his cast. "I can't even set type."

Herb shrugged. "Hire a typesetter."

"That's what I figure on doing," Andy said. He turned toward Herb, a determined look in his eyes. "What I need is somebody who already knows the operation."

It took a moment for Herb to realize what Andy was saying.

"Boy, that sounds awful close to a job offer."

"If you can still spell," Andy said.

He snorted. "'Course I can spell. But I haven't set type since Moses was a pup."

"Still the same equipment," Andy told him. "Mr. Parsons ran the paper the same way his father and his grandfather did. He never changed anything but the lightbulbs."

Back to *The Observer*. The idea had its merits. When Herb had quit the paper, he'd been a young man who couldn't stand being cooped up all day, a two-legged horseman with a long stretch of rodeos ahead of him. Now the notion of a sit-down job wasn't so terrible anymore. He could be indoors in cold weather. His back wouldn't ache from heavy lifting. He wouldn't have to work a shovel anymore.

"That's an interesting proposition," Herb admitted. "I'll give it some thought."

Andy smiled. "Don't take too long," he said, rising to his feet. "We've got an issue to put out on Tuesday."

As Andy walked out the front door, Mildred peered out from the bathroom.

"Dr. McKinney will see you now," she said and shut the door again.

Herb pushed himself up from the creaking couch and took a few stiff steps toward the examining room. He pushed open the paneled door, but paused at the threshold. Wally sat shuffling through papers at his desk. He wore a dark three-piece suit, probably for the funeral that afternoon, with the familiar gold chain of his pocket watch dangling stylishly from his vest. More than once Herb had thought of choking him with that gold chain.

"Come in, come in," Wally said, glancing up from the papers. Then he turned his scrutiny to the yellow form Herb had filled out when he arrived. "So what seems to be the trouble?" he asked, his tone jovial, practiced, his eyes still fixed on the piece of paper.

"I think it's time for a new leg," Herb said, and Wally looked up at him, his mouth open.

"Why, Herb Gatlin," he said, the false good humor draining from his voice. He looked back to the yellow form, presumably to verify his patient's name. "I didn't even recognize you."

"Clothes make the man," Herb said.

"I suppose that's true to some extent," Wally said. He leaned back in his chair and rubbed his chin. "Especially when a prosthetic leg is part of the outfit."

"I want one that bends at the knee," Herb said.

"They all bend at the knee nowadays," Wally said. "You should have upgraded a long time ago." He scribbled something on the yellow form. "I'll give you a catalog to look at. You come back next week and we'll fit you for a new one."

"What's a good leg go for these days?" Herb asked.

Wally swiveled back and forth in his chair. "You don't need to worry about that," he said. "I'll take care of it."

"I'm not looking for a free leg," Herb told him.

Wally regarded him for a long time. "Nothing's free," he said, and Herb understood the bitterness in such a simple statement.

"What I mean is, Wally, you can stop trying to buy me off."

Wally shifted uncomfortably and returned his attention to the yellow form.

"I don't know what you're talking about," he said.

"I'm through digging your holes," Herb told him. "You and me are square."

Wally eyed him suspiciously. Herb couldn't blame him for that. A lot had gone unsaid the past twenty years—feigned ignorance had been a necessary part of the deal. But Mary Jean was grown now, with a man of her own. It was time for Wally and Herb to cut each other loose.

"I appreciate everything you did," Herb told him. He meant it. He could never have given Mary Jean a proper life—or Ellen, either, for that matter—even if he hadn't been crippled.

Wally laced his fingers over his vest and rocked back in his chair. "You have no clue what I did," he said, still smug and defiant.

"You took off my leg when you didn't have to. Because I had Ellen."

Wally froze. "That's slander," he said.

Herb turned toward the examination table. It looked old—probably the same one he'd lain on so many years ago. He stepped over to the white-sheeted edge and sat back against it. "It was all I could do to keep from killing you back then. Even lately, if you want to know the truth."

Wally stared down at his desktop, his hands clenching the arms of his chair like it was a carnival ride. He looked like he might throw up.

"But hell," Herb said, lightening his tone, "I ain't the pope, I could be wrong. Maybe it had nothing to do with Ellen. Maybe you were just a lousy doctor who should've sold hats for a living."

"I can sue you for saying that," Wally said, but the fight had gone out of his voice.

Herb laughed. "It's just you and me talking, Wally. I don't plan on calling witnesses."

"Every doctor makes mistakes," Wally said, finally looking up. "That's just something we have to live with."

Herb tilted forward and, for the first time in two decades, looked Wally square in the eye.

"That's what I'm telling you, Wally. I don't care what the reason was anymore. It's time I learned to live with who I am."

Wally shook his head, as if none of this made any sense to him.

"Ellen was right to choose you," Herb went on. "I was a bad prospect from the get-go. Cowboys don't last; it's just too hard a life. I'd have turned out the same no matter how many legs I had."

Wally let his face sink into a genuine frown. "There are things I regret," he said, finally easing toward the truth. "Things that won't let go." He leaned forward onto his elbows and rubbed his temples with both hands. "I just don't know what to say to anybody anymore."

"It's been a long war," Herb agreed. "Time we quit on it."

"I don't even know if that's possible."

"You've done right by people I care about. I'm willing to let it go at that."

Wally took a long breath and looked up at Herb, his eyes rheumy and pale. "I've not had one happy day in twenty years," he said.

Herb shrugged. "Happy ain't all it's cracked up to be." He knew Wally wouldn't understand that, but it was true—happy could be flimsy as a ghost. The home-run ball, the bright box under the Christmas tree, the new foal, even the kiss on the courthouse lawn, they were all just temporary breathers in the onslaught. The game could still be lost, the box could open on a disappointment, the foal could die for no reason, the kiss could break its promise as easily as glass. Four aces at midnight, and a man could still go home broke in the morning.

No, people who pined after happiness were the ones who found what bitterness was all about. Now Herb was done with both. He was a man back from the dead, and that counted for something. Peace: that's what he'd somehow stumbled into and what he was determined to keep.

On the long walk to the cemetery, Herb had plenty of time to think. He'd had a big week. Talking to his daughter had been the highlight, even better than surviving the twister. He wished he could remember more about the twister, though. That must have been some ride, probably the wildest of his life, and yet he'd slept through it. But he liked knowing it had happened to him, just the same—knowing he had soared like a kite above the treetops. He'd flown in dreams before, when he was young, gliding over the grass, skimming the rooftops. Those had always been his favorites. Maybe he would dream like that again, now that some buried part of him knew what it was really like.

Of course, what it was really like was probably better forgotten. He'd been pretty banged up by it all—still was, in fact—and waking up in a drainage pipe in a trickle of icy water was certainly no treat. Maybe some things were better left in dreams.

As he passed beneath the wrought-iron archway at Rose Hill, he could see Sammy and Moody in the distance working in the Parsons family plot, putting the finishing touches on Mr. Tom's grave and positioning the bier above the open hole. He climbed the hill slowly, trying to minimize the discomfort from his damaged leg. As he neared the gravesite, before his friends even noticed his approach, he saw that the hole where Mr. Tom was to be buried was the same hole they had dug for Herb only a few days earlier. Or for his leg, rather. Now Sammy and Moody had enlarged the grave to accommodate a full-sized casket. Herb squinted up at the sun. Almost one thirty, he reckoned. The service would start in about half an hour. The hearse would arrive any minute now.

Moody sat on the pile of dirt next to the grave, swigging a coke. Sammy leaned out over the hole and pressed his weight on the bier to check the stability. The last thing grieving family members wanted to see at a funeral was the coffin toppling prematurely into the hole. Satisfied that the bier was secure, Sammy stepped back from the grave to admire his handiwork. That's when he spotted Herb, who was just then stepping across the rock wall into the Parsons' plot.

"Mr. Herb," he called, a smile breaking across his face, "You looking mighty sharp today."

The long climb had winded him. The knee joint in his good leg had a bad twinge in it, and the other was rubbed raw from new cracks and splinters, so all Herb could do was grit his teeth and raise his hand in greeting.

Moody looked up from the dirt pile and aimed a crooked finger in Herb's direction. "I know that suit," he said. "That suit was a close personal friend of mine."

"Mine too," Herb said.

Moody nodded his approval. "Makes you look half civilized."

"Then I guess I ought to keep wearing it," Herb said, easing himself down on a sturdy Parsons tombstone. "Half civilized is just about right for me."

"I been drunk with that suit more times than I can remember," Moody said. "Good to see it moving around again."

Herb pulled a clean handkerchief from his breast pocket and blotted his brow. "Sammy," he said, "I hear you were the big hero out at the Starlight."

Sammy narrowed his eyes. "Don't know about that," he said.

Moody smiled. "Sammy's a little nervous about being in the spotlight. He thinks certain folks might take a dim view of what he did."

"From what I hear, he stopped a crazy man on a killing spree," Herb said. The thigh muscles on his bad leg began to spasm, so he pressed his fingers into the knots to work them out.

"That's true for now," Sammy agreed. "But a story changes every time somebody tells it. Pretty soon it starts to be about a black man who brained a white preacher from behind."

Moody put his arm around Sammy's shoulder. "He thinks the Klan's going to be modeling bedsheets in his yard."

Herb knew that for some folks in Sammy's position, Klan backlash would be a real possibility.

"Don't waste your worry on cross-burners," Herb said. "You've got friends who won't let that happen."

"Just glad I didn't kill him," Sammy said. "I woulda been on somebody's list for sure."

Moody pushed himself up from the pile. "If I'd got to him first, that loony sumbitch would be laid out right now at the dime store." He shook his head. "I talked to Sheriff Tune this morning. He says Tyree's lawyer wants to argue it as a traffic accident."

"Nobody better hold their breath on that one," Herb said.

Sammy picked up his shovel and stuck it in the ground at his feet. "First Baptist's already looking for a new reverend," he told them.

"Maybe your Nolla Rae ought to apply," Moody said, grinning. "She's got connections in the spirit world."

Sammy put up his hands. "That ain't a joke no more. She says them Tarot cards told her to get out of her tent right before Tyree drove through."

Moody laughed. "Like you said, Sammy, every story chang-es. That one probably started out with Madame Zubu taking a bathroom break. Now it's all about haints."

"I didn't say nothing about haints," Sammy said. "Just may-be there's more going on than we know about."

"There's always more going on than we know about," Herb said.

Moody stepped to the edge of the hole and shook the bier, double-checking Sammy's efforts. Then he turned to Herb, his eyes narrowed to a squint. "Say, what about that dead body?" he asked. "The one had your leg stuck in it. Anybody ever find out who that was?"

"Not that I know of," Herb answered. "Just some guy, I guess. Same as the rest of us."

The hearse swung in off the highway and entered Rose Hill.

"Here comes Mr. Tom," Sammy said, plucking up his shovel and stepping away from the gravesite.

Herb watched as the long line of freshly washed automo-biles, their headlights shining, crept slowly through the archway behind the hearse. There seemed to be no end to it. More than a hundred cars stretched all the way back around the curve at the edge of town. The procession crept along the cemetery pathway, winding its way up the hillside toward them.

Herb rose from the tombstone and stepped over to the far side of the fresh hole, next to the smaller tombstone of Miss Kate. Herb hadn't thought of Miss Kate in a while, but he remembered her now—a lively sparkle of a woman, tough enough to keep her husband in line. Mr. Tom had lost a lot of his momentum when she died. Herb understood a little of what that was like. He'd gone through a rough patch himself when Ellen left him. But he got over it. Or at least he got used to it.

Now that he looked back on it, he'd had a lucky life—far luckier than Mr. Tom, who was always plagued by drink, and luckier than Wally, who had other weaknesses, and even luck-ier than Ellen, who had stiffened gradually into a pillar of salt, maybe the result of too much looking back.

He could still see some of the old Ellen in Mary Jean—the quick mind and the bright spirit. But the blind determination to go out and face the storm—that was Mary Jean's alone. A woman like that might manage to stay in love, even with a man who'd lost a good part of himself in a war.

Maybe someday, when Mary Jean's baby was older and she was settled in a solid life, he might talk to her about who she was and where she really came from. He might tell her about her father's brush with love, the simple touch that branded him for life.

The hearse pulled up before them and Charlie Monahan got out, dressed in his usual smartly pressed black suit. He walked to the rear of the hearse and opened the door wide, then stood there, emotionless and still, waiting for the pallbearers to emerge from the trailing automobiles. Mr. Tom was coming home to his family now, and there was peace in that.

But Herb couldn't help wondering about the naked man the twister had brought to town. Who were his kinfolk? How much had they loved him? How were they grieving his mysterious loss? And what had become of him, finally, in his crisp cowboy clothes from the dime store?

He expected no answers, of course. That was the way of the world, as Herb had come to understand it. Wars and whirlwinds at every turn. There would always be bodies unaccounted for, identities that never came to light.

Epilogue

Signalman 3rd Class Ronald Dawson—*Ronnie Boy* to his dead shipmates—tumbled clumsily along the bottom of the Tennessee River until the channel merged with the broader waters of the Mississippi. Spring rains had left both rivers brown and choppy with run-off, rife with storm debris, and his body took more beatings on the journey south. But the rough ride was a blessing overall, because the churning current delivered him from the catfish and turtles that scavenged the shallow eddies along the banks.

That might change, of course, when he slowed through the muddy delta, and if he bobbed too near the surface, the trolling gators might claim him on their rounds. But if he kept to the center channel, he might yet wash straight through into the salty tidewaters of the estuary. Beyond that he would run the risk of sharks and barracuda, but he might just as likely catch a riptide along the coast, one that would take him out into the bluer depths of the Gulf. And if his luck held for just a short while longer, maybe his bones would settle through the silt, all the way down to the ocean's rag bottom, to some barnacle-crusted hull in the still, cold waters at the edge of the world. There he might finally come to rest. He might take his proper place among the unsaved sailors of the sea.

Acknowledgments

Many thanks to the editors of the literary magazines where the following seven chapters first appeared:

The Gettysburg Review: "Mary Jean McKinney"
Colorado Review: "Patty Hatton"
Hunger Mountain: "Doc McKinney," "Jerry Lee Statten,"
    "Bobby Malone"
New Ohio Review: "Reverend Tyree"
Chautauqua: "Ellen Parsons McKinney"

Thanks also to Virginia Commonwealth University for allowing me the time to work on the manuscript; to Alan Davis for his early belief in what's here; to Mitchell Waters for so much legwork; and to Dawn Cooper, Bev Cooper, and Amber Timmerman for reading it all with a sustaining kindness.

Author Biography

Clint McCown was born in Fayetteville, Tennessee, a town severely damaged by a tornado the week of his birth. He has published three previous novels and four collections of poems, and his short stories, essays, and plays have appeared widely. Twice winner of the American Fiction Prize, he has also received the Germaine Breé Book Award, the S. Mariella Gable Prize, a Barnes & Noble Discover Great Writers designation, an Academy of American Poets Prize, and a Distinction in Literature citation from the Wisconsin Library Association. He is a past editor of *Indiana Review* and the founding editor of the *Beloit Fiction Journal*. He has worked as both a screenwriter for Warner Bros. and a creative consultant for HBO television, and he was once a principal actor with the National Shakespeare Company. As a journalist, he received the Associated Press Award for Documentary Excellence for his investigations of organized crime. He teaches in the MFA program in creative writing at Virginia Commonwealth University, as well as in the Vermont College of Fine Arts low-residency MFA program. McCown lives on a horse farm with his wife, Dawn Cooper.